BLOOD ON SHAKESPEARE'S TYPEWRITER

MARK EKLID

SPELLBOUND BOOKS.

First Published by in 2023 by SpellBound Books

Copyright © 2023 Mark Eklid

To Jane and Mark,
Proof that good things do happen to good people in the end.

CHAPTER
ONE

Ronnie Bridgeman was in a filthy mood. He paced the edge of the pavement outside the restaurant, flicking angry glances up and down the road. It had only been five minutes since he called for the taxi but his patience was already being stretched. He was not a patient man at the best of times and this was not the best of times.

Vanessa Bridgeman purposely stood five yards away, so still that she might have been mistaken for a mannequin dressed up to display glamorous and eye-wateringly expensive evening wear. She stared unseeingly straight ahead, lips pursed in silent fury. She couldn't even bear to look at him.

It was meant to be their special night. Their twentieth wedding anniversary. It had not gone as she had hoped it would.

'You couldn't behave like a civilised human being for one evening, could you?' The words had been simmering so intensely deep inside that they had to come out, popping like sulphurous bubbles through the surface of hot lava.

He ignored her. He stopped pacing and thrust his hands into the trouser pockets of his new suit, tailored especially for the occasion. He thought the bold check navy and white three-piece

1

made him appear edgy and dapper. She thought he looked ridiculous.

'Where's that bastard taxi?' he cursed and pulled out his phone from his jacket inside pocket in case that could offer him an answer.

Vanessa was not about to let him shut her out. She had to spell out how angry he had made her.

'We'll never be able to eat here again. So embarrassing.'

Ronnie rubbed his hand over his shaven head three times, trying not to rise to the bait. He knew full well he was in enough trouble as it was.

'I never *want* to come here again. Michelin star, my arse! They can't even cook a steak.'

A car was approaching from their right and Ronnie squinted keenly towards it to see if it was their cab, but it did not slow down and drove straight past. He swore under his breath.

'And what makes you such a bloody expert? You can't even cook an egg.'

'I know when a steak is rare, like I asked for it,' he barked back, without turning to face his wife. 'Not raw, not medium. You'd think when they're charging forty quid a pop they'd get it right. I gave them two goes.'

'You didn't have to throw it at the waitress! She was only a young lass! It wasn't her fault! She was in tears.'

'Well...' He wasn't about to admit his reaction might have been a bit excessive but when it was put like that it did sound like his temper had got the better of him. Again.

'I gave them two goes at getting it right,' he repeated. It was still the best he could muster in an appeal for mitigating circumstances to be considered.

'You didn't have to threaten the manager either! And you didn't have to announce to everybody that you've had better food at the pub. You showed yourself up and you embarrassed me.

2

One night without you behaving like a dickhead. That's all I wanted.'

Ronnie pushed his hands into his pockets again and hung his head. She was the only one who could talk to him like that and get away with it.

'That wine was bad as well. Sixty-five quid a bottle!'

'There was nothing wrong with the wine,' Vanessa replied bitterly.

He turned his back to her and skulked away a few steps.

'Tasted like piss,' he muttered to himself.

From behind him, a black cab pulled across from the opposite side of the road and chugged to a halt.

Ronnie spun and glared at it.

'About bastard time,' he said, striding quickly to wrench open the back door and climb in. Vanessa followed, struggling to pull the door closed without allowing the grey satin shawl to fall off her shoulders.

The cab pulled up on one of the more desirable streets in one of Sheffield's most affluent areas. The twenty-minute journey had passed in frosty silence. The driver took one look at them in his rear-view mirror, sat at extreme ends of the back seat with their eyes fixed in opposite directions through the side windows, and decided not to ask if they'd had a good night.

Vanessa climbed out while her husband waited for his change. The exact change. He didn't believe in tipping. She pressed the code into the access control keypad on the sturdy white pillar and the heavy wooden security gates stirred with a buzz before beginning to swing open. By the time she was halfway up the drive towards their home, Ronnie had pocketed his change and was following close behind.

She opened the outer door and headed straight for the burglar alarm to turn it off before it began to sound its alert. Her finger was poised to deactivate it when she realised it was not primed anyway.

'You forgot to set the alarm,' she chided.

Ronnie looked at the control disbelievingly. 'I did not. I *remembered* to set the alarm. I never forget.'

'Well, it's not bloody set.' Vanessa flounced away, leaving him to absorb the irrefutable evidence before him.

'I did set the alarm. I know I did.'

He was wrestling with the strength of his conviction when a call from the lounge startled him out of his musings.

'Get in here, quick! Somebody's been in. We've been robbed.'

Ronnie spun on his heels.

'What?'

He was numb for a moment but then headed into the lounge with purpose.

'They've taken the sixty-five-inch Ultra HDR,' Vanessa announced. He stared at the space on the wall where the large TV had once been, dumbfounded. He turned to the wall opposite. The spot reserved for his pride and joy.

'They've taken my signed Damien Hirst as well!'

Ronnie's face was starting to turn a shade of puce. Anyone in the know knew that was a sign of upcoming danger. Vanessa had not even noticed. She was heading upstairs to check out the master bedroom.

'The jewellery's gone,' she called down. 'And my laptop. And your Rolexes.'

'Fuck!' he cried and stomped up the broad polished wooden stairs to inspect the scene for himself.

Vanessa sat on the bed, her shoulders slumped, holding one of her empty jewellery boxes. The one where she kept her rings.

Whoever did this had not made a mess, though several drawers had been left open. It had been efficiently done.

Ronnie was too close to the verge of an explosion to think about offering her comfort but he did retain the presence of mind to realise he might have an even greater problem.

The office!

He headed back across the landing to the room he had made the nerve centre of his many operations. *Surely they can't have got into the safe.*

The signed, framed Lionel Messi Barcelona shirt which had hung over the wall safe had been taken down but the safe itself appeared unbreeched. He pulled at its door to make sure. It was still locked. That was a relief. He looked around to see what else had been taken.

The heavy black frame which had housed the shirt was on the floor, it's glass broken. The shirt was gone. So, too, was his autographed Muhammad Ali boxing glove from its glass showcase. Some of the antique office fittings he had collected, in the belief that it would give the place an edge of sophistication, had also been taken. This was almost too much. He had never been on the receiving end of criminal behaviour before. It was not a good feeling.

Ronnie leaned forward, pressing both hands against the surface of his hefty Georgian mahogany desk, barely able to contain his seething anger. He wanted to break something. Or somebody. His eyes scanned for an inanimate object to help him vent some of the intolerable pressure mounting inside his skull. He snatched up the brass paper knife and launched an immediate frenzied attack on the surface of the desk, raining down blow after blow and gouging out chunk after chunk of dark wood as his anguished yell echoed off the walls.

The assault lasted only half a minute but it exhausted him. He dropped the knife. The brass guard, where the blade met the handle, had cut into the flesh of the side of his hand through the force of the blows and a sparkling trail of blood ran down towards the cuff of his shirt as he held up his arm to inspect the damage.

The desk had definitely come off worst, however.

The violent attack had served its purpose. Ronnie felt appeased. He turned to leave the office and check what else might have been taken, the glass of the broken frame scrunching under his shoe. Then he noticed the pale blue jewellery case on the floor, under the safe. It was the one for the diamond necklace and matching earrings he gave Vanessa for their tenth anniversary. Because it was the most expensive set she owned she kept it in the safe. He picked up the case. It was empty.

'Have you had the Tiffany out?' he shouted through to the bedroom.

Silence fell between them for a moment, but then Vanessa called back.

'You mean the necklace and earrings I've been wearing all night, even when I was sitting opposite you in the restaurant?'

He heard the barb wrapped up in those words and winced. He hadn't noticed.

'Yeah,' he bluffed. 'Them ones. Why didn't you put the box back in the safe?'

'I did,' she responded, emphatically.

'Are you sure?'

'Course I'm fucking sure!'

The blue case in his hand suggested otherwise but Ronnie knew better than to push the point further. Irritatingly, she was never wrong in matters such as this. She could be, just this once. But then, what if...

He cast the case down on the pitted desktop and hurried back to the safe, pressing the ten-digit code into the keypad. It beeped its assent and he pulled open the door.

It was empty.

Everything was gone.

Documents, cash, the other jewellery, deeds. Everything.

Ronnie stared at its emptiness, barely able to take in the evidence of his own eyes. How could this be? He and Vanessa were the only ones who knew the code. The only place it was stored was in their heads. The safe door was locked when they left that night, he trusted Vanessa absolutely on that. It was still locked when they got home.

'They've been in the safe,' he called.

'What?'

'They've emptied the safe. There was more than forty-eight grand in there and all our passports and...' A realisation dawned with a sickening thud. 'Oh, shit!'

He ran his fingers along the inner edge of the safe and into its corners, in case it had miraculously been missed, unnoticed or perhaps discarded because it was so unobtrusive. It was not there.

'They took the flash drive,' he announced, his voice quietened by the gravity of the discovery. Vanessa heard him well enough and came rushing in.

'You certain?' She scanned the debris on the floor, trying to spot the small silver rectangle that was so valuable to them. It was nowhere to be seen.

'It's not the only copy, right?'

'Of course not,' he replied. 'There's another one in the bank safety deposit, but that's not the point. We can't afford for it to be out there.'

They both stared into the empty safe.

'I don't know why you decided to keep it in the house,' she said at last.

'You know full well I needed it at hand sometimes. I didn't think anybody would be stupid enough to break into my house! The safe's top of the range. I never took it out of the safe unless I needed to. Only I know the encryption code. It was secure.' He felt the glare of her retrospective disapproval boring into him.

'You're not helping, you know.'

'So what are you going to do about it?' she challenged.

Ronnie drew a deep breath. His temper began to rise again as he considered his response.

'I tell you what I'm going to do. I'm going to find whoever did this. I'm going to get back every last thing they've taken from us and then I'm going to rip their bastard arms off. That's what I'm going to do.'

CHAPTER
TWO

DAN STOOD BEHIND HIS GIRLFRIEND, SHANNON, HIS HANDS ON HER shoulders, guiding her in faltering small steps through the open door to the main room of their flat. She had a scarf tied over her eyes and held her arms in front of her for extra early warning reassurance.

'Nearly there,' said Dan, barely able to contain himself. He had been building up to this all afternoon, counting down the hours until Shannon came home from her shift at Asda, and had intercepted her as soon as she got back. He hadn't even given her enough time to take off her coat before declaring 'I've got a surprise for you' and brandishing the blindfold.

Shannon grinned broadly. She liked surprises. It pleased her when Dan made the effort to prepare something special for their tea or brought back a small bunch of flowers from the shop. He didn't usually go to this much trouble, though. This was even more exciting.

'What is it?' she squealed. He could not possibly lead her much further. The whole flat could be covered in a few strides. They must be almost there.

'Nearly, nearly...' He inched her a few shuffling steps further before clamping his hands a little more firmly on her shoulders '... and stop!'

Shannon allowed her arms to fall to her side and stood totally still, as instructed.

'Are you ready?' teased Dan.

'Yes, I'm ready, you daft sod,' she answered, almost bursting into a giggle.

He unfastened the loose knot in the scarf and released her from the blindfold with the panache of a magician at a children's party.

'Ta-dah!'

It took only a second for Shannon's eyes to readjust to the light, a further second or two for her to process exactly what her focus had now fallen upon and a few more for her to realise, with a sinking feeling of anti-climax, that what she saw before her *was* the big surprise.

It wasn't quite the exciting treat she hoped it might be. It certainly wasn't something she could claim to have always wanted. It wasn't even a pleasant little gift to brighten her day. It was... Well, it was a pile of junk, as far as she could tell.

Underwhelmed would be putting it mildly.

'Oh!' She could not disguise the disappointment in her voice.

Undeterred, Dan allowed her a few moments more to absorb the sight. His grin held firm. He knew there was more to come.

'Do you know what it is?'

'Some kind of very old machine,' she responded, flatly.

The small, battered rectangular flat pack table appeared to sag under the weight of it. Metal glinted where many years of use had worn away some of the black enamel and chipped at the edges, but someone had clearly spent hours lovingly restoring it close to its original glory. It sat proudly upright, a well-cared-for relic of an age long before computers or more modern touch-sensitive versions, with four rows of round button keys ready to be pressed into clattering action and, on the face of the casing behind them, the word *Imperial* embossed in white. On top, two round spools sat like chopped-down horns and fed the ink ribbon, which waited for the impact of each proud metal character to strike it and impress words, lines, whole fabulous stories on to blank paper fed by the smooth black roller of the carriage.

It was a superb machine but, as Shannon stared at it blankly, the question foremost in her mind was not *what* it was, but *why* it was on the table in the living room of their tiny flat.

'It's a typewriter!' Dan confirmed.

She shook her head. 'What the fuck, Dan?'

'I know what you're thinking,' he said. He didn't expect her to get it straight away.

'What I'm thinking is "why is this old piece of shit cluttering up my living room?" That's what I'm thinking. Where the hell did you get it from? You know what – I don't care. Just take it back. I don't want this thing taking up space in the flat.'

Dan was not put off. He stepped from behind her and put his hands on her shoulders again to gently turn her to face him. He had inherited skin the colour of roasted almonds and his sparkling dark eyes from his father, who was second generation British South Asian, and his placid nature from his mother, whose family line had not nudged beyond Sheffield's boundaries for hundreds of years. His parents had split up when he was very young, twenty years or so ago, and he did not see either of them much these days.

He was slenderly built and a few inches short of six feet but was a little taller than Shannon and leaned forward to plant a loving, reassuring kiss on her forehead.

'Just wait till I tell you a bit more about it,' he said. 'Then you might change your mind.'

Shannon's blue eyes narrowed. She trusted him and was

ready to be won over but shot him a look that suggested his explanation had better be good.

'You've heard of William Shakespeare, right?'

'Of course I've heard of William Shakespeare!' she retorted, slightly offended by the suggestion she might not have. 'I'm not a complete thicko!'

'So you know he wrote loads of plays and poems and stuff?'

'Yeah...'

'Well this...' Dan eased her around to face the hulking black machine again. 'This is the actual typewriter he wrote them on.'

Shannon was not often lost for words, but she was then. She was stunned into silence, struggling to comprehend what she had just been told. Did he *really* just say that?

'You're having me on, right?' she said at last, still gazing at the machine. 'Who spun you that one?'

Dan had been itching to share his discovery all afternoon but this was the one part of the story he was wary of telling. He had a feeling it would be the hardest part of the sell.

'Fingerless Frankie.'

Shannon rolled her eyes.

'You bought this from Fingerless Frankie? It'll be nicked. Where do you suppose he got it from?'

'He does some legit stuff as well,' Dan felt compelled to add in defence. 'He goes to antique fairs and all that. He told me he came across this when he was doing a house clearance.'

'Did the owners know he was clearing it?' quipped Shannon with spite.

He was undeterred.

'And, get this, the house was in Stratford on Avon, where Shakespeare used to live, right?'

She shook her head, unswayed. She was not about to let him off the hook that easily.

'How much did you give him for it? Please tell me you didn't pay more than a fiver.'

Dan swallowed. 'Fifty quid.'

'Fifty quid!' she roared. 'Fifty quid! For this? He's taken you for a mug!'

'Ah, well, no, actually. Look at this.'

He picked up a yellowing envelope from off the table, at the side of the typewriter, and carefully pulled out a sheet of ageing, brittle writing paper.

'Here. Read it.'

Shannon took the sheet and unfolded it, answering his encouraging look with a sceptical stare. She broke the exchange and read the short note, hand-written in blue pen ink.

> *Letter Of Certification*
> *This is to certify that this typewriter really did belong to the Bard himself, William Shakespeare, and that he used it to write all his plays like Hamlet and King Lear and the rest of them.*
> *Signed,*
> *Professor C M Jonson*
> *Head of English Literature at Oxford University*

'See?' said Dan, waiting for her to concede that his judgement was right all along.

Shannon read the words again. It certainly appeared genuine. For the first time, she began to soften. Could it be the real thing?

'But fifty quid, Dan! We haven't got fifty quid to spare.'

The point struck home. She was right. Ever since he lost his job at the food-packing company five months ago they had struggled to make ends meet. Shannon had taken on all the extra hours she could at Asda but money was still tight.

'I get that,' he conceded. 'I do, honest, but I reckon this could turn out to be a great investment. Shakespeare's still, like, really popular, so I reckon this could be worth two, three – ten times what I paid for it. Who knows? Frankie said it was a special price because it was me.'

'What did he mean by that?' asked Shannon with a knitted brow.

'It was because he knows I like books.'

She paused, puzzled. 'Do you?'

'Yeah!' He was surprised she thought the point needed clarification.

'You remember when I found that Harry Potter book on the bus? The one they based on the third film?'

She did now recall how Dan had become so wrapped up in reading it, even preferring it to watching *Gogglebox* on the telly for a whole week.

'Oh, yeah!'

'I sometimes took it with me to the pub and Frankie must have seen me. It was, like, a really thick book but I got through it all. It was brilliant. It felt even more alive than the film. Something changed for me when I was reading it.'

He edged closer to her, gently touching the soft skin of her cheek with the back of his left hand and brushing a stray wisp of dyed blonde hair off her face. He had fallen for her pretty features the moment he first spotted her in the late bar up town. Though they were both fairly pissed at that stage of the night, he knew she was his special one. They were only nineteen then and she moved into the house he shared with three mates four months later. That was partly because she had a huge bust-up with her parents, who were hostile towards their relationship because, they openly admitted, of Dan's racial heritage. Six months after that, they pooled everything they had so they could move into their own tiny, one-bedroom rented council flat on a run-down estate. That was just over four years ago. They still didn't have much, but they were blissfully happy together.

'Reading that book made me wonder if I could do something different with my life,' he explained. 'I wondered if I could be better. It's funny but I remembered my old form tutor at school and I used to tell him some ridiculous stories as excuses for why I was late or why I hadn't turned up at all and he never called me out. I'm sure he could have got me in trouble if he wanted because I don't suppose he believed a word, but it was like he enjoyed listening to me making up all these daft excuses, and the wilder I made them, the more he enjoyed them. He once said to me: "Do you know, if you learn to put that imagination of yours to good use one day, you might be on to a winner" and I thought he was taking the piss, but it was like he was telling me he reckoned I could make something of myself, you know? I never got that from anybody else when I was growing up, even my mum. Reading that book made me imagine what it would be like if I could write a story like that one day, but I kind of pushed it to one side because, you know, how could I write a book? Then when Frankie showed me the typewriter in his van outside the pub I had this really strange idea. I thought "what if some of Shakespeare's spirit is trapped in this old typewriter?" I know that sounds a bit weird, but could there be something in it? If he used this to write all them plays that people still talk about all these years later, maybe I might be able to write something great on it as well.'

Shannon pulled herself tight to him in an embrace. She could not say she understood him, but she wanted to show she believed in him. They had been through so much together and had emerged stronger, unbreakable.

'I don't want this poxy little flat and boring, dead-end jobs to be all we can get out of life. I want more. JK Rowland started out with nothing and look what happened.'

He kissed the top of her head again.

'If he can do it, then why can't I?'

THREE

There were three things you needed to know about Fingerless Frankie.

The first was that his nickname was misleading. He did have some fingers.

The second was that if there were particular goods you wanted and you didn't ask awkward questions, Frankie could get them for you for less than you'd find them in any shop. It had to be understood that what he offered was pre-owned and it was fair to say their previous owners hadn't necessarily parted with them by choice, but those were the terms you had to accept.

It was during one of his missions to source fresh supplies, three years earlier, that he earned his nickname.

Frankie had identified a promising domestic target and established that access wouldn't challenge him. It was a large house on a well-off estate. He favoured the higher-class neighbourhoods because the quality and variety of goods was generally high, the prospect of being spotted by neighbours was generally low and because the possibility that one of his potential customers lived on one of these posh estates was practically zero. By taking the precaution of keeping the source of his stock well away from where he sold it, Frankie's business flourished without attracting too much unwanted attention from law enforcement.

However, on this particular night, three years ago, he made a crucial oversight.

After waiting until he was sure the middle-aged couple who lived there were sound asleep, he made his move. Finding a house so large without an alarm system was as good as asking him to break in, but Frankie soon discovered why these householders had been lax in their electronic security protection.

It was a fully-grown, fiercely protective, and wide awake Doberman Pinscher called Cassius.

Cassius believed in the bite first, bark later, form of defence and though Frankie did manage to stick out an arm to shield himself from the dog's first lunge, it cost him the little finger and half the ring finger on his left hand. Cassius was momentarily distracted by the detached digits, long enough for Frankie to make his escape and so potentially avoid even greater damage, but his troubles were far from over. The police found more than enough DNA evidence to secure a conviction.

The case caught the interest of national press because of its part-gruesome, part-comic nature and earned Frankie an unwanted brush with fame as the burglar who left with less than he broke in with. Frankie was not amused and neither was the judge, who sent him to prison for a year.

While he was inside, Frankie decided he needed to diversify his business practices and planned to take the radical step of adding some activities that were almost legal. This didn't involve giving up those that were definitely not legal, of course, but he figured if he gave the impression of going straight, it might deflect away some of the heat he was bound to attract as a recently convicted burglar.

So he came out of prison with a plan, as well as a new nickname, and soon business was booming again. Of course it was.

You see, even though he was not necessarily the smartest and although his business practices were distinctly dubious, Frankie had a talent. He was a natural salesman. If ever there was a man who could sell sand to the Arabs or ice or the Eskimos, it was Frankie.

This was unquestionably his greatest asset, but it was also what made it dangerous to be in his company.

Which leads us to the third thing you needed to know about Fingerless Frankie.

If ever he called you 'mate', beware!

Worse still, if he said to you: 'Buy me a pint, mate. I'm about to do you a huge favour,' you knew you were in serious bother. The only sensible course of action in those circumstances was to turn him down flat and move as far from his predatory grasp as possible because if you allowed your curiosity to let him draw you in, the loss of a price of a pint was the least of your worries.

Dan Khan should have been reminded of this advice on his previous visit to The Swan, which was both his closest pub to home and one of the key outlets in Frankie's empire. If he had, he might not have returned to his flat that afternoon weighed down by an old cast iron typewriter but lighter in the pocket by fifty pounds.

The following day, Dan was back in The Swan.

It had been a tough morning. Dan had been for his latest interview with his Work Coach at the Jobcentre Plus, a thin-lipped woman called Joy who appeared to take very little of it from her role. She had threatened to stop his Jobseeker's Allowance unless he actively did something about seeking a job very soon. He was faced with the prospect of having to take on another soul-destroying, poorly-paid position he didn't want and his inability to break out of that cycle left him flat. He decided to drop into The Swan in the hope of cheering himself up with a couple of games of pool.

Apart from the attraction of a pool table, there was little else about The Swan that was likely to gladden the soul.

Neither the inside nor the outside had felt the frequent touch of a damp cloth, let alone the freshening stroke of a paint brush, since the landlady, Rita, ran off with the man who delivered the pub's crisps, nuts and pork products in 2009. More as a result of laziness than a deep sense of loss, her estranged husband, Roger, had neglected the place since, though, to his credit, he did quickly find a new company to provide bar snacks.

Behind the permanently tacky and stained wooden bar at the centre of the public room stood a row of six taps (two keg bitters, three lagers and a cider), with a range of spirits optics on the mirrored back wall beside the till. In the middle of the cork-tiled facia above the bar was mounted a small ship's wheel; the significance of which, if it ever had any, had long since been forgotten. Three rickety stools to the left of the bar, topped with red velvet cushions that were worn almost threadbare, were rarely trusted to take the weight of any of the few remaining regulars. Most of the half-dozen tables and chairs were arranged to the left, too, with the pool table in a small alcove to the right, so close to the dartboard on the wall that it was both impractical and dangerous for both to be used at the same time.

Dan was able to play safely at this time because the pub was almost deserted. The only other customer was an old man who, every day, dragged in his ageing arthritic Jack Russell terrier midway through their post-lunch walk and made a pint last an hour as he read his Daily Mirror quietly in the corner.

Roger the landlord had taken pity on Dan and handed him the key to the pool table, to play for as long as he liked without having to pay. Roger had then disappeared into the back room. There was little point hanging around the bar waiting to serve. The place was usually quiet these days, even on Friday and Saturday nights. Ever since another of those large chain supermarkets had popped up practically overnight where the bingo hall used to be, the lure of staying in with the telly and cheap tinned beer rather than trudging out to the pub had proved too strong for many of his former regulars. The Swan, like so many other out-of-town pubs, had since struggled on, under permanent threat of the brewery calling time for good.

Right now, quiet suited Dan's mood down to the ground. The pool table and the way the red and yellow balls were positioned on it was the only thought he was allowing to hold his attention. The frustrations of his morning faded with every satisfying clack of the balls against the plastic back of the pocket, the haunting spectre of failure fading every time they rolled away into the belly of the machine, ready to be set up again once the black was potted last of all. He didn't even notice the creak of the pub's front door as he crouched, lining up a long red to the top right-hand pocket, but his seclusion was shattered as he drew back the cue to take the shot.

'Danny boy!'

Even the Jack Russell opened its eyes and raised its dozing head off its front paws at the sudden disturbance.

Dan froze, mid-shot. He exhaled, like all the effort he had made to reinflate his punctured self-esteem had escaped in a rush. There was no need to turn to see who had called to him. He knew.

Fingerless Frankie stood, pointing towards the pool table with his outstretched right arm, grinning at the magnificence of his own grand entrance as the door closed slowly behind him.

Because he was no longer the age or shape to carry off the look, some might have considered he appeared faintly absurd in his designer grey hooded tracksuit and immaculately white trainers. He would not have agreed. To Frankie, the way he dressed was all part of the pitch.

I am a man at the top of my game. Like what you see? Say the word and I can sort you out with gear like this, too.

Even setting aside the intrusive force of his personality and his dress sense, his height and physique made it hard not to notice Frankie. Even in his early forties, his middle no longer able to conceal his appetite for good living, he remained brawny enough to haul bulky goods in and out of his van, yet agile enough to ease himself into buildings through tight spaces when the situation demanded. His combed-back hair remained thick and dark. His ravenous eyes and seductive wide grin could still be switched on in an instant, like a garish neon sign, at the first scent of an opportunity to sell. In many ways, Frankie possessed the instincts of a dangerous predator, luring in the unwary and stripping their wallets to the bone before they had the chance to realise he had them in his unforgiving grip.

'Just the man I wanted to see!' he bellowed and began to move closer to Dan's corner of the room in long, stalking steps. 'How you doing, mate?'

Dan stood and drew the cue in both hands across his chest in an intuitive gesture of self-defence.

'All right, Frankie?' he courteously replied, the counter-arguments of how he had already spent more than he should and had no more to give, no matter how alluring today's great bargain was, already forming in his mind. Surely that was reason enough to be left alone? You cannot feast from a cupboard that is empty. Frankie didn't believe in offering credit terms.

'You and me need to talk,' said Frankie, flashing that smile again. 'Let me get you a drink. Pint of lager?'

Dan was instantly disarmed. Frankie never offered to buy a drink. He sometimes had to resort to buying his own, but showing generosity? That was unknown.

'Thanks,' he replied timidly, confused.

Frankie strode to the bar and rapped on the wooden surface with his knuckles.

'Roger! Get your arse out here!' he yelled to the closed door at the back of the bar. 'I wouldn't have thought it was possible to die of thirst in a pub.'

Shortly, the landlord emerged, haggard and dazed from having been rudely awakened mid-snooze, blowing his nose into a grubby handkerchief.

'Have you decided to go self-service? It's no wonder this place is going to the dogs.'

Roger ignored the gibe and stuffed the hanky into his trouser pocket.

'Now then, Frankie. What you having?'

'Pint of lager for Danny boy and I'll have a soda with lime. I assume you've got ice.'

The drinks were poured and paid for. Frankie carried them to where Dan had been standing and watching, wondering with trepidation where this unexpected show of largesse was heading.

'I need a favour,' said Frankie, setting the drinks down on a table which rocked slightly and dribbled lager froth down the side of the glass.

'This is a bit awkward and I don't normally do this kind of thing,' he added and picked up his drink to take a sip. Dan gulped, even more wary of what he may soon be about to face.

'It's about that typewriter I sold you yesterday. You see, unbeknown to me, my business partner had already promised it to an important client and – I'm not saying you aren't important as well – but it's put me in a difficult position.'

Dan tried to edge closer to the table as casually as he could and snatched up his pint in case there was any chance it could be taken away again.

'I see,' he said, though he didn't.

'I need to buy it back from you. Don't worry, I'll see you right. How much did you pay me for it? Forty?'

'Fifty,' Dan confirmed.

'Fifty, right.' Frankie nodded to himself, taking the opportunity to marvel at how profitable a deal he had driven. 'Well, as I say, I appreciate this is my mistake and so, as a gesture of good will, I'm willing to give you your money back and a bit on top for your trouble. How about seventy?'

Dan paused, pint in one hand and cue in the other, considering the offer. His eyes narrowed. It sounded like a fair exchange. He could certainly use the extra twenty and though Shannon had appeared to understand his reasons for wanting to buy the typewriter, he was sure she wouldn't miss it if he gave it back.

And yet...

'No deal.'

'Eh?' Frankie hadn't anticipated that response. His mask slipped momentarily but the smile and the glint in the eye were soon restored.

'You're driving a hard bargain, Danny boy! I respect that. Make it seventy-five.'

Dan drew the glass to his mouth and took a drink.

'Nope.'

'Eighty, then.'

He shook his head. 'I don't want to sell it.'

This was totally unexpected. The Frankie charm was failing him. This could not be.

'Look, mate. I'm in a bit of a hole here. I'm asking you to help me out. I'm being more than fair. Come on! For me! Ninety. Last offer.'

Dan was resolute. It wasn't just that he was enjoying the switch in the balance of power, though it was novel to see Frankie squirm like this. It went further than that.

'I'm not selling. At any price. Find another one for your important client.'

'It's a piece of junk!' cried Frankie in exasperation. 'A hundred!'

'If it's junk, why do you want it back so badly? No deal.'

Frankie was temporarily dumbstruck. This was supposed to be straightforward. He had promised it would be. It might involve taking on a small financial loss, but he could always recoup that when he sold it on next time. He didn't think the kid would dig in his heels and want to keep the damned thing. That was unforeseen. How dare he!

'Listen, you don't know what you're getting yourself into here. I need it back or there's going to be trouble, and if I'm in trouble, it's going to come down on your head as well. Do you get what I'm saying? So I'm asking you one more time to be reasonable. Sell me back the typewriter and we all just move on. A hundred and twenty.'

This was the wrong day to use threats. Dan had had enough of people telling him what to do and that he'd be punished unless he did what they said. He didn't want to take some crappy job on minimum wage which would leave him not much better off than if he was out of work and he didn't want to sell the typewriter back to Fingerless Frankie.

That 'piece of junk' typewriter was special. It used to belong to a man who made it big. A man whose name was still well known, even though he'd been dead for years. Dan wanted to make it, too. That typewriter could be his way to escape.

And so he held firm. He stared Frankie straight in the eye, defiance etched over his face, and spelled out to the world that he wasn't going to be walked over any more.

'No. Deal.'

Frankie knew he had been beaten and he did not like it. People like Dan were on this earth for him to take advantage of. They weren't meant to cause him grief. He was furious.

'You'll regret this,' he spat out behind a wagging finger. 'This is going to bring you big trouble, believe me, Danny boy. Big trouble. Just you see.'

He flounced out of the pub, kicking over the uneven table in his rage as he turned to go, sending the remains of his glass of soda with lime spilling over the already sticky carpet. The old man looked up over his newspaper and his dog yapped its disapproval at such poor behaviour. Then Frankie was gone.

'Wow!' said Shannon as he finished telling her the tale over their evening meal of sell-by-day chicken and pasta. 'He really threatened you?'

Dan scooped in the mouthful that had been poised on the end of his fork for a while and nodded as he began to chew.

'I'm not scared of Fingerless Frankie,' he was able to say at last. 'What's he going to do? Refuse to sell me any more of his knock-off stuff?'

Shannon raised her eyebrows in a 'suppose so' kind of way and turned back to her plate. They ate in silence for a minute.

'Still,' she said, unable to contain the thought any longer. 'A hundred and twenty quid.'

He laid down his knife and fork with a clatter.

'But don't you get it, Shan? Frankie was willing to give me double – more than double – what I paid him only the day before. He doesn't give money away. I don't believe this promised-it-to-somebody-else bullshit for a minute. He must have realised what that typewriter is *really* worth and that's why he wanted it back so much. He's realised he's missed a trick. Didn't I tell you, Shan?

That typewriter could get us a lot more than a piddling hundred and twenty quid.'

He paused.

'Besides, you know it ain't just about that.'

Shannon looked sympathetically back at him, like a mother biting her tongue so as not to crush her child's fanciful dreams. She couldn't do that.

'That's all well and good, hun,' she said. 'But what are you going to do about it? If we don't start bringing in more money soon, we'll be in bother. I don't want to lose the flat.'

She was right. He shared her fears. If he was to prove that taking on another low-paid job was not the only long-term solution, he had to set about it straight away.

Dan glanced over to the typewriter, sitting as heavy as expectation on the table, and then turned back to Shannon.

'I'll make a start tomorrow. I promise.'

CHAPTER
FOUR

THE SCREWED UP SHEETS OF PAPER FILLED TO THE TOP OF THE PLASTIC carrier bag. Dan had to compress the waste even more before he could tie the handles of the bag to stop the crumpled balls from spilling out.

Progress had not been as rapid as he wanted. Even with the spirit of the world's greatest playwright at his shoulder, it turned out writing a book was harder than it seemed. Especially, it turned out, when attempting to do it on a machine so unfamiliar and ancient that he might as well have been challenged to produce yarn on a Spinning Jenny.

The first setback to Dan's aims for the day came as soon as, with high hopes and steely determination, he sat in front of the typewriter for the first time that morning. That was when he realised he would need some paper.

He could find none in the flat, apart from the back of an old Asda employees' safety at work document in a plastic folder, but he wasn't sure if Shannon still needed it and, besides, there wasn't enough of it for what he had in mind.

So Dan's first task was to head to the shop in the precinct

where everything cost a pound. The best he could find there was a one hundred-sheet children's sketch pad. The paper wasn't great quality and there was a cartoon picture of a smiling pink unicorn printed in the top right corner of every sheet, but he reckoned it would be good enough to enable him to make a start.

There were not many more than half a dozen sheets left in the pad now. Most of the rest were screwed up in the carrier bag but two of them were laid out, neatly and proudly, beside the type-writer, waiting to be presented to Shannon when she returned home from her shift.

It may have amounted to only one and two-thirds pages of type and they were dotted with multiple scribbled-out mistakes, but Dan was exceptionally proud of them. He had rarely felt such a sense of achievement. He was an author.

Twenty past four. Only ten more minutes until the time Shannon could usually be expected to walk through the door. The anticipation was unbearable! He was sure she would like it, but he needed her approval. She didn't say anything about working overtime today, did she?

Finally, on time, he heard the rattle of the key in the lock and eased back in the sofa seat, attempting to appear as casual as he could.

She was wearing a black shop uniform fleece over a bright green polo shirt and had her hair tied back. As she reached the door to the living room, she flashed the bright smile he loved and brandished a white and green shopping bag.

'I got us a broccoli and cheese quiche for tea,' she announced.

'Nice,' said Dan, stretching to cup his hands behind the back of his head but then quickly putting them down again because he thought that was overdoing the casual look.

'Good shift?'

'Yeah, not bad.' Shannon put the bag on the floor while she

took off her fleece. 'Some guy dropped a jar of pickled onions which smashed all over the floor at the till I was on, but all right apart from that.'

'Big jar or little jar?' asked Dan, trying to appear interested.

'Big enough to make the whole place stink of vinegar for the rest of the afternoon.' She laid the fleece over the back of the sofa as she carried the bag through to the kitchen.

'What about you? How did you get on?'

'Yeah, pretty good,' he replied. 'I started my book.'

'Ooo!' Her voice was slightly masked by the buzz of the fridge as she opened the door to put away the quiche, but he then heard it close and Shannon headed straight back into the living room.

'Can I read it?'

Dan was still playing it cool.

'Sure. If you'd like.'

Please read it. Now.

'It's over there.' He gestured towards the typewriter.

'Exciting!' She walked quickly and stood in front of the machine.

'Love the unicorns.'

'It was the only pad I could get.' Dan was a little disappointed she had commented on the unicorns.

Shannon picked up the two sheets and flicked them to make sure there were not others stuck together. She scanned the table, wondering if there were more.

'Is this all of it?'

He knew she wasn't being deliberately unkind, but Dan took it as a veiled criticism. Heightened anticipation had left him more sensitive than usual.

'It's not that easy,' he pleaded. 'It took me ages to figure out how the typewriter worked. I couldn't get the paper in at first and then how was I to know that the bar thing on the side was what you used to go on to the next line? I had to Google it.'

The frustrations of his creative process were bubbling to the surface.

'The letters are in the same order as on phones, which is a help, but it's difficult getting used to having to press down on the keys and you can't just press them, you have to really bang them down or it doesn't make a big enough mark on the paper. It really hurts the end of your fingers after a bit. There's no predictive text and you can't back space to delete stuff, so you have to think about what you're writing all the time. As well as that, there's something wrong with the 'a' so that it's dead faint unless you go back and go over it two or three times and sometimes when you press the 'p' it gets caught up with the 'o' and you have to untangle the metal levers. Honestly, it's a nightmare writing on that thing. I don't know how those guys got anything done before they invented computers.'

Shannon let him get it off his chest. She didn't think she was coming over as harsh. Perhaps this was what it must be like to live with a writer.

'I didn't mean... This is great, to say you've never done it before. I'm proud of you, hun.'

Dan relaxed and leaned back in the chair again, appeased.

'Do you want me to read it, or would you rather I didn't?'

'No, I'd like you to,' he mumbled. 'Please.'

She nodded and began to read.

The police detectives were getting kind of worried as they watched through one of them two way mirror things in the police station interrogation room.

'Oh! I thought you were going to do something like Harry Potter.'

'I couldn't come up with an idea for that, so I decided to do one about cops and crime. There's always cops and crime stuff on the telly.'

'OK. Makes sense.'

The police detectives were getting kind of worried as they watched through one of them two way mirror things in the police station inter-rogation room. They only had a few more minutes to get a confession out of Mad Charlie Smith or they were going to have to set him free, even though they knew it was him what had done all them murders. They hadn't got enough evidence to have him bang to rights.

'What are we going to do? He's not telling us nothing. The guvnor, who always makes my life a misery because he's a bit of a dick, says we'll have to turn him loose soon and I bet he'll go straight out and kill a few more innocent folk,' said Sergeant Black.

'How about I go in there and rough him up a bit to make him talk?' said Constable Jones.

'No. I don't go in for that kind of stuff. If we did that, we'd be no better than the criminals,' said Black, who was a good copper.

'Then what can we do?' said Inspector Patel. 'We're running out of time and that. Our situation is getting desperate.'

Just then, the door opened and in walked Detective Peaches McPlenty. All the men looked around at her because she was dead gorgeous and they all fancied her.

'Hello boys. I hear we have a problem,' she said, all sexy like.

'Yes Peaches,' said Black. 'We've got to make Mad Charlie Smith confess to all them murders or we'll have to cut him loose. The streets of our town are not safe with him wandering around them and we might never get a better chance to throw him in prison for the rest of his life. What can you do to help us?'

She walked up to the two way mirror and stared at Mad Charlie, who was sitting in the interrogation room looking like a really nasty piece of work. She took out her bright red lipstick and put some on.

'Leave him to me boys. I'll have him singing like a bird.'

Peaches wiggled back through the door in her tight skirt.

'Good luck Peaches. We're all depending on you,' said Black.

Mad Charlie snarled when he heard another copper coming into the room because he hated coppers. He'd not told them nothing and he knew they'd not got nothing on him, so they were going to have to let him out of jail really soon. He was looking forward to celebrating beating the system again by getting dead pissed at some sleazy club with his criminal mates.

But when he saw Peaches in her low cut blouse and her short skirt with suspenders and all that, his jaw dropped open.

'Hello Charlie,' she said. 'I hear you've been a naughty boy. Why don't you tell me all about it?'

Charlie was right gobsmacked because he'd never seen a woman that sexy but he really wanted to be set free so that he could carry on being a criminal mastermind.

'I'm not telling you nothing,' he said.

'Don't be shy,' said Peaches. 'I won't tell anybody else. It's just you and me now. You scratch my back and I'll scratch yours.'

Charlie knew what she meant and it was nothing to do with scratching backs. His heart started pounding dead fast and he started sweating as Peaches moved closer to him.

'You're sweating,' she said. 'Mind you, it is kind of hot in here.'

She undid another button on her blouse. Charlie gasped. He was ready to crack.

Peaches leaned forward towards him and looked down at the bulge in his trousers.

'So that's why they call you a hardened criminal,' she said.

Charlie was powerless now. He'd do anything to be able to have sex with Peaches.

'I'll tell you what,' she said. 'You confess to all them murders and I'll let you play with my big bouncy boobies.'

. . .

'Big bouncy boobies? Seriously?'

Shannon held up the two sheets of paper in one hand and put the other on her hip. Dan, who had felt too on edge to be able to watch her while she read, glanced up and recognised the disapproval in her expression. She looked deeply let down, like he had dropped the f-bomb in front of her grandma.

'I mean, this is a joke, right? You've hidden the real one away, haven't you? Please tell me this isn't it.'

'What's wrong with it?' he asked. He knew what he'd written was a bit close to the bone but hadn't expected that reaction. 'I wanted her to be a sexy character. None of the women detectives you see on telly are sexy like that. I thought it'd be something different.'

She was unable to talk as she attempted to put the rush of her opinions into order of priority. Where to start?

'It's insulting, Dan. What are you saying – women aren't smart enough to do a job like a police detective without flashing their big bouncy boobies? Is that what you think? If you do, then I'm not sure I know you at all. This...'

She shook the papers at him, accusingly.

'This makes me angry. It's no wonder women can't get the same kind of chances to get on in this world when there's stuff like this giving men the excuse to carry on thinking we're just sex objects with no brains. It's rubbish, Dan. It's insulting. It's pathetic. If this is the best you can do, then you should just pack it in.'

Shannon tossed the two pages away with a flick of the wrist and they fluttered across the room as she turned to head out.

'I need a shower,' she said and was gone, leaving behind a shocked vacuum in which the only sound was the faint crackle of the two sheets in the air followed by the heavy thud of the bathroom door being slammed shut.

Dan sat stunned on the sofa.
She didn't like it. He didn't see that coming.

CHAPTER
FIVE

Once the initial shock had subsided, Dan was angry and hurt. He knew the story probably needed some fine tuning before it was ready to be published, but he didn't think it was that bad. He'd worked really hard on it all day. She should have been more supportive. She shouldn't have gone mental at him like that. If she'd only have read on a bit further, she'd have seen that Peaches tricks Mad Charlie into confessing but then doesn't let him get his hands on her after all.

Who's the clever one there, eh? She's sexy, smart and cunning. Surely, women would all be rooting for Peaches McPlenty, the beautiful ace detective who gets results.

Dan and Shannon ate their broccoli and cheese quiche with oven chips and peas together, but in silence. Shannon decided she would rather have an early night than watch the next episode of *Stranger Things* on Netflix with him. They didn't even kiss goodnight.

That was fine by Dan. He was still on the defensive. He decided to use the time to himself to work on his book some more. He'd show her. She'd soon change her tune. But he made no progress. He just sat there, mocked by the cartoon unicorn on the

blank sheet of paper in the typewriter, and ran theoretical argu-
ments over and over in his mind until he had the script right to
completely convince Shannon she had totally overreacted. In
theory.

His disgruntlement so absorbed him that Dan hardly noticed
darkness falling. When he did, he decided he didn't want to get
up to put the light on. He sat in the growing gloom until he could
barely see the typewriter keys. The darker it became, the more his
pique subsided and regret began to take its place.

They hardly ever fell out. He hated it when they did. They'd
never had a serious row, like a proper potential break-up set-to.
He hoped they never would. She was his world.

Perhaps he should have been more understanding. Shannon
had only just got in from her shift, after all, and it can't have been
easy putting up with the smell of pickled onions all afternoon.
She was a bit stressed from work, that's all.

Maybe she also had a point about Peaches McPlenty. Maybe
he had overdone the sexy stuff. The more he thought about it, he
could see how the character's methods might be misconstrued.
He should tone it down a bit.

Dan certainly didn't want to write anything that was
insulting to women. That wasn't what he intended at all. He
never thought of women in the way Shannon suggested. He
always regarded Shannon as a lot smarter than he was and,
looking further back, he had total respect for his mum practically
bringing him up on her own. They had clashed all the time before
he moved out, just after his nineteenth birthday, but, as he experienced for himself the harsh realities of trying to eke a living on
very little money, he could recognise that it would not have been
easy for mum. Especially looking after a kid who made a habit of
attracting trouble.

He ought to get in touch more often.

The room grew darker and darker and Dan's eyelids grew

heavier and heavier. He needed to sleep but couldn't face the possibility of waking Shannon and making her even crosser with him, so he pushed the typewriter to one side and lay his head on the table. He'd stay there for a bit; have a short doze. He'd go to bed later when Shannon was properly asleep.

He thought of making up with her. He'd fix her a cup of tea and take it to her in bed before the alarm went off. He'd explain that he hadn't meant to insult anybody. She'd understand. They could never be angry with each other for long. It would be all right again.

He thought of making up with her and how nice it would be as he drifted into a deep slumber.

The click of the front door latch startled him awake. At first, disorientated, he didn't realise what the noise was, just that there had been a noise and he was now awake. He also became aware that he had dribbled in his sleep on to the first page of his Peaches McPlenty manuscript and he had to peel it off the side of his face.

Click.

There it was again. He had recovered his bearings sufficiently by this time to work out where it was coming from.

Somebody was trying to get into the flat.

Dan tentatively put the saliva-stained sheet back on the table, not daring to risk even the slightest noise. His senses were on high alert, like a cat picking up the sound of a fox close by.

Click.

Whoever it was clearly didn't have a key, which ruled out the highly remote possibility that Shannon had slipped out for a late-night walk. Who the hell was it? He had no appetite for a confrontation with a burglar. What if they had a knife or a gun? He willed whoever it was to give in and go away.

But there was a final click, click and the outside door began to creak gently open.

Shit! They're in! What do I do?

Dan thought about shouting to try to scare them off – but what if they didn't run away? What if they decided to silence him? They might have a knife or a gun. He'd already considered that. There might be more than one of them. Two or three, even.

Shit!

He jumped to his feet and bolted as quickly, as silently, as he could towards the kitchen. He pressed his body against the wall on the other side of the door, out of sight from the front room, and tried to think.

Hopefully, they would take a quick scout around and see there was nothing worth stealing, then leave.

But what if they went up to the bedroom, where Shannon was sleeping? He'd have to confront them then, to protect her.

Shit!

He could hear nothing. No conspiratorial voices. Dan realised he would have to risk taking a look, so he could be sure they were in the main room and had not made straight for upstairs. He had no choice.

Slowly, slowly he craned his neck until he could peek into the main room around the frame of the kitchen door.

There was movement. Through the almost total darkness, he could see a shape behind the narrow bright beam of a torch. It was in front of the typewriter. What was it doing?

The shape was small, childlike. Was it a kid?

It stayed at the typewriter, seemingly not even interested in anything else.

That was when Dan realised.

They were going to steal the typewriter. Whoever it was, they knew it held a unique place in the history of world literature and they were going to nick it.

39

The shape was far too small for Fingerless Frankie, so it couldn't be him. Perhaps he'd paid some kid to steal it for him. Steal it back. From their exchange in The Swan the previous day, it was obvious Frankie knew it was valuable and wanted it.

The thieving bastard! He's not having my typewriter!

He was going to have to take positive action. There was only one intruder, as far as he could see, and Dan could tell he was bigger than them. That was good.

But if they *did* have a knife or a gun... Best not to just rush in and take that chance. He needed to have some sort of weapon of his own. He looked at what was close at hand.

The cutlery drawer, with their two sharp knives, was over the other side of the kitchen, too far away. On the work surface next to him was a dirty mug, a half-full packet of Coco Pops and *(oh, yes!)* the round, wooden chopping board Shannon constantly reminded him to use every time he had to cut up vegetables or slice bread.

That will do nicely.

Dan picked it up. It was reassuringly sturdy in his hand. He counted to three in his head, spun quickly into the door frame and hurled it, frisbee-like, towards the figure who was still at the typewriter.

The intruder didn't stand a chance of recognising the danger or averting it. The wooden chopping board struck the figure on the head and deflected with a clatter into the wall.

The force snapped their head back and the intruder reeled unsteadily, then slumped forward, on to the typewriter. It lay there, arms strung over the carriage, motionless.

Shit! I've killed them!

Panic filled Dan's being with a rush of cold blood to his face. He had acted in self-defence, but would the police see it that way? In only a few brief seconds, he could see the full scope of horrible repercussions that were the consequences of what he had just done.

But then the figure groaned and moved. The intruder lifted its head groggily and weaved away, heading towards the outside door. Dan thought about pursuing them and maybe restraining them until the police could be summoned but decided to let them go.

It wasn't worth the hassle and, besides, he had triumphed.

The attempt had been thwarted.

When he was sure the intruder had staggered into the night, he closed the outside door again and wedged one of the wooden chairs from the main room against the handle, for extra peace of mind.

His heart thumped loudly so that he could feel it in his throat. He had got into one or two scrapes in the past, but nothing like that. That was properly scary.

Dan dropped to his haunches panting, trying desperately to clear his head.

The phone buzzed on the cabinet next to where Shannon lay and she stretched out an unwilling hand to tap it into still quiet again. Seven-thirty had come around so quickly. It had taken her a while to get off to sleep and she had spent ages going through all her favourite sites on the phone but, when she did drift off, she had been dead to the world.

She woke with a lingering sensation of unease. Why had it taken so long to get to sleep?

Oh, yeah! That.

She didn't like falling out. Once she had stopped being angry with Dan it had made her cry and she didn't like being made to cry. That's what weak people do. She was tough. Toughish.

She wasn't angry at him anymore. Perhaps her reaction was a

bit over the top. He was trying his best and had never done anything like this type of thing before. Allowances had to be made. She would make it up to him.

Shannon could sense Dan's presence heavy on the other side of the bed. They had twenty minutes until she needed to start getting ready for work. That was enough time to start the making-up process. She rolled over and...

What the fuck?

Dan was still asleep but sat upright. His head slumped to the left with his chin stuck to his chest, but his posture wasn't the most unusual thing that caught Shannon's eye.

It was the thing on his lap. That bloody typewriter.

'Dan! Wake up!' She nudged him sharply.

'Wha?' His head jerked straight as he shot out of a dream about being chased through town carrying a vintage piece of office equipment. His neck hurt from being too long in an unnatural position.

'Hey. What time is it?'

'Half seven. What you doing, bringing that to bed with you?'

Dan was still not fully aware. But then he looked down to the heavy weight blocking the circulation to his lower legs. She must mean the typewriter.

It all came flooding rapidly back. The intruder. The wooden chopping board.

'Oh, yeah.'

He explained what had happened. Shannon was horrified.

'Why didn't you wake me up?' she asked.

'I didn't want to after, you know.' She knew. 'I blocked the door to make sure they didn't try to get back in, but I think they were in no state to try it again anyway. I gave them a pretty good whack with the chopping board. I wanted to keep a close eye on this anyway, so I thought...'

Shannon gazed at the black machine like it had developed a

life of its own. It had only been in their lives for a couple of days and already it had commanded so much of their attention... *Hang on! What's that?*

She leaned forward for a closer inspection.

'Is that blood?'

Dan moved his nose close to the typewriter and sniffed. It smelled of nothing much but the evidence was there before his eyes. It was not completely obvious against the black enamel but it was unmistakeably there, dark and sticky. On the cover. On the carriage. Spots on the carriage return lever. Spatters on the keys. The 'f', 'h' and 't' had been coloured deep red.

'Oh, shit!' he exclaimed. 'What a mess! We'll never get that off!'

Shannon gave him a look.

'Don't be daft. It'll come off with cold water and a cloth. The point is, this is serious, Dan. If somebody really broke into our flat just to try to steal this, like you said, they might very easily try again. The fact that you hurt them might make them even more determined.'

'You're right,' he acknowledged with a solemn nod. 'What it means as well is this thing really must be valuable.'

They both stared at the machine, lost in the gravity of the situation it had plunged them into.

'I'm going to Google it,' said Shannon, suddenly, turning to snatch up her phone. 'There must be something out there to tell us what it's worth.'

She keyed in *Shakespeare typewriter value* and pressed return.

That brought up a load of nonsense about an infinite number of monkeys, so she decided to try again.

'People buy this kind of valuable stuff at auctions, right?' suggested Dan.

Good point. 'Yeah!' She keyed in *Shakespeare auction*. Return.

Her eyes widened.

'Shit, Dan!'

'What you got?' He tried to shuffle closer, despite the restriction of the weight on his lap.

'It's something that was on the BBC in 2020. It says: 'Shakespeare First Folio fetches a record $10m at auction.' Ten million dollars! What's that in pounds?'

'Fuck! Don't know, but it's got to be a lot.' A thought crossed his mind.

'What's a first folio?'

Shannon scrolled down the article to a picture.

'It looks like a book to me. Shit, if that's what one of his books is worth, what would you get for the typewriter he wrote it on?'

The dizzying possibilities of the question sent them silent.

'We could be multi-millionaires, Shan. We could get out of this flat and buy one of them posh places in Dore or Frecheville. We might never have to work crappy jobs in a factory or a supermarket ever again.'

They were quiet again. Contemplating.

'Should we put it into one of them auctions?' Dan asked.

'Hmm.' The suggestion made sense. 'I guess so, but I don't really know anything about them. We'll have to find out how to do it. In the meantime, I reckon we'll have to take this somewhere safe, away from the flat. We can't risk anybody breaking in again to nick it. They're not going to give up when this thing is worth millions.'

Dan nodded. 'Where?'

'I don't know yet. One of my friends might be able to help. I'll have a think. We'll have to do it today, though. We can't leave it here.'

'Aren't you working today?'

She glanced at the time on her phone. 'I'll have to call in sick. Come on. Let's get ready. We've got to act quickly.'

CHAPTER
SIX

FINGERLESS FRANKIE WAS A WISER MAN FOR THE FATEFUL NIGHT, THREE years earlier, that left him with fewer fingers and a new nickname.

He learned the importance of assessing a break-in target more thoroughly, instead of simply looking around the outside of the house for potential access points and signs an alarm had been installed.

He learned that fame – or infamy, call it what you like – is not all it's cracked up to be.

He also learned a lot about his pain threshold. It was not, it turned out, very high. He couldn't stand to be in it. So, instead of biting the bullet, tending his own wounds and keeping a low profile after escaping the jaws of Cassius the Dobermann Pinscher, Frankie panicked and drove himself straight to the Northern General Hospital, demanding all the pain relief they could possibly give him.

When A&E staff heard his story, about an allegedly random dog attack in the middle of the night, from a man who was either dressed to deliver a box of Milk Tray or because he was up to no good, they called in the police. The police, dealing with the

45

bloody aftermath of an attempted burglary at a domestic property in Chapeltown, quickly put two and two together and Frankie's already calamitous night took another turn for the worse.

The two men who surprised Frankie three years later, as he pulled up outside his home from a day at an antiques fair in Doncaster, didn't know how little pain he could stand. It wouldn't have made much difference if they had. Inflicting pain through violence was a way of life for them, so when the instruction came through to pick up the man their boss was particularly keen to have words with, they didn't for a moment think of politely asking him to accompany them. They kind of took it as read that they were meant to rough him up a bit first. It was part of the job and, if the truth be told, the part they enjoyed quite a lot.

Frankie had just stepped out of his battered white van when the men, with necks as thick as grizzly bears' thighs and faces as ominous as a gathering storm, pounced. One of them grabbed the back of his head and slammed his face into the side of the van with such force that his vision swam with red and green blotches and his ears rang. The second man aimed a short jabbing punch with his large fist into the soft flesh of Frankie's lower back, in the left kidney area, making his knees buckle and forcing out a low, guttural cry.

Frankie was completely suppressed. He did not resist when one of the men wrapped gaffer tape around his wrists to secure them behind his back and made no objection at all when the other fixed strips of the tape over his mouth and his eyes. They bundled him towards their vehicle and he willingly allowed them to. Once they had pushed him on to the back seat, he sat up, arching to his left to try to ease the ache from the punch, he was not even thinking about what he had done to deserve such rough treatment.

He was just relieved they were not hurting him anymore.

Whatever comfort that brought him soon passed. Twenty minutes later, secured to a chair in a cold, silent room God knows where, Frankie was giving plenty of thought to what had led him to his current predicament.

He had no idea why he had been snatched, manhandled and, basically, imprisoned. Though he hadn't lived a blameless life and had, unquestionably, upset a few people along the way, he couldn't imagine who those men might be working for and what they wanted with him. They had told him nothing. They hadn't spoken at all, not even to each other.

But as he waited to face whatever lay ahead, tormented by the silence and the mystery of his surroundings, Frankie was starkly aware of one likelihood.

This was probably going to be painful.

They left him there for what felt like an eternity. He may have been alone. It was hard to tell. In his mind's eye, he could visualise the two hired thugs standing to attention opposite him, exuding menace, waiting for the slightest excuse to hurt him again. He was desperate not to provide one. Just in case.

The only noise he could hear was the sound of his own shallow, frantic breathing through his nose as he drew in the stale air. His right leg twitched, involuntarily, up and down like he was keeping the beat for a thrash metal track. His guts rumbled and churned. As he battled against the compelling urge to relax and empty his bowel, there and then, he was punished by stabbing cramps. He fought the urge anyway, both to preserve his dignity and so that he did not upset his captors.

He had never been so scared. Compared to this, the first night in prison was like visiting a nice Airbnb in the countryside.

He was almost at the stage where he craved someone – the thugs, their boss, whoever – to tell him what he had done to offend them this badly. At least then he would know. Then he could explain how it was all some sort of misunderstanding. Turn on the Frankie patter. Try to wheedle his way out of the situation. Offer recompense if needs be. He just wanted to end the misery of uncertainty.

But then he heard a door opening in front of him and he suddenly wasn't so sure he wanted to know anymore.

His breathing quickened further as heavy footsteps approached. One pair of feet. They stopped right beside him, to his left. He wanted to scream, sob. A dark patch of urine spread on the front of his crimson tracksuit bottoms.

He felt the faint touch of rough fingertips on his cheek before the gaffer tape was ripped from his mouth, seeming to take all the skin off his dry lips with it. A yelp of pain barely had time to escape his throat before the second strip of tape was torn from across his eyes. Frankie winced, feeling as if half his eyebrow hair had been removed, and his eyes swam with tears.

Slowly, he became aware that he was in what seemed to be an empty stock room, windowless and stark, with the only light coming from a single bare bulb in the centre of the ceiling. Most alarmingly, as his vision cleared, he realised there were now three men in front of him.

The two thugs who had snatched him stood as foreboding as the guards to the gates of hell, sturdy arms crossed over their broad chests.

Between them was the newcomer. He was shorter and less physically imposing, but only by comparison. Alone and without knowing his reputation, he presented an intimidating enough figure in his own right, with his shaven head, lean body and fixed scowl. Once you knew his reputation, the impact of his appearance increased manyfold. And Frankie knew his reputation.

You didn't mess with Ronnie Bridgeman. He was the biggest name in Sheffield's criminal underworld. Would-be mobsters dare not challenge him. Small-time crooks like Frankie knew not to cross him. His status was such that he appeared untouchable, out of reach even of the law enforcers.

Frankie recognised him straight away and only then realised the dizzying scale of the danger he was in. Ronnie Bridgeman would not normally go hands-on with someone so clearly beneath him. He had plenty of underlings to administer whatever punishment he felt necessary.

Yet here he was, carefully draping his tailored pale blue pinstripe suit jacket over a chair and beginning to roll up the sleeves of his crisp white shirt. Seemingly getting ready to go hands-on in person.

So, Frankie understood then he was in big trouble.

What he still didn't understand was what he had done to deserve personal attention from the most feared man in Sheffield.

He began to cry. Uncontrollably.

Bridgeman paused, midway through rolling up his second sleeve, and surveyed the pitiful sight before him.

'Oh dear, oh dear!' He glanced either side to his two minders, who still stared impassively straight ahead at nothing in particular.

'What have you brought me here?'

Bridgeman stepped forward, finishing rolling the sleeve and unfastening the top button of his shirt to loosen his tie.

'I told you the man I'm looking for was able to disable my security gate *and* my very expensive intruder alarm *and* my home CCTV system, then crack the code to my supposedly impenetrable state-of-the-art safe and make off with close to half a million pounds-worth of my personal possessions. The man capable of doing all that must be a bastard genius and must have balls the size of watermelons for even thinking about breaking into my house in the first place.'

He turned to face the thugs with an expression of mock confusion.

'I think you must have got the wrong guy, lads. This can't be him, pissing himself all over my floor and blubbing like a soft tart. Are you sure this is the right guy?'

Neither reacted. They knew they were not meant to.

Bridgeman walked up to Frankie and leaned toward him until their heads were at the same level.

'You must forgive my boys, Frankie,' he whispered, conspiratorially. 'As you can probably tell, they're men of action, rather than words. Not very much going on up top if you get my drift. I don't employ them to think. So tell me; have we got it wrong? Was it you who broke into my house and stole my stuff?'

As the charade was playing out before him, the full horror of his situation became clear.

The big house they hit two weeks ago. His associate hadn't mentioned whose house it was. All he was told was that it would be a very lucrative night and so it was. Very lucrative. Had he realised whose house it was...

He wasn't there because of a misunderstanding. He had stolen from Frankie Bridgeman. He was doomed.

There was only one option open to him. Bluff it out.

'It wasn't me, Mr Bridgeman, I swear. I would never. I swear on my eyes.'

Bridgeman stood upright and sighed, shaking his head ruefully.

'That's very disappointing,' he said, turning to walk back towards his two henchmen.

Without need for a signal or a word, one of them sauntered towards a battered holdall close to the door and reached in, pulling from it a large pair of heavy duty bolt cutters. Frankie's eyes widened as the man carried the tool towards him and around the back of his chair.

Perhaps he was going to use them to cut him loose?

Then he felt the cold steel close around the little finger of his right hand, followed by a surge of excruciating agony as the jaws of the bolt cutters snipped through bone like they were being used to trim a twig off a rose bush.

Frankie screamed a scream to wake the dead. Every muscle of his body tensed in reaction to the savage intervention.

As his cries, unheard by anyone outside the room, died down and the initial shock gave way, Bridgeman's voice reached him again.

'That's what happens, see, when you lie to Ronnie Bridgeman. Now you can only count to seven and a half.'

He prowled in front of his wretched captive.

'You see, while you might have been smart enough to get past my security system, I've got friends who were able to show me other footage. That's how I knew it was your shitty van driving away from my place, full of my stuff, and I could see it was you and your little apprentice sitting there in the front seat. So let's try again, shall we? Was it you who broke into my house?'

There was no point trying to brazen it out further.

'Yes,' Frankie whimpered.

'Now we're getting places,' said Bridgeman with a smile.

'Next question. Where have you put all my stuff? I want it back. Every last bit of it.'

This presented Frankie with a new difficulty. He's already sold some of his share of the property they stole.

'I will, I will. I just need a bit of time.'

'Time?' Bridgeman screwed up his face as if he didn't comprehend. 'You haven't got any time. I want my stuff back and I want it *now*. Straight away. Understand?'

The rage in his tormentor's stare burned through Frankie. He would have given anything to be able to hand everything over there and then but wishing for that made it no easier a task.

'I'll get it, I swear. It's... It's just not that simple.'

Bridgeman's whole head had been pulsing through the many

shades of red on its way to purple, but he drew a deep breath and an eerily ominous calm descended over him.

'I'm normally a patient man,' he professed, though he would have been hard pushed to come up with examples to illustrate his claim. 'But, you see, the problem is this.'

He leaned in again until their noses almost touched.

'Not only did you take my Damien Hurst and the Barcelona shirt Lionel Messi's agent gave to me personally, not to mention my watches, the upset you caused my missus by taking her jewellery and the close to fifty grand in cash you snaffled. It's bad enough that you broke into my house and took all that, but what you also took was something that's even more valuable to me – something you probably didn't even realise was so important when you took it. That's what I want back more than anything else and the longer that's out of my possession, the more anxious I get. The more anxious I get, the more likely I am to hurt people. Do you get my drift? That's why my patience is wearing thinner than usual. That's why I want you to tell me where I can get what you took from me straight away. No time. No negotiating. It really is that simple.'

He took a step back.

'Now are you going to show my boys where you've put my stuff or do I start cutting off more fingers from your thieving hands?'

The man with the bolt cutters readied himself to step into position again.

'In fact, fuck it!' said Bridgeman, stopping his henchman with a raised palm. 'You swore to me on your eyes you wouldn't lie to me and you lied. I'm going to pluck your bastard eyes out!'

Frankie felt Bridgeman's left knee braced against his chest and left hand pressed against his shoulder. Helpless, terrified, he gazed deeply, for what could be the last time, into a crimson face of fury and saw the claw of Bridgeman's free hand poised to strike.

A natural ability to cajole his customers into buying what they didn't previously realise they really needed was Frankie's great talent and had served him most profitably through his criminal career.

Yet he had never been inspired to words so precious as in that moment of his greatest need, there in that dingy room, faced by a psychopathic lunatic who was about to pluck out his eyes.

'The flash drive!'

Bridgeman froze.

'What did you say?'

'The flash drive. That's what you want, isn't it? That's what's so valuable to you.'

He had Bridgeman's undivided attention now.

'What do you know about it?' he snarled.

'Nothing. I mean, I don't know what's on it. I just know it was among the things we took. It was put somewhere safe. I know where you can go to get it back.'

'Where?' It was clear to Frankie from the tone that he was far from out of imminent danger.

'We hid it in the old typewriter we took from your office. We thought it would be safe there, but then...'

Confession time.

'Then what?'

Deep breath.

'I sold it.'

Bridgeman reddened to new darker hues.

'You have got to be bastard kidding me.'

'I forgot,' pleaded Frankie. 'I forgot it was there – but it's OK. The kid I sold it to has no idea. He's not the brightest bulb, if you know what I mean. I could take you to his place and you can get it back. He's got a flat on Blackstock Road. I'll take you there now.'

Bridgeman released Frankie from his hold and stood back. He needed to think. Every instinct in his body told him not to take the word of this pathetic worm, but he had no choice. He had to get the flash drive back.

'What's his name, this kid?'

'Dan Khan. As I said, he has no clue and you'll only have to lean on him to make him give it back. I'll take you to him, then I can get you your other stuff – or most of it, at least. There's other items I might have already moved on, but if you'll give me a couple of weeks I can –'

'Quiet.'

Frankie stopped talking.

Bridgeman was still thinking. The first thing he needed to do was to dispatch the boys to see this Dan Khan and get the flash drive back. If Frankie was telling them the truth and the flash drive really was in the typewriter, he was back in full control. He was still calling all the shots.

But what if Frankie *had* seen what was on the drive? It was encrypted to protect the contents from prying eyes, but what if he'd found a way to open it? Though he gave the outward impression of being an idiot, he had managed to bypass an expensive home security system and open the safe. He must have been curious to know what was on the drive and he'd surely not say if he had opened it and had seen what was on it. He might even have made a copy. If he had seen it, he would surely realise the contents carried rich currency.

It came down to one question, as Bridgeman saw it. Could he afford to take a chance that the power of the flash drive had been compromised on the word of a man who would say anything to get out of a tight corner?

He could not. They would have to take care of Frankie. However you looked at it, he knew too much.

If that meant giving up the plan to get all his property back, then so be it. It was only stuff. The flash drive and the sway that gave him was all that really mattered.

But first things first.

'Cut him loose,' said Bridgeman. 'You're going to show my boys where this Dan Khan lives.'

CHAPTER
SEVEN

'I MESSAGED MY FRIEND HERMIE. SHE SAYS SHE'LL HELP US,' SAID Shannon.

Dan was in the bedroom, getting dressed after his shower. He stood, finely balanced with a foot halfway down one leg of his skinny jeans.

'Oh, right,' he acknowledged, pulling up the jeans and fastening the waist button. 'Who's she?'

He wouldn't normally have cared to ask, but this was an unusual situation. They had to be careful.

'We've known each other since we were five, at Primary School,' Shannon explained. 'We used to hang around together all the time, but we haven't seen each other much in the last few years, what with lockdown and everything. She lives up Walkley now. We're still in touch on WhatsApp.'

Dan remained uncertain. He was still disturbed by the previous night's brush with danger.

'And we can trust her, then, this Hermie?'

'Absolutely!' Shannon heard the ping of another message landing and took her phone from her back pocket to see who it was from.

'She can come across as a bit unfriendly, but that's just her way. Once she's your mate, she'll do anything for you and I'd trust her with my life. She's quite handy as well. She teaches women's self-defence classes. This is her now, actually.'

Shannon read the message.

'She says we can leave it at her mum and dad's house. They've got a big, converted loft. Hermie's got a car and she says she'll come to pick us up this afternoon at three.'

That certainly sounded like the kind of solution they were looking for. He had been concerned at the prospect of having to take the typewriter somewhere by bus. Dan nodded at the plan.

'What did you tell her? You know, about the typewriter?' He spoke in hushed tones with a secretive glance towards the machine where he had left it, on the bed, as if he didn't want it to appear too obvious they were discussing it and arouse its suspicions.

'I told her it was an antique left to you when your auntie died and that we didn't want to leave it in the flat because there's been a lot of break-ins around here recently. I said we wanted to take it somewhere safe until we can get it valued because we think it might be worth a few quid.'

He approved. 'That's good. No need to mention who the real previous owner was.'

'Of course not.' She sensed he was in major need of reassurance and walked around the bed to hug him.

'It'll be all right,' she said. 'I know Hermie's mum and dad and they're lovely. Fingerless Frankie would never think to look for it at their house. Once it's safe, we can find out about places that do auctions and, hopefully, we'll get enough money from the sale to take us well away from here.'

She broke the embrace to kiss him on the lips.

'I really think this can be it, Dan. I get the feeling our lives are about to change for the better.'

. . .

At just before five to three, Shannon watched from the front room window of their flat as an ageing silver Ford Fiesta pulled up on the street below.

'She's here!'

Dan perched on the edge of the sofa. He had been unable to shake an uneasy feeling all day. The typewriter was beside him in a sturdy box that had originally contained bottles of bleach. Shannon had brought it home from work one day full of groceries.

He sighed. It was time. He felt as if he would be unable to relax until the precious typewriter was safely stored away.

Shannon scooped up her house keys, ready for them to leave, but then faltered and turned to Dan. She had been thinking about this. It was best to tell him.

'You know I said Hermie can seem a bit... intense.'

'Yeah...' Something about her tone left Dan concerned about where this was going.

'Well, it's mostly for show. She just likes people to keep their distance. She's great really. Only she's particularly wary with men, especially ones she doesn't know. I once saw her smash this guy's nose with the heel of her hand just because she thought he touched her arse in a bar. I don't know if she just doesn't like men. I always kind of suspected she preferred girls, you know, but I've never known her go out with a boy or a girl. I think she just likes to keep herself to herself.'

Dan was beginning to wonder what he was letting himself in for.

'Anyway, you'll like her when you get to know her. Just don't try to give her a hug or anything, that's all.'

With that, she headed for the door. Dan stayed in his seat for a couple of seconds more, absorbing the advice, before picking up the bleach box and following her.

Hermie was leaning against the car, drawing on a cigarette. Her hair was so close-cropped as to be almost down to the scalp and was dyed shocking pink. She had piercings around practically the full curve of both ears, two rings through her left nostril and studs through her right eyebrow and bottom lip. A neck tattoo of a dagger piercing a bleeding heart peeked just above the folds of a baggy grey hoodie which had the logo of a martial arts club printed on the front. Her black jogging bottoms were loose fitting and their elasticated ankles rode just above a pair of hefty black Dr Marten boots.

Dan dared take no more than a few stolen looks. There had been no need for Shannon to warn him that Hermie wasn't the touchy-feely type. Everything about her appearance said it for her.

Stay away if you know what's good for you.

Shannon clearly knew the warning signs didn't apply to her.

'Hey, Hermie, how's it going? This is so good of you.'

She extended her arm for a fist bump. Hermie held the cigarette in her lips and returned it.

'Shan,' she said, flatly.

'This is Dan,' Shannon added, beckoning him forward.

Dan wasn't sure if he was expected to risk a fist bump as well, but the heavy box in his arms made the decision for him, so all he offered was an apologetic smile.

Hermie glanced him up and down with searching green eyes.

'Dan.'

She took the cigarette between her fingers again and sucked deeply on it before casting it contemptuously down and crushing it beneath her boot sole.

'We should go,' she said, turning to the back of the car to open the hatchback door so that the box could be put in the boot. Without saying another word, she headed back towards the driver's seat.

Dan read the unspoken invitation, glad of the chance to set his burden down, but he found no space in the boot. It was crammed with chest pads, boxing gloves, headguards and what appeared to be a weapon made of two short sticks linked by a thick chain.

'Is it OK if I move some of your stuff out of the way?' he asked. It was better to ask.

'Yeah,' came the weary reply. 'I've got a class later.'

Balancing the box on the tailgate, he struggled to make enough room to fit everything in and slammed the door shut before anything else could fall out.

Dan sat quietly in the back seat while Shannon filled her friend in on everything she had learned about their mutual acquaintances since the last time they met. Hermie lit another cigarette.

Dan was more at ease once they had stowed the typewriter in the loft but was never at his most comfortable in the company of strangers in a strange place. Hermie's parents were welcoming and friendly, as Shannon promised they would be, and insisted that their visitors stay for a meal.

Shannon and Hermie's mum, Melissa, did most of the talking at the table, with her dad, Simon, chipping in with the occasional quip and Shannon occasionally, unsuccessfully, trying to draw Dan into the conversation. There seemed to be a general acceptance that Hermie would not be required to join in.

After the meal, Simon made the excuse of having a work-related email that needed attending to and took himself away upstairs as the rest of them went through to the living room with coffees. Dan sat stiffly, nursing his cup, while Shannon and Melissa continued their catching-up and Hermie distracted herself with her phone.

Shortly, Melissa announced she was going to load the dishwasher with the pans and crockery they had left in the kitchen after the meal and Shannon volunteered to join her in the task. With view, no doubt, to talking some more.

Dan was abandoned. Worse than being left alone, which he would not have minded in the slightest, he was left alone with Hermie.

If the awkwardness affected her at all, Hermie did not show it. She remained absorbed by whatever was on her phone, apparently oblivious to the presence of another, acutely self-conscious, person in the room.

Three and three quarter strained minutes later, Dan could stand the sound of silence no longer.

'Cool hair.'

The sudden disturbance made Hermie look up from the screen.

'What?' The word was issued like a challenge.

'Your hair,' he explained, defensively. 'I think it looks cool.'

She stared at him for a few seconds as if working out the threat level of the observation, before turning back to her phone in acceptance that the words were relatively harmless.

'Oh,' she said, adding as an afterthought, 'Thanks.'

'Like the tats as well,' he ventured, feeling bolder, though he drew the line at asking if she had other tattoos, apart from the ones he could see on her neck and what he imagined to be the end of a full-arm sleeve seeping beyond the cuff of her hoodie. That might have been deemed too intrusive.

Hermie ignored the compliment.

Dan thought about what he could say next.

'Your name's unusual,' was the best he could manage under the pressure of otherwise returning to an uneasy silence. 'I've never heard of anybody called that before. Is it short for something?'

She sighed. This was becoming an irritation. She considered for a moment saying it was short for something random, like hermaphrodite or hermit crab, just to see if this bloke was really as gormless as he seemed but couldn't be bothered making the effort.

'Hermione,' she replied through gritted teeth.

'Yeah?' The revelation brightened him. He found that genuinely interesting. 'Like the girl in Harry Potter?'

'Yeah, like the girl in Harry Potter,' she confirmed, wearily dragging the words out.

This was the closest Dan had felt to having something in common with her. He wasn't about to let the topic rest there.

'So, did your mum and dad decide to call you that after watching the films? Or did they read one of the books? I bet it was weird watching the films yourself when one of the characters had the same name as you.'

The sting of a million childhood taunts and a million stupid childish jokes made her prickle for the first time in a long time. Having that name had contributed heavily to many miserable school days.

'Never seen them.'

'You should,' added Dan, totally failing to recognise the sensitivity of what he had stirred up. 'I've seen four of the films and I read one of the books. It was brilliant.'

There was another brief lull before he added: 'You know what, though, I didn't expect your name to be spelt like that. If I'd read it before I'd seen the films, I think I'd have said it completely wrong. I'd have said it Hermie-wan – you know, like Obi-Wan.'

That was as much conversation as she could stand.

'Look, I've got to get ready for my class. If you and Shan want a lift back, we'll have to go now,' she said, getting to her feet and pushing the phone into the pocket of her jogging bottoms.

Without waiting for an answer, Hermie headed towards the kitchen to give the same message to her friend.

Dan watched her go, a momentary urge to protest dying in his throat. He was a bit miffed the chat had been cut short. Just when they seemed to be hitting it off as well.

EIGHT

Q<small>UARTER OF AN HOUR LATER, THE THREE OF THEM WERE IN</small> H<small>ERMIE'S</small> car, heading back to the flat. It was a quiet trip. Shannon, normally the one to take the lead, appeared to have talked herself out and neither of the other two showed any inclination to fill the role.

Hermie chain-smoked all the way, making up for being deprived of nicotine stimulus for too long at her parents' house, and Dan spent most of the journey trying to avoid the cigarette fumes which blew back at him in the rear seat whenever she exhaled towards the wide-open driver's side window.

Shannon idly watched the city landscape change from desirable Totley to less desirable Gleadless Valley through her side window, lost in thought, until the sight of flashing blue lights snapped her out of her contemplation. The fading early evening haze made it hard to be sure, at first, but as they drove further up the hill she could tell two police cars were parked near to their flat.

'What's going on?' she asked.

Dan craned forward to peer between the front seat headrests. It was not unusual to see police activity in the neighbourhood, but this time it was too close to home to disregard. As they drew nearer, they could see for sure the two cars were right outside their four-story block.

Hermie turned off the main road and on to a side street, past the two police cars, to find a space to pull in. Their piercing lights made the three of them squint.

'I'll wait here,' she said, turning off the engine.

Shannon and Dan climbed out of the car without replying, anxious concern tying tight knots in their stomachs. Whatever was at the focus of the activity, it most likely involved someone they knew and was almost certainly not good news.

They stepped rapidly towards the flats. A small cluster of neighbours had gathered on the pavement, sharing whatever little information they held as they awaited the latest developments. Shannon recognised one of them as the elderly lady who shared the flat above with her no-good grown-up son. Had he got himself in bother again?

'Hi, Mrs Nelson. What's happening?'

The old lady, wrapped in a well-worn long green coat which covered her almost to the tops of her pink carpet slippers, reacted to the voice as if she had heard a call from beyond the grave, but then threw her hands and eyes to the skies when she recognised the familiar face.

'Shannon, my love, thank God you're both safe.' Though she had lived in Sheffield since the late 1970s, she had not lost her Jamaican twang. 'I was thinkin' somethin' awful must have happened to you.'

Dan had moved past the group to try to get a better view of what was holding everybody's interest.

The blue and white tape stopped him getting as close as he would have liked. It cordoned off the approach to the central stairwell; the one they used to get to their flat on the first floor. One end of the tape was tied to a drainpipe and the other to the front door handle of one of the police cars. Dan took hold of it as it flapped in the wind.

POLICE LINE DO NOT CROSS

He peered upwards at the chipped white paint of the railings of their tiny balcony and tried to spot any signs of activity inside. There wasn't any, as far as he could tell, but it was hard to be sure. He scanned the outside of the other flats and couldn't see any clues to suggest which one the police were taking an interest in.

'Could you step back from the tape please, sir.'

A young officer in a peaked police cap and a yellow hi-vis vest was walking towards Dan, gesturing with the flat palms of both hands for him to move away.

'I live here,' he replied, letting go of the tape but standing his ground.

Shannon appeared at his shoulder. She was flushed, agitated. She spoke to the policeman.

'What is it? Our neighbour said she dialled nine-nine-nine because she heard noises from our flat like the place was being taken apart and then heard screams. You've got to let us in.'

The officer realised this was not a couple he should be moving on.

'Could I ask which flat is yours?'

'That one,' said Dan, pointing to the balcony. 'Number twenty-nine.'

'Sarge.' The officer spoke into the radio fixed to the left shoulder strap of his vest.

'Yes, Jamie' came the reply after a short delay.

'Two people who say they are the flat's occupants have just arrived at the stairwell.'

Another pause.

'I'm on my way.'

The policeman nodded at Dan and Shannon. There was no need to keep them informed. They had plainly heard the conversation. They both turned to face the stairwell.

A middle-aged woman with short, dark hair and brown-framed glasses was making her way down the steps towards them. She was dressed the same as her colleague, except for the three stripes on her epaulettes and the blue disposable gloves on her hands.

'My name's Sergeant Thackeray. You say you live in flat twenty-nine.' The words were issued almost as if they were a challenge requiring proof.

'We do,' confirmed Shannon. 'Can you tell us what's going on?'

'In good time,' said the Sergeant, firmly. 'Let's begin by you telling me where you've been for the last few hours.'

'With my friend at her parents' house in Totley. What's that got to do with anything? My neighbour said there were people in our flat.'

'There appears to have been a break-in, yes.' She was prepared to concede that much but little else. 'Are you able to corroborate your story about where you've been?'

'Of course we can.' Shannon was getting irritated and snapped out the reply.

'And apart from what your neighbour has just told you, do you know what might have taken place here?'

'We've only just got back, how could we –?'

'When the report was called in to control we were given the impression a suspected assault was taking place. Has there been anyone else staying in your flat?'

'No. Just the two of us.'

'Have you any thoughts as to who might have wanted to break into your flat? Are you involved in any ongoing disputes?

Have there been any other attempts to enter your property recently?'

Dan and Shannon's eyes met. Their thoughts remained unspoken, but they were the same.

'Someone got in,' Dan stammered. 'Last night. I scared them off. They didn't take anything.'

'I see.' The Sergeant reached for her notebook and gave a deep sigh. 'And did you report this to the police?'

'Not yet. We...' Shannon was on the defensive now. 'We were going to, only...'

'They didn't take anything,' repeated Dan.

The Sergeant was allowing no benefit of doubt in her stare. Any call-out to this part of town automatically spelled hassle in her experience. No such thing as a straight answer from anybody and ingrained mistrust on both sides. No doubt this pair had something to hide as well. They all did.

'Look, I'm going to need you to make a statement about last night, but first I'm going to take you upstairs to see if you can tell me what might have been stolen. It's a bit of a mess up there, but you can't touch or move anything, understand? The Scene of Crime Officers are on their way and I don't want anything disturbed.'

She held the two of them in an icy glare, defying them to disobey her command. They shrunk, subdued, and prepared themselves for whatever lay ahead. The Sergeant turned to lead them up the stairs. They ducked under the tape and, instinctively, reached out to each other to hold hands for comfort.

Even the ever-present stale urine smell of the stairwell did not get to them this time. They followed the officer as if they were being led to their doom.

The front door to the flat was still slightly ajar and the Sergeant met resistance as she pushed it wider open. Shannon and Dan held back as she took a first step into the flat and gave a sharp flick of her head to gesture them closer.

They took the cue, edging forward with trepidation, and held their breath as they turned to see the scene for the first time.

A bit of a mess, the officer had said. *Appears to have been a break-in*, she said before that.

Appears to?

The flat was completely trashed. Nothing was as they had left it. Nothing looked to still be intact. Furniture was toppled, drawers emptied and their contents scattered. The cushions of their sofa were slashed, yellow foam spilling from its gaping wounds.

This was only one room. What was the rest of it like?

Shannon could not take it all in. It was overwhelming. Yet in among all the mess, her eye was drawn to three small shattered pink figures. The three ceramic flying pigs she had brought home from work one day because she saw them on display and they made her smile. Dan had hung them on the wall, in formation, on panel pins. She loved her pigs. They'd even knocked her pigs off the wall and smashed them.

It was too much. Not just the pigs. Everything.

The flat wasn't a grand one, by any means, but it was their together home. Their little nest.

Now look at it. Ruined. Forever sullied.

She burst into tears.

Dan was shocked beyond any sort of emotional reaction by the sight of the room but having to watch his Shan's heart break like this was more than he could bear.

Tears welled in his eyes, too, but they were angry tears.

He wanted retribution.

And he knew who should pay.

'I know who did this,' he blurted. The Sergeant glanced up at him and read the deep fury in his face.

'Fingerless Frankie Aston. He's the one. He sold me something but then he wanted it back and he got mad when I wouldn't sell it him. It wasn't him in the flat last night, but you can bet it was somebody he sent. He's behind this. I'm sure of it.'

The Sergeant was taken aback, not only by the sudden unexpected burst of cooperation but because of the vehemence in the accusation. She was familiar with Aston's reputation. He was a thief, a wide boy, but wanton destruction wasn't his usual m.o.

'You need to find Fingerless Frankie and arrest him. That's what you should do. He did this.'

Dan had been addressing only the tangled mess of his front room as he delivered his revelation, but he turned to glare straight at the officer. His expression, already grim and enraged, blackened to even deeper shades of wrath.

'But I'll tell you what, you'd better find him soon because if I find him first, I'm going to fucking kill him.'

One stern lecture about the perils of taking the law into your own hands and one brief joint statement later, the Sergeant advised Shannon and Dan to pack a few things in an overnight bag and find alternative accommodation for the night. It was half past nine and the Scene of Crime team had only just arrived. Faced with such a tangled mess, they would be a while yet.

They were happy to take the advice. Every room of their small two-storey flat was the same. Destruction. Devastation. It was as if the whole building had been tipped upside down and shaken. The heartbreak of it all drained them to the point of exhaustion. They certainly could not face hanging on for the police to finish so that they could begin the long tidying-up process. That would have to wait for another day. They just needed to get out of there now.

But where could they go?

Dan carried the small gym holdall into which they had crammed a few essentials as they trudged silently down the stairs. The blue tape had been taken away and one of the patrol cars had left, but there was another police vehicle in its place; the one used by the white-suited SOCOs. The small huddle of neighbours had long since dispersed.

A biting wind met them as they stepped out onto the road, as if to remind them they were now temporarily homeless and vulnerable. It chilled them to the bone. They were rooted to the spot, unsure which direction to turn.

'Hey!'

The call startled them. They turned towards it. Stood beside a battered silver Ford Fiesta with a cigarette glowing in her hand as she waved it above her pink head was Hermie.

Shannon was so glad to see her friend she felt she might cry again. Dan was so relieved he wanted to hug her.

Maybe best not, though, thinking on.

With a new spring in their step, they headed towards Hermie like she was handing out free money at a shopping centre.

'What are you still doing here? You had a class,' said Shannon.

'I phoned in and cancelled.'

'But you didn't have to do that. We didn't expect you to wait for us.'

Hermie shrugged, as if any course of action other than waiting had not occurred to her.

'Is it bad?' she asked.

'Wrecked,' Shannon replied, sadly. 'They've taken the place apart.'

Hermie nodded.

'You can stop at mine if you'd like.'

'Could we? We've nowhere else. It'll only be till we're straight again.'

The truth was Shannon was already wondering if she could face living in the flat anymore. It could never be the same.

'Course.' Hermie opened the driver's side door and flicked away her cigarette. 'You'd better get in then.'

'Thank you, Hermie,' said Shannon.

'Thanks, Hermie,' added Dan, as he took up his place in the back.

The Fiesta sparked into life and the car pulled away with its grateful cargo.

Twenty yards further back down the road, on the opposite side, the driver of a white Range Rover also started the engine and pulled out, holding back just behind but within close watching distance of the small silver car ahead.

CHAPTER
NINE

RONNIE BRIDGEMAN POURED WHISKY INTO HIS EXPENSIVE CRYSTAL GLASS tumbler and slugged it back in one gulp. The shock of it hit the back of his throat and caused him to break into an involuntary grimace, but it did the job. He needed that. He tipped out another half-glassful from the decanter.

It had been a trying day. Trying and, ultimately, fruitless. The flash drive was still out there. Somewhere. He had believed working his powers of persuasion on Fingerless Frankie would resolve the matter, but that pathetic, lying sneak thief had led them on a wild goose chase.

He won't be doing that again.

The situation would have to be accelerated now. Bridgeman had wanted to avoid doing that, if at all possible, but he could see no alternative. He took a sip of whisky and carried his glass upstairs to his office. Vanessa was out, so he could make this call without her listening over his shoulder and then, after he had hung up, pointing out how he should have handled the conversation better. He hated when she did that.

The office was considerably more spartan than it had been. He had made no effort to get new stuff, to replace all that had been stolen from him in the break-in. He had believed he would recover it all. That might not happen now. The person who knew where all his stuff was stashed was no longer in a position to impart such information.

Bridgeman had, however, bought a new desk to replace the one that had felt the brunt of his frustration and the furious assault with a brass paper knife. The new one was vintage oak with a green leather writing surface. As soon as he saw it, he knew it was classy, befitting a man of his standing. He set his tumbler of whisky down on it and eased himself into the Chesterfield swivel chair. The leather groaned as he leaned back into it and took his phone from his inside jacket pocket.

He hesitated. No. Not this one.

Bridgeman tossed the phone onto the desk and opened the top drawer to his left. He reached in and fumbled under the lip of the desktop to where he had secured his other phone with tape.

The content of this conversation would be sensitive. It needed to be made on a phone that was untraceable, in case anybody was listening in. You can never be too sure.

There was only one number programmed into it. He pressed 'dial'.

He knew he would have to leave it ringing for a while. He could picture the scene at the other end. There would be a scramble and curses as the identical phone was dragged out from wherever it was hidden. Bridgeman smiled to himself at the thought of the disruption he was causing to an otherwise peaceful evening at home.

'What is it?'

He wasn't pleased. Of course he wasn't. There was only one person it could be when that phone rang and he never had the slightest desire to talk to that person. It was never good news.

Bridgeman knew that. He revelled in the power he held in

their relationship. Bridgeman called and the other one had to jump. That was so gratifying.

'I need you to do something,' he said.

An undisguised groan sounded on the other end of the line.

'What now?'

Bridgeman would normally have said something to deliberately rile at this point, but not this time. This was too serious and he was partly to blame for the scale of the problem.

'We have an issue. One of the flash drives is missing.'

'What!' The word erupted with much more force than he intended. 'What do you mean, missing?' he hissed in his more usual secretive whisper.

'It was stolen from me.' No need to fill in the details of how. That might undermine his authority.

'Jesus Christ!'

There was a pause. He was rattled.

'What are you going to do to get it back? You must be able to find out who took it.'

Bridgeman appreciated the unintended compliment. For someone in that position to acknowledge the scope of the influence he wielded fed his ego.

'I know who took it.'

'Then what's the problem? Find him and take it back.'

'It's not that simple. I picked him up but he says he doesn't have it anymore. He said somebody else has got it and gave me a name.'

The voice at the other end of the line was becoming increasingly exasperated.

'Do what you have to do. What are you telling me for? This is your problem. Handle it.'

Bridgeman felt his temper rise. Somebody needed to be put back in their place.

'No. I'm making it your problem now. My information is it

was hidden within an item that was also stolen from me and that the new owner wasn't aware what it contained, but that person has gone to ground. I had my boys give his place a good going-over this afternoon and the flash drive wasn't there. Neither was the item it was hidden inside. To my mind, this means one of two things. Either the story I was told from the thief who stole the flash drive was a pack of lies, or the person it was passed on to has scarpered. I've seen stronger men break under the kind of duress I put the thief under and still he stuck to his story, which leaves me inclined to believe he was telling the truth. That leaves the second possibility. The one who now has it has got wind of the situation and has taken off. He knows something. Why else would he do a runner and leave behind everything else he owns apart from this one item that contains the flash drive, eh? He might not have twigged the full significance yet, but I need you to get your people to track him down before he realises what he has and does something stupid which exposes us. I don't think we want that to happen, do we?'

Neither of them wanted that, for sure.

'OK. I'll do what I can. What's the name?'

'I'll text it you.'

'Right. What about the other guy – the one who stole from you? What are we going to do about him?'

Bridgeman drew a breath.

'That situation has been resolved.'

Silence. Realisation.

'Jesus Christ! You can't just go around –'

'Mind what you're saying!' Burner phone or not, Bridgeman's concern about the possibility of being under surveillance bordered on paranoia.

'You just can't do that. There's only so much I can protect you against.'

76

'Don't tell me what I can and can't do. You do what I bastard tell you to do and that's all, got it?'

The words hung menacingly in the air between them.

'Text me whatever you have on your man.' The other one knew it was an argument he could not win.

'Find him, tell me where he is and leave the rest to me. I don't want your lot getting involved any more than that. And I want it done straight away.'

Silence.

'Understood?'

He sighed. 'Yeah, got it.'

Bridgeman hung up.

It still irritated him that he needed to involve people outside his organisation, but Dan Khan didn't move in circles that would make him known to those who normally acted as his eyes and ears. This needed to be sorted quickly and he had this resource at his disposal, so why not use it? To try to manage without would be like leaving his Aston Martin on the drive and taking the bus.

All that mattered was getting the flash drive back. Once he had it, he could tidy up the remaining loose ends. Khan's silence would have to be guaranteed. He had no idea who this kid was, but that was the way it had to be. Khan shouldn't have got involved in the first place.

Bridgeman picked up his tumbler and drained the rest of the whisky.

CHAPTER
TEN

From the first floor flat window, Sergeant Alice Thackeray watched as the young couple climbed into a waiting silver car and were driven away.

She had done the right thing by suggesting they leave and was relieved they apparently had somewhere else to stay. It had been tough to see how distraught they were at the sight of their flat in such a state of complete desolation. They didn't deserve that. They weren't as bad as some of the toerags she often encountered on this estate. She had run their names through the Connect system to check if they were caught up in anything that might explain why they were targeted this way and the check had come back clean. Maybe they really were innocent victims of a pretty savage attack on their home.

So she took pity on them. She noted their details, jotted down a brief statement and told them to leave. It was the kind thing to do. They had been told to come into the station to give a formal, complete statement in the next couple of days when they had their heads back together.

Frankie Aston. The notorious Fingerless Frankie. It would be well worth hauling him in for a chat in the next day or two as well, to see if he really was behind this. The male resident, Mr Khan, had fervently insisted he was. He had no proof, though. It was never a bad thing to put the squeeze on slippery customers like Frankie Aston, all the same, but this didn't feel like his handiwork.

Sergeant Thackeray turned back from looking out of the window to face the turmoil of the small living room again. She would have liked to have been able to get away herself when she sent the couple on their way, but they had to stay while the SOCOs did their thing. Her young PC, Jamie Farrell, was supervising upstairs.

With luck, the SOCOs would quickly take their photos and try to lift a few prints at the key access points and then they could all get out of there. There really was little point picking through all this debris for clues, especially as nothing appeared to have been stolen. Maybe something among all this might give them something to pin it on Fingerless Frankie, but the chances of finding that were minimal. It would mean a lot of effort with the remote potential of reward.

She checked her watch. It was approaching the end of the shift. She didn't want to be here on her own time.

'Excuse me, Sergeant.'

The SOCO in her white, hooded all-in-one suit and purple gloves was on her knees close to where a table had been tipped over.

'There are blood stains on the carpet. There's quite a bit of it here and here and I think it's quite fresh.'

The Sergeant moved to take a closer look over the shoulder of the SOCO.

'I noticed it when I moved this paper out of the way. There's blood on it, see?'

The SOCO held up a pad of A4 sheets which had a cartoon smiling pink unicorn printed in the top right corner. At the bottom of the sheet were three crimson blotches, still wet from where it had, until a few seconds before, lay face down on the stains on the carpet.

Thackeray took out her torch and shone it where the SOCO was pointing. There was one larger patch about the size of a side plate, still glistening in the light of the torch, and half a dozen or more smaller spots.

'Document it and take whatever samples you can. Could you try to clear a larger area around here as well, to see if there's any more blood?'

The SOCO nodded. 'Sure.'

Thackeray stepped back. This could be getting more serious than she expected. She remembered that the call from control specified cries had been heard coming from the flat, suggesting to the person who reported it that an assault might be taking place. That was why two cars were dispatched straight away. An ordinary break-in, especially in this type of neighbourhood, might not have drawn such an urgent response.

'Oh!' said the SOCO. 'You're going to want to see this.'

It was within two feet of the blood stains. It lay partly underneath the toppled table but could plainly be seen because the table was propped up by having fallen on a discarded seat cushion. As the Sergeant shone her torch on it, she would have guessed index and almost certainly a male's. But it was definitely severed and it was definitely a human finger.

CHAPTER

ELEVEN

THE JOLT OF THE CAR BEING BUMPED UP THE LOW KERB OF THE PAVEMENT awoke Shannon and Dan as if from a dream, though neither had been asleep for any part of the 20-minute drive. How could they sleep? Both spent the full journey lost in their thoughts, each reliving the nightmare they had driven away from but could not leave behind. Images of their ransacked home had burned deep into the back of their eyes.

Hermie pulled on the handbrake and turned off the engine. She stepped out of the driver's door and on to the pavement almost before the seatbelt had recoiled back into place.

Shannon unclipped her seatbelt and checked to make sure no traffic was heading down the narrow road towards her before opening the door and climbing wearily out. She sighed deeply and turned for the pavement around the back of the car but stopped when she noticed her friend, rigidly still and staring intently down the hill. Shannon followed the direction of her gaze towards the red taillights of a large white car picking its way carefully through the slender gap left by vehicles parked on either side.

'What is it?'

Only when the car had disappeared from view did Hermie break the apparent thrall the white car had cast on her.

'Nothing,' she replied, dismissively.

Dan emerged from the back seat, clutching his black holdall. Hermie locked the car.

'This way.'

She headed for a passageway that cut between two of the houses in a terraced row. Such was the steepness of the hill they had clung to for well over a century that the front door and windows of the house on the left of the passage was staggered, the height of four brown stone bricks, lower than its neighbour to the right. It was late evening now and the terrace was illuminated by the streetlamps on the opposite side of the road. Shannon looked around her to take in her new surroundings. It was nothing grand, but it was nice. Better than the area around their flat. She sighed again. Their flat.

'You OK?'

Dan touched her shoulder and squeezed lightly. She forced a smile and nodded.

'Let's go inside.'

They took each other by the hand again, even though it was only for a few short steps along the path between the slender strips of neglected front yards in front of the terrace. The passageway was only wide enough for one person at a time. They emerged from it before two neat, narrow gardens, hemmed in by high privet hedges and separated by a wooden fence. The door of the house to their left was open and welcoming lights shone brightly from inside. Dan gestured for Shannon to go in first.

She stepped into a tidy modern kitchen and turned to go through a doorway to her left. Hermie was at the far end of the living room, glancing up and down the road outside between the slats of a blind. When she realised she was no longer alone, she stopped the surveillance and drew the blue curtains closed, as if that was the purpose of her being there all along.

Shannon was too absorbed by the décor to notice her friend's behaviour. If she had taken time to imagine what the inside of Hermie's home looked like, it would have been nothing like this. The fresh pale walls, the dark wooden flooring, the brown leather sofa stretching along the length of one wall opposite the wall-mounted TV and old-style wood burner fire set into a crimson-backed fireplace. In her eyes, it looked like a show home.

'Hermie, this is lovely!'

Dan stepped beside her and blinked.

'Yeah. Lovely.'

Hermie did not allow herself the moment of pride she had been invited to share.

'I like it,' she said with a shrug. 'I'll show you where you can sleep.'

She grabbed the white painted handrail of the open staircase leading from the corner of the room, beside the front door, and they followed.

'There's an air mattress. You'll have to pump it up,' said Hermie as she came to a halt beside a small back bedroom. 'Just move the boxes out of the way. I'll get the spare quilt and some pillows for you in a bit.'

Shannon and Dan caught her up. It was a small room but it was fine. They edged inside and Dan put down the holdall.

'Hermie, I can't thank you enough for this,' said Shannon, turning, but Hermie was already walking away.

'S'all right,' she muttered.

They looked around. By the look of the wallpaper, it used to be a small child's room quite a long time ago, but its role now was as a store for everything that had no place in the rest of the house. The deflated air mattress was rolled out over a tatty blue carpet and almost completely hidden under plastic storage boxes, piles of unwanted clothing and spare combat training gear, suggesting Hermie didn't often accommodate overnight visitors.

Dan began stacking the debris at the side of the room to clear the space. The foot pump was still attached and he pressed down on it three times, reassured to hear the hiss of the air going into the mattress.

Shannon stayed at the door, showing no sign of being about to help get the room in shape for their stay. She could not muster the will. Dan glanced up to see her standing, motionless, and could tell the mattress wasn't the only thing in the room feeling flat.

'It'll only be for a day or two,' he said, setting down a stack of ring binder files.

'Hmm,' she replied, unconvincingly.

He took a step towards her, but she turned to go.

'I need a wee,' she said, her fragile voice disappearing down the hallway.

By the time she returned, Dan had fully made the room habitable and had inflated the mattress. He was concerned. She was not right. He searched her face as she stepped back into the frame of the door. She had clearly been crying.

This time, she welcomed his approach and fell into the offered embrace.

'It will be all right, Shan,' he whispered softly.

'But it won't, though,' she sobbed. 'It's not all right. Our home has been wrecked. Everything we had has been trashed. We've got to start all over again and we're going to have to find another place to live. I can't move back into that flat. Not after this. I'd never feel safe again.'

The tears were flowing again. Even though he knew he was blameless, Dan felt he had let her down.

'We'll find somewhere new. Somewhere better. Once we sell the typewriter...'

'That fucking typewriter!'

The sharpness of her reaction pierced him.

'I wish I'd never seen that fucking typewriter! All this is because of that. We were fine before you brought that thing back home. It's cursed. Now look at us!'

'Shan, you don't mean that. It's not the typewriter's fault, it's that bastard Fingerless Frankie. He's to blame for...'

'Why didn't you just sell it back to him, Dan? Even if you'd just given it him without getting your fifty quid back we'd have been better off than we are now. You can never mess about with criminals. They can turn nasty if they don't get their way. What if we'd still been in the flat when he came round with his heavies to tear the place apart? He could have killed us both. You don't get on the wrong side of people like that.'

Dan understood her unease. He shared it, but if she was right about it being his fault, how the situation had gone so badly wrong, it was his job now to try to dispel the worst of her agitation.

'He won't get away with this, Shan. We know it was him and when we go to the police station, to give them a proper statement, they'll arrest him and they'll lock him up. He's gone too far this time and the police will make him pay. They'll get him.'

'And then what?' Shannon pulled back from him. Her eyes were red and watery but ablaze. 'What happens when he's done his time? He'll be in prison for what – a few weeks? A couple of months? Do you think he'll just forget about us after he gets out? He'll come for us. He'll want revenge. It doesn't matter if we get a flat somewhere new, we're always going to be looking over our shoulders, waiting for Frankie to find us. His type doesn't move on.'

'The police are going to protect us.' Dan was dredging for every ounce of faith in their future wellbeing. 'They can put orders in place to stop him coming anywhere near us. Besides, he'll know that if anything was to happen, the police will come and get him and put him away again. Even Frankie isn't that stupid.'

From Shannon's expression, looking over his shoulder, he could tell they were no longer alone. Dan spun around to see Hermie at the door with a pile of pillows and bedding.

'I need to get the duvet,' she said. Dan took the pile from her and Hermie quickly made her exit.

Dan lowered the load onto the mattress.

'We have to tell her,' said Shannon. 'We might be putting Hermie in danger by being here. She has to know the full picture and then she can decide if she's still willing to let us stay.'

He nodded. It was the right thing to do.

Hermie was sitting at one end of the brown leather sofa as they walked hesitatingly down the stairs to the living room. She was upright, with her arms folded and head cocked slightly to one side, studying a mixed martial arts bout on the TV with intense scrutiny like it was an information film on international shipping law. Her stare remained fixed on the screen, even when Shannon eased herself down at the opposite end of the sofa. Dan remained standing and shuffled uncomfortably.

It seemed rude to interrupt and Shannon waited for a sign that it was appropriate for her to speak. Hermie did not flinch, even as the TV commentator exploded into hysterics when a hapless competitor was sent spinning into unconscious oblivion by a blow from his opponent's foot to his jaw.

'Can we talk?' Shannon offered, tentatively.

Only when the victor began celebrating over the prone body of his defeated foe did Hermie acknowledge the request. 'Fire away,' she said, turning off the TV with the remote on the chair arm.

Shannon told her how they had acquired the typewriter they had left with Hermie's parents in a deal with a sordid crook called Fingerless Frankie and that it was not part of a recently departed aunt's legacy, as they had originally suggested. Before they came down to have the talk, she and Dan had agreed not to divulge the more exotic details of the typewriter's history just yet. They did, however, explain how their suspicions of its value as an antique were seemingly confirmed by Frankie's attempts to buy it back. They revealed how Frankie had sent an accomplice to break into their flat to steal it back the night before and how Dan had valiantly fought off the raider. They then went into the full sorry detail of how Frankie and his gang had vented his fury on their flat following a second break-in and how that had left them fearing for their safety until they could be sure Frankie was securely in police custody.

Hermie listened without a flicker of sympathetic emotion.

'So you've already told the police who's responsible?' she said after carefully absorbing the information.

'We have, but they said they want us to give a full statement in the next couple of days,' Shannon replied. 'I don't know if that means they can't arrest him yet.'

Hermie considered the possibility. 'It shouldn't make a difference. They'll want to pick him up for questioning. Get his side of the story. Once you give them yours, he'll be arrested. Do you want me to take you to the station tomorrow?'

'Maybe.' Shannon and Dan exchanged a glance. 'Can we see how we feel? I'm not sure I'm ready for it yet.'

'Up to you.' Hermie picked up the remote again and turned the TV back on.

'The thing is,' Shannon interrupted. There was still an important point to raise. 'We don't want to put you in danger. Frankie doesn't know we're here with you, but what if he does find out? He's a bad man.'

Hermie stalled. The white Range Rover. She was sure it had followed them from the flat.

'I can handle it. You're safe here.'

She folded her arms and gave her full attention back to the MMA.

Intuitively, Shannon and Dan both also turned their eyes to the screen, but their minds were not on the action. They wanted to be assured but could not escape the dreaded fear that it could be them who would soon be pummelled by a violent assailant, like the man on the TV.

TWELVE

THE BEEP-BEEP-BEEP OF THE REVERSING GREEN AND WHITE TRUCK pierced the thin early morning light like the unwelcome shrill of an electronic alarm clock. It had been many hours since everyone in the supermarket service yard had been rudely stirred from their slumbers, though. The deliveries of fresh produce had been arriving at the yard to be unloaded, unpacked and stacked since it was still dark. It was like that every day. The vast store had an insatiable appetite and the driver now backing up to loading bay three would be followed by many more before the last shoppers made their way from the tills at midnight.

It was almost seven and, for Vaclav, that meant it was almost the end of his cleaning shift. He stifled a yawn as he leaned against the heavy security door to prop it open with his hip while he pulled out a shopping trolly full of rubbish bags. He didn't mind being the one who usually made the trip to the bins. He was the only man in the cleaning team and the lids on the large bins were too heavy for some of the others. Where he came from, it was considered the right thing for the man to take on the most physically demanding tasks.

The trolly rattled as he pushed it across the rough concrete surface of the service yard, past the tightly-bound piles of compressed cardboard boxes and the stacks of blue plastic pallets. It was chilly and there was a mist of drizzle hanging in the air. Vaclav was looking forward to getting done and getting away. Home was a twenty-five minute walk from there, but he would be back to have breakfast with the kids before seeing them off to school. Then he liked to doze in the chair for an hour before getting ready to leave for the second of his three part-time jobs, at a warehouse on the little industrial estate just off London Road.

There were two large red general waste bins in the far corner of the yard. Even though the rest of the enclosed area was well lit, that corner always seemed to linger in shadowy darkness. That was another reason why the others were happy to leave this task to Vaclav. It spooked some of them.

The following day was when the bins were due to be emptied and Vaclav knew that the one to the left was practically full already. There was room in the one on the right. He pushed the trolly forward using one hand and his belly to steer while he reached with the other hand into his trouser pocket for the keys. The bins were always padlocked. Not this day, though. As he picked out the correct key and went to insert it, he realised the lock was already open.

Somebody on the late shift has messed up. The store manager would not be happy. Vaclav considered for a moment if he should report this but he didn't want to get anybody into trouble. It was only a bin. It was not as if there was anything worth stealing in it. He lifted the bulky black lid high until it flopped back, fully open, and turned to take the first two bags from the trolly.

As he flipped in the first of them, he stopped. The large blue bag at the top of the rubbish pile in the bin was not like the type they used in the store. It was more like the heavy-duty sacks used by builders. As he looked closer, Vaclav could tell it was actually two bags, bound together with a thick swathe of lots of grey gaffer tape. It was unusual for anything this big and bulky to end up here. Perhaps somebody who worked there had decided to use the company's large bins to get rid of their private waste because they couldn't be bothered to take it to the council tip.

The store manager really wouldn't like that.

Vaclav shrugged. It was none of his business. He tossed in the second of the bags he was carrying and went back to the trolly to get the rest.

As he was stretching to pull down the lid, he noticed there was a hole in the bottom of the large blue sack. That would not have bothered him at all normally, but what caught his eye was the shape. It was familiar. A white outlined figure with a ball at the end of an outstretched arm.

His curiosity was stirred. He pulled at the hole to make it bigger. He was right. It looked and felt like the blue and black sole of a training shoe and the white figure was the Air Jordan logo. Judging by the soles, they were pretty new. Certainly not worn out. Who would want to throw out a perfectly decent pair of Air Jordans?

If it is a pair.

Vaclav took a sneaky look over his shoulder. The shadows were protecting him. If he could make the hole big enough to pull out this shoe and then locate the other one, it could be quite a find. With luck, they would be close enough to his size. If not, he could sell them. People loved these shoes. They cost a fortune back home.

He grabbed both sides of the hole and tried to prise it apart with all his strength. The fabric was hard to rip but it began to give. He could see the white leather of the shoe itself now. It appeared almost pristine. Vaclav was even more intrigued. There must be the matching shoe here as well. He pulled harder and the tear opened wider.

That was when he realised there was a leg attached to the shoe.

CHAPTER

THIRTEEN

SHE WAS ACTUALLY NERVOUS. SHE HADN'T EXPECTED THAT, BUT MAYBE she should have. It was, after all, the first time she had been named to lead a major crime investigation. Her promotion to the rank of Detective Chief Inspector had been confirmed only two days earlier and she had found out she would be Senior Investigating Officer little over an hour ago, so a few butterflies was a perfectly reasonable reaction.

Nevertheless, Clare Larson gazed sternly at her reflection in the mirror of the ladies' toilets at South Yorkshire Police Headquarters and gave herself a telling-off.

'Don't be so soft.'

She tugged at the lapels of her jacket to pull it straight and brushed the shoulders in turn. She then checked the front of her yellow blouse to make sure there were no stray stains and adjusted the waistband of her trousers. They were tight. She was aware she had been eating too much junk food and drinking too much beer lately and vowed – again – to do something about that.

Must buy bigger trousers.

It had been a whirlwind few weeks. When it was

announced there was a vacancy for a DCI she decided she might as well go for it. Nothing to lose. After missing out on promotion from Detective Sergeant to Detective Inspector a couple of times, however, she didn't expect to get it. She knew there were no stronger candidates within the department but thought it was more likely they would appoint someone from outside, transferred in from another force. The interview went well, but she reckoned her relative lack of experience – aged thirty-five and only three years as a DI – would count against her. When she was summoned to hear the verdict, she expected a consolatory 'Maybe next time, Clare' and to be sent back to her DI duties.

Being offered the job was a very pleasant surprise. It seemed her work in finally untangling the Abie Moran murder case impressed them more than she realised.

However, in a few minutes she had to walk into a packed briefing room and prove the top brass had made the right decision. It was an intimidating prospect. Everybody had been good to her since the announcement was made, but you could never be sure how much simmering resentment might lay just beneath the surface, prying for a sign of weakness to seize upon. People could be like that. Coppers were no different.

She drew a deep breath and stood erect, head back.

You've got this, Clare.

What would Jim Pendlebury have done? He would have stepped boldly into the room, demanded quiet and established control straight away. There would have been no superiority complex, no belittling of colleagues, but nobody would have been left in doubt that he was in charge. He was a leader by word and deed. Everybody respected Jim when he was DCI.

Over a year later, she still missed him. He was still the invisible presence at her shoulder, offering guidance whenever there was a judgement call to make.

Maybe he would be there to help her through this. Whatever. It was time.

'OK you lot.'

Larson's long strides ate up the distance from the door to the front of the room. The rest of the team were in groups, chatting, most sat on blue chairs and the others standing by the wall. They were all aware the new DCI had been appointed SIO for this case and twenty-two pairs of eyes watched as she took up her position and laid a hastily-gathered small bundle of notes on a table beside a blank wall-mounted white board.

'Glad you got the gig, boss,' called out a voice from the back and a small spontaneous round of applause broke out.

'Thanks,' she replied, fighting the blush that was welling in her cheeks. The default setting in the department was usually the well-natured piss-take and she would have been more comfortable with that response, if the truth be told. She appreciated the gesture, all the same.

'Let's get down to business, shall we?'

The room settled; their attention engaged.

'This morning at just before seven a.m. a body was discovered by a cleaner in a large refuse bin at the back of the Asda superstore on Chesterfield Road. The bin is situated in one of the less well-lit areas of an enclosed service yard behind the store and our initial viewing of the CCTV doesn't show us much regarding the actual dumping of the body. It does, though, show a bundle being manhandled over an eight-foot wall at the Derbyshire Lane side of the site by two large males at just before two-thirty. They were, naturally, dressed to not give anything away regarding identification, so not much to go on there, but we do have an i.d. on the body. Before the pathologist took him away for the post-mortem, we were able to recover the wallet from his pocket and establish that he is Francis Aston, aged 43, of Gaunt Road in Gleadless Valley. He was a convicted burglar and trader in stolen goods, known to all who were unfortunate enough to encounter him as Fingerless Frankie.'

Larson picked up a black marker pen and wrote on it:

FRANCIS ASTON (43)
'FINGERLESS FRANKIE'

'We already have a lead as to Frankie's whereabouts in the hours leading up to this morning's discovery. Ryan.'

All eyes turned to DI Ryan Nickle, who had been leaning against a wall while Larson was talking. He stood straight to deliver his contribution to the briefing. He was lean and athletically built, tall and good-looking. The type who could never slip unnoticed into a room. The type who would never want to slip unnoticed into a room.

'We do. At around five p.m. yesterday evening, our communications room took a call from a member of the public reporting a disturbance and the sounds of a suspected assault at a flat in the same block where she lived, on Blackstock Road in Gleadless Valley. Two cars were dispatched and when they arrived at the premises, they found no one at the flat in question, but it had been given a proper going-over by whoever had been there when the disturbance was called in by the neighbour. In the process of investigation by the SOCOs, areas of recent blood loss were found among the debris and, close to the blood, three severed male fingers. We were able to use these to make a fingerprint identity from our records and the match came back as Francis Aston.'

'I should add at this stage,' interrupted the DCI at the front of the room, 'that we know our man was already missing the little finger and half the ring finger on his left hand when an attempted burglary went wrong three years ago, for which he earned a custodial sentence and his nickname.'

She tapped the white board.

'Could I ask anyone who has not already turned off their irony meters to do so now.'

There was a ripple of appreciative laughter around the room at the joke.

'Seriously, though, it does look as if our hapless victim was the subject of some pretty horrendous treatment before he was killed, so I think we can assume we are looking for dangerous people here. It also raises the question of whether Frankie knew something our murderers were very keen to learn. I don't think this is the consequence of an argument over a dodgy rip-off laptop but, as far as we know, Aston had never previously been involved in anything other than the petty crime end of the market. He'd clearly trod on somebody's toes he shouldn't have.'

Larson allowed a moment for the room to digest that thought.

'The flat where the fingers were found is to be regarded as a possible murder scene and has remained secure since the time uniform arrived on the scene yesterday evening. Forensics have been asked to give us quick turn-around on the samples they took in case not all the blood was Aston's. As regards potential suspects, what can you tell us about the occupants of the flat, Ryan?'

'It's a council property rented to –' Nickle looked to a pad to check his notes '– a Mr Daniel Khan and a Miss Shannon Rafferty. They're a young couple who have been at the address for four years now. Neither has been in trouble in the past, bar a minor youth offence for Mr Khan in 2014. Sergeant Thackeray, who was one of the uniform officers first on the scene when the disturbance was called in, reported that Mr Khan and Miss Rafferty turned up forty minutes or so after they got there. They told Sergeant Thackeray they had been at a friend's house through the afternoon. She said they appeared distressed when they were taken in to see the damage caused to their flat and that after taking down a brief account and their contact details, she allowed them to leave to find somewhere to stay for the night. She asked them to come in to provide a full statement in the next couple of days. It was after they'd gone that the SOCOs discovered the areas of fresh blood and the severed fingers.'

'We'll need to talk to them sooner rather than later,' said Larson. 'We've got numbers for them, so we need to call them this morning and send a car round to wherever they're staying to collect them, if necessary. DC Short, can you get on to that, please?'

DC Hannah Short nodded a little too enthusiastically and scribbled a reminder on her notepad.

'If we're treating their flat as a potential murder scene, we need to have their prints and possibly blood samples so that we can identify theirs among the ones picked up by the SOCOs. In the meantime, I want us to find out if there are previous links between our couple and the victim to explain why he ended up in their flat having his fingers cut off. It seems likely at this stage that the two men picked up on CCTV in the Asda service yard dumping the body could have been with Aston in the flat when the injuries were inflicted. Were they the ones who ransacked the place as well? If so, who are they and what were they looking for? Hopefully, our young couple will be able to provide the answer there.'

Larson turned over a sheet of her notes.

'I also want us to knock on every door in the flats and all nearby properties to ask neighbours what they saw. I can't believe three big blokes, if that is the case, could have got into and out of a block of flats unnoticed in the middle of the day, especially as one of them might have been dead when they left. At the very least one of them will have been bleeding all over the place. Somebody must have seen them and the vehicle they arrived and drove away in. DS Senior, I want you to take three DCs to get what we can from the good residents of Blackstock Road flats. We also need to check all the CCTV we can lay our hands on for the streets close to the Asda store at and around two-thirty this morning. DC Cook and DC Doyle, I'm afraid that task falls to you.'

She glanced around the room, to absorb the moment. It was a good team. She'd known most of them for years. She knew they were all with her. This was her investigation. Her chance to really shine. She knew they would get this right. Together.

'That will do us for now. Let's reconvene this evening at six to review what else we've learned by then. Hopefully, by that stage we'll have statements from the couple, an initial report from the pathologists and maybe a few clues from forensics. Thank you, everyone.'

The briefing came to an end in a flurry of disturbed chairs and communal chatter. Larson gathered her notes. The first briefing was out of the way and she felt better for that.

CHAPTER
FOURTEEN

THE PHONE BUZZED IN HIS TROUSER POCKET. RONNIE BRIDGEMAN HADN'T returned it to the hidden place in the desk drawer where he usually kept it. He'd been expecting this call.

'What took you so long?'

It was only just after nine in the morning. Bridgeman had just poured a second cup of tea into one of the fancy china cups his wife, Vanessa, insisted on setting out for breakfast. Two cups equalled a proper mugful, he reckoned. The call had come through earlier than he anticipated, but he wasn't about to dish out praise for efficiency. Not to him.

'I'm texting you an address.' The tone of the reply was joyless. Grudging.

'Hang on.' Bridgeman stood up from the table. He wanted to finish this conversation in his office. Vanessa carried on buttering a slice of toast and pretended not to notice or care. She knew what this was about. She'd press him for details later to make sure he didn't mess anything else up.

Bridgeman threw himself into his Chesterfield leather swivel chair slightly out of breath after sprinting upstairs, two steps at a time. He opened the text and scowled.

'That's the address we went to yesterday. He wasn't there. That's why I told you to find out where he is now.'

There was a muttered curse down the line.

'I've got a mobile number as well.'

'Well?' Bridgeman expected more. Nothing more was offered. 'Use the bastard number to find his current location.'

'It can't be done. Not without leaving a trace and arousing suspicion. We can't just press a key on a computer and everything's there on the screen for us, you know. There are procedures limiting this kind of thing. We have regulations.'

'Fuck your regulations!' Bridgeman was becoming irritated. 'What bastard use is a number to me? What am I supposed to do – call him and ask him where he is?'

Icy silence.

'You'll figure it out. You're the criminal mastermind.'

He was getting bold. Bridgeman didn't like that. It reflected the fact that his position was weakened by the situation he was now in.

'Just send me the number.'

He expected the phone to go dead, but it didn't. There was no response for a second or two, then the other one spoke.

'Couldn't you have taken care of things more discreetly? They found it this morning.'

There was anger in the voice. It wasn't his place to question, but Bridgeman resisted slapping him down.

'So?'

'So there's already a full-blown investigation. If you'd disposed of it more carefully you could have bought more time. This makes things very awkward.'

Bridgeman admitted to himself he hadn't thought that part through properly. One of the benefits of being untouchable was that he didn't have to be cautious. The bins at the back of the supermarket was a perfectly good place to get rid of the rubbish.

'Just you deal with your end and I'll deal with mine.'

An exasperated sigh came down the line.

'You don't get it, do you? You'll have to act on this information very quickly or else you might find your man has already been picked up.'

He got it now.

'Text me the number.'

Bridgeman hung up. Within half a minute, the phone pinged as the text landed. He read it.

What the hell am I supposed to do with just a phone number?

Then he realised. Sometimes the simple solutions are the best.

He picked up his other phone and speed-dialled a number.

'Faz. Go to collect Gammo. By the time you get to his place I'll have an address for you where you can pick up the target. This has to be done now.'

Bridgeman hung up. He didn't need confirmation. It would be done.

Soon he would have the flash drive back. For sure this time.

CHAPTER

FIFTEEN

SHANNON AND DAN WOKE EARLY. MORE ACCURATELY, SHANNON WOKE early and then woke Dan because she wanted to him to find out what was causing the noises that had awoken her.

It was not only the clang of metal, followed by a heavy thud that vibrated through the floorboards, that disturbed her. There was also the rhythmic blowing as if a small steam engine was gathering speed and the stifled grunts which sounded like a mountain lion in the early stages of giving birth.

When Dan was dispatched to investigate, he realised it was Hermie in her bedroom doing her morning workout. After reporting his findings, the two of them lay, silently listening and fully awake, on their air mattress until the workout was over. Only when Hermie closed the door to her room again following a swift shower did Shannon rise and tip-toe her way to the bathroom.

Dan waited until he heard Hermie go downstairs before he dressed and went in search of breakfast.

Hermie sat at the small dining table in the living room, scrolling over pages on her phone. She had a large plastic water bottle two-thirds full of a protein shake the colour of a muddy puddle and drew a mouthful of it up the straw as Dan made his way tentatively down the stairs. He stood awkwardly beside the end of the banister in expectation of an exchange of morning niceties, but none were offered.

'Hi,' he said, without response. He dallied a few seconds more before taking three timid steps towards his host.

'Er, can I get some breakfast?'

Hermie took another slurp of her shake. 'Help yourself.'

Dan pressed on towards the kitchen. After a fruitless search for Coco Pops or Cheerios, he unenthusiastically tipped a serving of wheat bran into a bowl. The splash of almond milk did little to make it more to his taste and there was no sign of a sugar basin, so he added a spoonful of organic honey and put the kettle on, ready to make a cup of tea when Shannon joined them.

When Shannon did head down the stairs, there was urgency in her step.

'Oh my god, you'll never guess!' she announced. Dan peeked around the kitchen door and Hermie peered up from her phone.

'I've just called into work to tell them I can't come in because of the break-in and Ayesha in the office says there's been a murder! Apparently, one of the cleaners found a man's body in one of the bins in the service yard.'

Even Hermie's eyes widened at the news. She turned back to her phone to hunt for confirmation.

Dan was about to ask what made them so sure it was a murder when his phone rang and he retreated back into the kitchen to answer it.

'I can't believe it,' Shannon added. 'A murder! They can't open the store because the police won't allow any deliveries until they've finished.' She eased herself down on to the brown leather sofa to gather her thoughts.

Hermie offered an update. 'There's a few posts on Instagram

about it but nothing official that I can see yet. Early days, I suppose.'

Shannon also took out her phone to join the search of social media, but both of them stopped when Dan leaned through the frame of the kitchen door with his phone to his ear.

'Er, what's your address please, Hermie? It's the police. They said they want to come here to interview me about last night.'

'Bit early, isn't it?' Shannon looked at the clock on the wall. Just before quarter past nine.

'Thirty-three Eagle Street,' said Hermie.

Dan relayed the information and, seconds later, hung up.

'Do they want to talk to us both?' Shannon asked.

Dan shrugged. 'Said just me. Told me to not leave the house until they get here.'

He went back to the kitchen while Shannon tried to work out if she should be offended by the apparent snub. Dan re-emerged shortly after with tea for them both and sat on the sofa to finish his now soggy bowl of cereal.

Ten minutes later, his phone rang again.

'Hello?' It was a local dialling code but not a number he recognised.

'Good morning. Is this Mr Khan?' It was a young, female voice. There was noise in the background, but not call centre noise.

'Yeah.'

'Hi. My name's Detective Constable Hannah Short from South Yorkshire CID. It's about the break-in at your property on Blackstock Road yesterday. There are a few things we need to talk to yourself and Miss Rafferty about and we need to see you this morning.'

Dan was confused. They'd already told him this.

'Some guy from your place just called me to say you're coming round.'

'Sorry?'

'Some guy from the police. I can't remember his name. He said they were coming here.'

It was Hannah's turn to be confused. The first hours of an investigation were usually a bit chaotic but she had specifically been given this task. Why would anyone else call?

'I'm sorry about that, sir. There may be crossed wires here. What we actually need is for you and Miss Rafferty to come in to the station and I'd like to arrange for a car to come to pick you up. Could you let me know the address where you are at the moment, please?'

'What, again? I already gave it to the other guy.'

Dan and Shannon exchanged an exasperated look, but, close by and listening intently, Hermie was suddenly on high alert, like an animal sensing impending danger. She stepped across the room with purpose and lifted the slats of the blind to peer outside.

Across and a little further up the steep road, she spotted a parked white Range Rover.

Dan gave the address again and the phone conversation ended.

'Said they'll be here in ten to fifteen minutes. You'd think get their act together, wouldn't you? What a waste of time to be phoning twice.'

Across and a little further up the steep road, the driver of the Range Rover noticed the movement of the blind and set off at speed

'Do either of you know anybody who drives a white Range Rover with a black roof?' she asked, without taking her eyes off the vehicle as it disappeared from view.

Shannon and Dan glanced at each other and shook their heads. Their hearts began beating a little faster as Hermie continued her hawk-like surveillance.

'I don't like it. Something's wrong. We should leave. Now.'

Shannon stood. 'Hermie, what is it? You're scaring me now.'

Dan's brow wrinkled. 'But the police said we should wait.'

Across the road, a sleek black Mercedes SUV rolled slowly down the hill and pulled into the space the Range Rover had just vacated. Hermie darted to grab her Dr Marten boots from where she had left them next to the front door and began to pull them on while keeping both eyes on the new arrival.

'This isn't good. You two should go upstairs and get ready so you can get out of here when I tell you to.'

The couple were motionless, bemused.

'Go!' Hermie shot out the command and they did as they were told.

While she laced up her boots, two large hulking figures emerged from the black SUV. The driver had skin the colour of mahogany and gazed searchingly through dark glasses for the numbers on the houses of the sloping terrace before them. The passenger wore blue mirror shades perched on top of his pale, shaved head and ran his fingers through his thick beard as he, too, checked to locate the house they were looking for. Both were dressed head to foot in black, making them look like muscular undertakers, though the simmering menace in their bearing left no doubt they were men more likely to cause a funeral than supervise one.

With barely discernible nods, they confirmed their target and skulked towards it, checking up and down the street for the presence of anyone who might have noticed their arrival. Hermie shrank from her position to press her back close to the wall, from where she could still observe through the chink of a gap at the side of the blind and remain out of sight from outside.

The two men stalled beside her house. Blue Shades barely broke his stride as he headed for the passageway towards the back door. The driver took off his sunglasses and slid them into the breast pocket of his knee-length overcoat, hitched up the cuffs of his black leather gloves and stepped up to the front door. He hammered it three times with such force that it took Hermie's breath.

She composed herself, blinking her eyes shut for three seconds. When they opened, the fire had been ignited behind them. She knew what she had to do.

'Yeah?'

The man towered over Hermie, even though her feet were a step level higher than his from her position inside the house. She folded her arms and leaned against the frame of the door; eyes fixed defiantly on his to show she was not intimidated.

'I'm here for Dan Khan.'

He looked her up and down. She was not what he expected. Obviously a feisty one. A bit quirky. Was this the girlfriend?

'Never heard of him.' Hermie was deadpan. Unflinching.

He sighed. 'Don't fuck us about, darling. He's here. He's coming with us and it doesn't have to get messy for you. Let me in.'

Darling? Not a word to use to get on Hermie's good side.

'There's no one of that name here and you're not coming in.'

The man pursed his lips and nodded.

So that's the way it's going to go.

Tension crackled in the stare that locked them together until he broke it first, easing a half-step back and sucking his teeth with another nod of the head. Suddenly, he sprang forward again, pushing the palms of his huge hands against Hermie's shoulders. She was not braced to absorb the blow and tripped backwards in a faltering stumble until she fell with a heavy bump onto her bottom. By the time she had skidded to a halt, the man was in her house.

'In here!' he yelled and Hermie heard the back door handle being tried.

'Open it! Now!' There was no pretence of tolerance in the

man's glare this time. Hermie rose slowly to her feet and crouched below her full height in supplication.

'I don't want any trouble. Please don't hurt me. There's nobody in the house except me. Just leave or I'll call the police.'

She reached into the pocket of her jogging bottoms to take out her phone. Fury filled the man's eyes. He stepped forward to grab it. Mistake.

It was just the opportunity she wanted to provoke. As the man lurched with his right hand to snatch the phone, Hermie pivoted on her left foot and shot a straight right arm towards his throat. The prominent middle finger knuckle of her clenched fist sank into his Adam's apple and he buckled, with a stunned gasp, at the waist. As his head dipped, her right knee rose to connect with a sickening crack against his chin and he toppled, dazed, struggling for breath, to the floor. It was a technique she had taught dozens of times in her self-defence classes.

At the back door, Hermie could hear the second man barging against it with his shoulder to break it open. They didn't have much time.

'Run!'

At the top of the stairs, Shannon and Dan had huddled together, quaking, as they listened to the drama unfolding in the room below them, certain the worst was about to happen. When Hermie cried out, they were startled into action, clattering down the wooden stairs with reckless haste to make the most of an opportunity they feared might not come. She was at the open front door, beckoning them forward with urgency.

'Go!'

They leapt out of the door towards the road. Hermie took a last glance over her shoulder to see the driver gaining the strength to lift himself with his arms as he recovered his scrambled senses. Then she heard the splintering crash of the back door finally giving way as the second man burst through into the kitchen. She slammed the front door behind her and sprinted to catch up her friends.

They had headed down the steep road. She began to close on them a little too easily. Shannon stopped, forcing Dan to do the same, and turned back towards the house.

'Quick, Hermie! They're coming!'

What have they stopped for? Keep running!

Hermie turned. Blue Shades was eating up the yards at a surprising pace. The driver was just emerging from the front door and was about to break into a trot. Her friends were waiting for her to catch up. Before they knew it, the men would be on top of them all. They wouldn't stand a chance. They had one option.

She pulled up.

'Run for the main road. I'll hold them off.'

Shannon heard the words but they made no sense. She couldn't possibly take on both of them. *What is she thinking?*

'Hermie! You can't! Come on!'

'Just move!' she yelled back, spinning to face her advancing foes. She began bouncing on the ball of her right foot, her left foot forward, and drew up her fists to either side of her chin. She was ready for them.

Dan watched with horror, powerless. He felt as if he, too, should make a stand but realised that even the three of them against those two was no fair match. Shannon had told him Hermie would do anything for a friend. The point was about to be proved in blood and pain. All they could do was make sure it was not spilled in vain.

'Come on! We've got to go!'

He dragged at her arm, beseeching her to move. The terror of what was about to unfold gripped Shannon and drained the power of movement from her, but the jolt from Dan stirred her legs, involuntarily, into action again.

'Hermie!' she called, despairingly, before she gave in to the attempt to tear her away and lumbered into a reluctant run.

Blue Shades slowed as he neared Hermie in her fighting stance. When he broke into the house, he saw his mate down and that shocked him. No one put Faz on the floor. That made him wary, but Faz must have let his guard down. No girl with weird hair was going to catch him out like that. He was going to make this swift and decisive.

They eyed each other for a second or two, but then Blue Shades feinted to the left and swung a big, arching right hook. Hermie was ready for him. She ducked low and sprung up at the knees to deliver a short-arm jab into his exposed ribs.

The air rushed from his giant frame. The blow stung him, but he was quickly upright. He prowled left and right in front of her, as if searching for a weak spot. She covered his movement, content to buy time, still limber and ready to counter.

The driver caught them up. He was properly angry now. The knee to his chin had made him bite his tongue and he was swallowing blood. The smart move would be to bypass her and leave her to Gammo while he pursued the others, but fuck it. She'd embarrassed him. He wanted to hurt her first.

Hermie's eyes darted from foe to foe. Even if both of them came head-on at her, it was almost impossible to hold them both off. It was time to get out of there. Run for it and back herself to outrun them.

But just as she edged backwards, ready to make a break, Blue Glasses lurched forward with both hands, trying to grab her. She fended off his left hand with her forearm, but, in an instant, a scything kick from the driver took both legs from under her and she hit the road surface with a jolting thud.

There was no escape then. All she could do was try to cover up as her body was rocked by the force of spiteful kicks from the two men. She was helpless. Vanquished.

The violent burst lasted only seconds.

'Come on!' barked the driver and they set off to catch up with the others.

Hermie half-heard the heavy beat of their boots fade as they ran down the hill. It was over. She slipped into unconsciousness.

A quarter of a mile away, Shannon and Dan came to a halt. Momentum, as much as anything, had carried them down the hill so far, but now the road split into two ahead of them. Both roads led sharply uphill.

'Which way to the main road?' asked Dan, breathlessly.

Shannon doubled up, her hands on her knees as she tried to draw air into her screaming lungs. Intense exercise was something she hadn't attempted in years and now they had come to a halt, her legs felt as if they were about to buckle.

'Can't do this,' she gasped.

Dan attempted to encourage her to stand upright again.

'We have to, Shan. They're coming for us.'

She shook her head. 'Can't run.'

He turned to check behind them. No sign of the men yet, but surely there soon would be. They couldn't rely on Hermie to hold them off for long. Could they hide? He surveyed frantically all around for likely hiding places.

The sound of a car behind him stretched his already frayed nerves further. It screeched to a halt at the junction of the side road they had just run past and tore off at pace towards them.

This was it. They were finished. Any attempt to escape now was hopeless.

The car pulled up sharply beside them. A white Range Rover with a black roof.

The passenger side window was down. Across from the driver's seat, a small figure was leaning towards them. It was such a tiny frame, with a head almost overwhelmed by a blue baseball cap, that Dan thought it was a child at first. He could not tell if the figure was male or female.

'Come on! Get in!'

He could not move. Beside him, he felt a tug on his arm as Shannon tried to pull him away, wary of the new presence. But then he glanced up the hill again and saw the two thugs in sight, bounding towards them.

'There's no time! Come on!' the newcomer yelled.

Dan had to think fast. Of his limited choices, there was no doubt which carried the least risk.

He looped his arm around Shannon's waist and opened the back door, bustling her inside the car. He dived in after her and pulled the door shut.

The car sped with a squeal of tyres up one of the roads ahead of them.

A hundred yards behind, their two pursuers gave up the chase.

CHAPTER
SIXTEEN

Both of them sat in stunned silence, drawing in deep gasping breaths to recover from the physical exertion and the emotional trauma of a morning that had so suddenly taken a dark, dangerous turn for the worse.

As their heads stopped spinning and their hearts stopped pounding, Shannon and Dan began to adjust to a new predicament. Certainly, it was less fraught with potential jeopardy than their last one, but who was this stranger who had saved them from the two men? Where were they heading?

From his seat to the driver's left, Dan could not see the stranger's face, but his eyes were drawn to the left hand on the steering wheel. Its skin was pale and taut, young-looking, but was stretched over enlarged knuckles on the back of the hand and over stiff, misshapen fingers. The hand gripped, pincer-like, a large button knob fixed to the steering wheel, moving it to manoeuvre the car through the side streets and on to the main road towards town. The stranger's right thumb was hooked on the other side of wheel with fingers around a lever which was pulled to accelerate and pushed to brake.

Dan watched the process with fascination. He had never seen

a car driven like this before. Shannon was not aware of what was holding his attention. She had other things on her mind.

'You've got to take us back to the house.' There was an edge of desperation in her tone. 'We need to help Hermie. She could be badly hurt.'

'It's too risky.' The voice from the front of the car was firm, but soft, feminine. 'I'm sure your friend will be getting the help she needs if she is injured. Your presence there would be unnecessary. It's more important that I get you somewhere safe.'

On top of everything they had already been through, the icy certainty in the words unsettled, rather than reassured, the two passengers. *What is going on?* It was as if they had stepped unwittingly into a plan that was already fully formed.

'What do you...? Who the hell are you anyway?'

Shannon was weighing up opening the car door and making a dash for it the next time they slowed down. It was a risky move, but could that be any worse than what they might soon be facing?

'Call me Em.'

'Em?' Dan's mind had already leapt to the character in the James Bond films. 'Why Em?'

'Because I prefer that to Emilia. Look, I'll tell you anything you want to know when I get you safe. Until then, just sit back and relax. We'll be there in twenty minutes.'

Shannon was not about to relax.

'No. We need some answers, or we want you to pull over right now and let us out. Who are you? Who were those men? Why were they coming for us? We've done nothing wrong.'

Em sighed. The impatience, more than the ingratitude, irritated her.

'Those men are heavies employed to do the dirty work of a gangster by the name of Ronnie Bridgeman. Have you heard of Ronnie Bridgeman?'

Two blank expressions in the rear view mirror told her they had not.

'Ronnie Bridgeman is an inhuman, pathetic piece of shit who dominates the Sheffield underworld and terrorises decent people trying to live decent lives through intimidation, cruelty, and violence. As far as he's concerned, he practically runs the city and nobody who is supposed to be enforcing the rule of law seems in the least bit inclined to stop him. He appears to be able to get away with anything and he'll stop at nothing to get his way. He and his two goons have already killed Frankie Aston.'

The shock wave caused by that news caused both passengers to recoil.

'Frankie's dead?' said Dan.

Shannon's eyes widened with another alarming thought.

'Oh my god! Was it him they found this morning at Asda?'

'I can only assume so,' confirmed Em. 'I was parked outside your flat yesterday afternoon and I saw two gorillas practically carrying him off into their car. He didn't look in a good way, but he was still alive. I don't believe he will have been for very much longer. He's not been seen since. I don't think for a minute they will have just let him go.'

'But why Frankie?' Dan pleaded. 'He was a bit dodgy, but why would they want to murder him? And why have they come after us?'

'Bridgeman believed Frankie had something that belonged to him. Something he wants back pretty desperately. He's coming after you now because you've got it.'

Shannon felt her stomach contents curdle and threaten to come spilling out. She and Dan gazed, horror-struck, at each other. *Surely, she didn't mean...*

'Look, I know this is a lot to take in and I will explain in more detail when we reach the safe house, but first I need you to do something. Have you both got mobile phones?'

They nodded.

'I need you to switch them off and take out the batteries. You can't use them.'

'What?' The situation was getting more and more bizarre for Shannon. 'Why the hell should we...? We need to let people know we're OK. We need to call the police and tell them everything that's gone on. We need them.'

Em took a deep breath.

'How do you suppose Bridgeman traced you to your friend's house this morning? I knew where you were because I followed you there last night, but who else did you tell?'

Dan considered the question. 'Nobody. Apart from the police this morning when they called. In fact, they called twice.'

'You gave the address both times?'

'Yeah, but...'

It was odd that they'd called twice. Both calls were quite different as well.

'You think one of the calls was Bridgeman?' said Shannon.

'That would be my guess. It's the only way I can think of that his thugs could have turned up so soon and knew to find you there. If they've got your numbers, it might not be beyond them to put a trace on it and we can't afford to take a chance that they'll track you to the safe house. That's why I must insist – switch off your phones and take out the batteries.'

Reluctantly, they complied.

'We need to keep our heads low for a few days. All three of us are in danger. You might not have heard of Ronnie Bridgeman before, but he certainly knows who you are. The only reason I can see to explain why he knows it's you who's got what he's so keen to get back is because Frankie must have given him your name. God knows what he did to poor Frankie to make him do that, but if he gave up you two I have to assume he has my name as well.'

'So how are you mixed up in all this?' asked Shannon.

'Let's just say Frankie was my business partner. It's a long story. I'll tell you all about it later.'

In the back seat, Dan pulled Shannon close.

'Shouldn't we just go to the police?' he said.

Em pulled off the ring road and past the Chinese stores and restaurants at the bottom of the narrower, busy, London Road.

'I don't trust the police. I wouldn't be surprised if they're trying to pin Frankie's murder on you right now. There must have been his blood all over your flat, judging by the state of him when he left. Let's see what they come up with before we go making their job easy for them by presenting them with someone to blame.'

'They couldn't do that. It would be ridiculous to blame us.' Shannon spoke the words with conviction, but doubt had already crept in. Could they *really* be certain?

'Anyway, why should we trust you?'

Em accelerated on through a traffic light that had just turned amber.

'Because we're in the same boat. Ronnie Bridgeman most likely wants to do to the three of us what he's already done to Frankie. I can keep you safe and nobody else, including the police, can promise you that. That means, right now, I'm the only person you can trust.'

CHAPTER
SEVENTEEN

'Problem, ma'am.'

DCI Clare Larson had been going over the details of the scene where the dead body was found only a few hours earlier with one of her sergeants, but when she saw the flushed face of the young DC beside the desk she realised there was a new issue which would demand her attention.

'What is it, Hannah?'

DC Hannah Short knew full well she could not have done more. She made the call to the potentially key witnesses practically as soon as the briefing had adjourned and had arranged for a car to be sent from the closest station to pick them up straight away. A car close by that had been returning from a call-out was diverted within minutes. It was all so straightforward.

So why did she feel responsible for it going wrong? Maybe it was just that nobody wanted to be the bearer of bad news so soon into a major investigation.

'I've just had word from the car sent to collect Dan Khan and Shannon Rafferty. They might have been abducted.'

Larson scanned around her to spot the two Detective Inspectors assigned to the team.

'Ryan. Gareth.'

She was more than happy with the choice of the two who would be her closest lieutenants on this case. Ryan Nickle and Gareth Powell were rock solid, experienced detectives. They and Larson had been on the force a similar amount of time and were around the same age, though Nickle was closer to forty than the other two. She knew them well enough to feel she could count on their complete support as she found her feet in her new role.

The two DIs stopped what they were doing and made their way over from different parts of the office. Powell, wiry and always irrepressibly keen, arrived first and took the chair. The more languid Nickle had to settle for the corner of an adjoining desk.

'The two witnesses are missing,' said Larson, bringing them rapidly up to speed. She signalled with an arch of her eyebrows that the young DC should continue.

'When the patrol car officers arrived at the address they said there were residents on the street around the scene of a serious assault. It turns out the victim was the owner of the house Khan and Rafferty had stayed in last night. She was conscious but had taken quite a beating, though her condition's not believed to be life-threatening. Witnesses reported seeing two men engaged in a confrontation with the house owner. One of them said she saw a young man and woman, who sound as if they are our couple, running away from the scene while the confrontation was taking place and said that after they had beaten up the house owner, the two men set off in the same direction as the young couple. There's been no sighting yet of any of them since.'

'Shit!' It was an early complication Larson could have done without, to say the least.

'The car must have arrived only ten minutes or so after I made the call to Khan,' said Short, feeling the need to deflect blame, even though none was heading her way.

'Could they be the same two men who dumped the body? Do we have descriptions?'

'All I have at the moment is that they were both tall and heavily built, one white with a beard, one black, both wearing dark clothing. The officers at the scene are gathering more detailed information.'

Larson turned to her two most senior officers.

'What do you think?'

They nodded.

'Sounds likely,' said Powell. 'Hard to be sure from the service yard CCTV, but maybe we'll pick them up on security footage or get something from witness sightings at the Blackstock Road flats. Whatever it was they were looking for at the flat, if they didn't find it, then it would make sense to suppose they went after the tenants.'

'DS Senior is out at the flats now,' confirmed Nickle. 'I'll make sure he knows to alert us as soon as he gets anything.'

Larson stood. 'We have to assume our couple are in significant danger and that they might have already been apprehended by the two men suspected of murdering Frankie Aston. Hannah, try the numbers we have for them. Hopefully, they found a place to hide.'

The DC returned to her desk with urgency.

'In the meantime, put word out for all available officers in the area to look out for them. I also want us to knock on doors of houses in the direction our couple and the two suspects were seen heading. Somebody must have seen or heard something. Start looking to see if they were spotted on CCTV. Time is crucial here.'

The two DIs left just as Hannah Short came scurrying back.

'Both numbers are dead, ma'am.'

'Shit!' Not good. Definitely not good.

'Listen everybody.' Everybody paid attention. 'Locating Daniel Khan and Shannon Rafferty is now our top priority. I need as many hands on this as we can get. We need to find them quickly or we might soon have three murders to deal with.'

'So let me get this straight.'

Ronnie Bridgeman was the type of angry that meant you really had to be wary. All was calm, on the surface, but you knew he was liable to explode into a burst of violent spite in a heartbeat. Then you *were* in trouble.

The two men in front of him were in enough trouble as it was.

'*You* got beaten up by a girl and while *you* were still fannying about trying to get into the house, the kid I sent you to pick up and his girlfriend ran away. Am I missing anything or did you two just completely fuck up an apparently simple task?'

Though it was not yet even lunchtime, it had already been a long and difficult day for Gammo and Faz.

Once the boss, the previous evening, had failed to extract the information he wanted from the guy they had picked up and basically dragged halfway across the city, it was their job to clean up the room at the depot and get the body ready for disposal. Torture was invariably a messy business.

To avoid the risk of being seen, they then had to carry the body half a mile across wasteland in the middle of the night, manhandle it over an eight-foot wall at the back of the supermarket, dump it, scramble back over the wall and hike back to the car. When they returned to the depot, they had to burn the clothes they had been wearing and virtually scald the car clean, inside and out, to leave no trace of evidence. Only then could they even think about getting some sleep.

Sleep? Some hope.

A couple of hours later, they were on their way to Walkley to collect the kid the dead guy had been talking about, but that had gone wrong.

What's more, when they went back for the car, the place was crawling with neighbours and coppers, so they had to abandon it, hide, and wait to be picked up.

But all that was nothing, compared to having to face the boss to explain how they had lost the kid. And the car.

'To be fair.'

Bridgeman shot Gammo a look that made it plain he had better choose his next words wisely.

'To be fair, the girl turned out to be quite handy. Some kind of martial arts expert.'

'I don't care if she was Conor McGregor's big fucking sister, how the bastard hell did she outflank the two of you?'

Faz tried to clear his throat. Swallowing was difficult because of the punch he had taken to his larynx, and his still-bleeding tongue felt three times its normal size after chomping down on it when Hermie's knee connected with his chin. Still, as the more senior ranked of the two, he had to say something in their defence.

'We took care of her.'

'So fucking what!' Bridgeman's colour was going through the puce scale. 'They got away! The fuckers I sent you to collect got away!'

He turned his back to them, close to the point of eruption.

'Maybe I should get rid of you two and hire the bastard kung fu girl instead.'

'To be fair.'

Bridgeman spun on his toes and pointed a stubby finger at Gammo.

'If you say, "to be fair" to me one more time I swear what I'll have done to you will be far from fucking fair.'

Gammo made a mental note of the advice and continued.

'We would have had them, but we couldn't have known about the car they were driven off in.'

'Did you at least get the plate?'

'Partial' lisped Faz. 'It started YP20'

'Might have been YR,' added Gammo, unhelpfully. 'We were quite a long way away.' He just managed to hold back on adding the rider 'to be fair'.

'So white Range Rover, of which there must be thousands, with a reg plate starting YP or YR, both of which are very common around Sheffield. How difficult can that be to track down?'

Bridgeman ran his hand over his bald scalp. The last thing he needed was another player in the game. Whoever this car driver was, the risk of outsiders gaining access to the flash drive had increased and that meant somebody else they needed to take care of. But they had to find out who the driver was first. They didn't have enough to go on. Even his source wouldn't be able to locate the car from what they had so far.

'I want word out to everybody in the organisation. Let them know it's high priority. I want everybody looking out for white Range Rovers that match what we know of the registration, especially if the occupants fit the descriptions of Khan and his girlfriend. I'll put up a grand for whoever makes the call that leads us to them.'

Gammo and Faz started to shuffle away.

'In the meantime, please tell me you at least took steps to make sure the car won't lead the coppers straight to you.'

Faz nodded. The one piece of good news.

'Cleaned after we disposed of the body.'

Bridgeman was calming down. He had to think.

'That's something, I suppose.'

He needed to make a call.

'Get out of my bastard sight. I've got to try to sort out your mess.'

CHAPTER

EIGHTEEN

HOW COULD EM BE THE ONLY PERSON THEY CAN TRUST? TEN MINUTES ago, they had never even met her. They still had no idea who she was, apart from that she was part of Fingerless Frankie's shady enterprises in some way. There was still no logical reason why they should trust her at all, let alone trust her and her alone.

Yet their ordinary, safe, comfortable, uneventful lives had crumbled around them in the last day and a half. Normal didn't apply anymore. It might lay buried in the debris of their ruined flat or could have been stashed with the dumped dead body in the supermarket service yard bins, but their usual ordinary, safe, comfortable, uneventful normal was elsewhere. Out of reach. Perhaps even gone forever. This was a new situation and they were nowhere close to coming to terms with it.

So, Shannon and Dan clung to each other in the back of the stranger's car and did not say another word as they tried to figure it out.

Could they really be suspects in a murder case? Was that why the police wanted to collect them so early in the morning from Hermie's – to arrest them? You do see TV programmes about innocent people who get blamed for serious crimes they didn't commit. It mostly seemed to happen in America, but who's to say that sort of thing doesn't go on over here?

They certainly didn't want to fall into the hands of the men who had attacked Hermie. That was for sure. Who was this guy Em told them had sent the men? This Bridgeman. Why was he so keen to get his hands on their typewriter?

At least Em had saved them from the men. Credit where it's due. They were in her debt for that and who else had they to turn to right now? Where else would they be safe?

With Hermie injured, dead – who knows? – maybe Em really was the only one they could trust. But there was still so much they needed to know.

They drove on, through a landscape of low-rent housing and the graffitied shutters of failed businesses, past the once glorious 1920s white Picture House and towards where the overhanging trees of a wood brought a welcome intrusion of natural green.

Beyond a short stretch of shops, Em turned off the main road. She veered to the right side of the side street towards a garage door, which began to roll up automatically as the car slowly approached. When it was fully open, she manoeuvred the car through the gap and into a yard behind the end shop of the terrace. Em pressed the button on a small plastic pad attached to a keyring in a shallow well between the two front seats and the garage door began to close behind them.

'We're here,' she confirmed.

Shannon and Dan did not question what 'here' was exactly. They shuffled towards the car doors in resignation. Worn down and weary. Whatever 'here' was, if it offered them temporary shelter from the outside forces that had buffeted them in the last day and a half, they were willing to give it a chance.

It took longer for Em to climb down from the driver's seat. She lowered herself cautiously onto her feet, as if the surface below her was formed of sharp rocks, and took her time rising from a crouch to her full height. Such as that was. At her full extent she was less than five feet tall and, in keeping with the impression Shannon and Dan took when they first saw her, tiny in the cabin of the large car, her delicate, slender, frame made her appear child-like. The rigidity in every movement was nothing like that of a child, though. She reached back into the car to pull out a black walking stick and leaned heavily with both hands on the wooden handle for support as soon as she pressed its tip against the ground. She stood still, like a tripod, gathering her poise, before finally raising her bowed head to her curious passengers with a broadening apologetic smile.

'You'll have to bear with me. I have rheumatoid arthritis. It takes me a while to get going again when I've been sitting for a while.'

Her mobility may have been as limited as a fragile old lady's, but her face reflected the true age of a woman in her late twenties. Vivid green eyes flashed with life in a setting of skin so pale that it practically glowed, like a polished porcelain doll. Her smile creased her cheeks into dimples. It was a pretty face, allowed to sparkle only briefly before Em dipped her head and it was hidden away again under the shade of the over-large blue baseball cap.

'OK now. Let's go inside.'

Em started to walk stiffly towards the worn wooden door at the rear of the shop, bracing her slight weight against the stick in her left hand and reaching into the pocket of her black jacket with her right to fish out her keys. Shannon and Dan followed slowly behind her.

She climbed the stairs with mechanical efficiency.

Stick on the next stair. Right foot. Left foot. Repeat.

Soon they were in the flat. It was bright and functional, but cluttered, like someone was in the process of moving in.

'Let me put the kettle on,' said Em. 'I imagine there's a few things you'd like to ask me.'

She tottered towards an open door to her right. Her movement more assured with every short step, she propped her stick against the wall before entering the kitchen.

'Tea OK? Please make yourselves at home.'

Shannon took up the invitation, lowering herself gratefully onto a wooden-framed sofa with mustard cushions like she had just completed an arduous trek. Dan finished a scan of his new surroundings before joining her.

They said nothing to each other before Em emerged back into the room, pushing a trolly crowded with cups and saucers, a teapot, milk jug and a sugar bowl, all in the same wildflower pattern. So, too, was the plate, though that was largely obscured by biscuits.

Em eased into a single chair which matched the sofa and smiled at her guests as if her next words should be: 'Well, isn't this nice?'

They weren't.

'What do you want to know?'

Where to start?

'Who are you?' asked Shannon. 'What's all this got to do with you and why have you gone to all this trouble to rescue us from those men? Even if this bloke Bridgeman is after you as well, like you say, how does helping us keep him from coming for you? I don't get it.'

'Well.' Em gathered her thoughts. How to put this? 'Honestly, I didn't set out to do the whole rescue thing when I left here this morning. That wasn't part of the plan. That said, having watched events unfold I wasn't just going to sit back and let those thugs take you away. That would have been inhuman. But you're right, in a way, in what you're saying. I wasn't just intervening out of the goodness of my heart. I suppose you could say it has become in my best interests to make sure you don't fall into the wrong hands.'

She could tell that had not made the position any clearer at all.

'Let me try to explain. We have actually met before. Briefly. Of sorts.'

The two on the sofa were even more bemused now.

'A couple of nights ago? In your flat?'

She took off her baseball cap. High on her forehead, beneath strands of dark brown hair, was a fresh wound, drawn together by three paper surgical strips.

'That was you?' The realisation hit Dan first. 'What were you doing breaking into our flat?'

'I'd better start from the beginning.' Em put the cap over the end of the chair arm. 'Could you do the honours please, Dan, and pour the tea? Help yourselves to biscuits.'

Dan began to set out three cups and saucers, while Em leaned back in her chair, in readiness to reveal all.

'This is actually my brother's flat. My twin brother's. We're very close, but quite different. Thankfully, he doesn't have the same physical condition as I have, but Anthony has always had plenty of issues of his own. He's always struggled with low self-esteem, right from being a child, but he's always been brilliant with anything electronic. He was fascinated by taking things apart and restoring them. He found it therapeutic, so our parents suggested that instead of doing it for a hobby, he should have a go at making a living of it. Eventually, we persuaded him to give it a go. Our parents put up the money to set up a shop and, three years or so ago, he was up and running. The shop under this flat was his. *Tech Two*, he called it. He'd buy up broken and discarded tech, like phones, computers, tablets, games consoles – you name it – and do it up as good as new to sell. He was taking on repairs as well. He loved it. I'd never known him to be in such a good place with his mental health.'

She paused as Dan handed her a cup of tea and she balanced it on the chair arm.

'Then, one day, a couple of youths called into the shop. They told him their boss ran this part of the city and that any businesses on his patch had to pay a monthly levy. It was a protection racket. He paid up because they frightened him. He's not the biggest, like me, but he decided to report it to the police. They came round to take a statement and he thought that might be the end of it. The police reckoned it was probably a couple of kids trying it on, you see, but the next day, three men came to the shop. They told him they knew he'd gone to the police and started smashing things up. They told him the levy had been tripled and that if he spoke to the police again, they'd put him in hospital.'

Shannon took a sip of her drink. They were rapt, silent.

'Anthony couldn't handle it. It wasn't just the merchandise they broke that day. Anthony put everything into every piece he brought into the shop. Fixing them was an obsession for him, even though he was making very little money when he sold it on again. They gave him his sense of purpose and when those yobs smashed the place up, they destroyed Anthony. He started self-harming again. Our parents had to put him back in care, for his own safety, but they decided to keep on the shop and flat so that Anthony would have something to return to when he was well again. To be honest, I don't know if he ever will come back here. I doubt it. Too many bad associations. We never heard from the police again.'

Em sighed. The light had dimmed in her green eyes.

'I was able to do a bit of asking around of my own and I was told by several sources that the man in charge of the protection racket bullies was Ronnie Bridgeman. I figured there was no point going to the police with this information. They're clearly in his pocket. How else could he have found out about Anthony reporting the first visit so quickly, eh? Everybody I talked to were of the same opinion. Bridgeman does what he likes and the police don't care. That's why I decided to do something myself.'

She carefully raised her cup in two crooked hands to take a drink and replaced it with a rattle onto the saucer.

'When we went into lockdown, I had a lot of time to myself. I had to isolate because I was clinically vulnerable, but I made that work in my favour. Anthony's skill is in repairing and mine is in computer programming. I started to devise a programme capable of dismantling even the most sophisticated security system. I decided I was going to break into Ronnie Bridgeman's home and steal from him. He thinks he's untouchable, but I wanted to prove to him that he's still vulnerable and how better to demonstrate this than to nick his personal effects from his own home? It was perfect. I was going to start a new career as a housebreaker!'

Em allowed herself a very proud smile.

'Writing the programme was quite easy, really. The more sophisticated the system, the more straightforward they are to disable, strange as that sounds. Being a thief himself, I reckoned Bridgeman would want the best security on the market and they operate on radio frequencies. You hit on the right frequencies and you can stop the sensors communicating with the control panel, stop it transmitting alerts to the mobile phone of the owner and scramble the CCTV, wiping its recorded images completely. Cracking the safe was harder, but, like everything else these days, it depends on an electronic chip. All I had to do was write a programme capable of enabling my computer to talk to the microchip in the safe and effectively trick it into revealing the combination. Simple. All I had to do then was spend a few nights outside his house, identifying and isolating the radio frequencies for the security system. When I had them, I just had to listen in to his phone for a short while to find out when the house would be empty. When I heard his wife booking the restaurant for a cosy anniversary meal together, I was in business.'

Lost in the technical details, Shannon was becoming impatient. 'I still don't see what this has to do with Bridgeman coming for us.'

'I was getting to that,' said Em with a tolerant glance. 'My problem was that I couldn't do the job on my own, because of my physical limitations. That was why I recruited Frankie Aston. I needed his muscle if I was to really hit Bridgeman where it hurt and I could tell Frankie was both willing and greedy enough to buy into the project without asking too many questions. Our arrangement was that I would keep computers and everything from the safe that could be pertinent to Bridgeman's twisted business enterprise and Frankie could help himself to anything else – big tellies, jewellery, cash, tasteless artefacts, the lot. The one condition I specified was that whatever we took, we would bring back to put into store here – '

She gestured towards the cluttered end of the room closest the window.

' – until the heat had died down. Only then would Frankie be free to take it away and do with it whatever he saw fit. Unfortunately, I underestimated how badly Frankie's judgement was hampered by his greed. When we'd unloaded all the stuff, we agreed that I'd get in touch with him when I thought the time was right for him to collect his contraband and off he went – so I thought. I headed off to the kitchen to sort out my meds and I didn't realise Frankie had sneaked back up the stairs because he'd decided to help himself to a little down payment. It turned out he had an antiques fair coming up and he reckoned some of the items would go down well with the punters. As I recall, there was an old-fashioned globe, a gilded skull with the top cut out to make it a pen holder, a few other tacky nick-nacks – and your typewriter.

'Now what Frankie wasn't aware of was that while he was hauling the stuff out of the van and up the stairs, I was sorting through the contents of Bridgeman's safe. That's when I came across the flash drive. What could be on an ordinary flash drive to make it valuable enough to keep in a safe, I wondered? My instincts told me it had to be something significant, so I decided to hide it away until I could investigate properly. I didn't want to take a chance on this place being burgled and it going missing. There are a lot of thieves about, right? I looked around and guessed that about the last thing anybody would want to steal was the big, heavy, ugly old typewriter.'

Dan shuffled uneasily in his seat.

'Those old machines can be stripped down so that the engineers can service them, so I separated the mechanism from the casing and taped the flash drive inside the casing. That way, you would only come across the flash drive if you knew it was there – and I was the only one who knew it was there.'

Em ruefully rolled her eyes.

'The best-laid plans, I guess.'

She took hold of the cup for another drink. Shannon and Dan gazed through widened eyes at each other. They shared the same thought.

Should we say?

'Er, you don't know about the typewriter, then?' ventured Dan.

Em froze, mid-sip. 'Know what?'

'You didn't realise it's, like, really valuable. Worth millions, probably.'

Clearly, she didn't.

'It used to belong to William Shakespeare. He wrote all his plays on it. It's iconic.'

Though she tried to suppress it, Em could not stop herself from laughing. She glanced guiltily towards the sofa. The joke was not shared.

'I'm sorry, but where did you get that from?'

Dan was nonplussed. Shannon stared at him in alarm.

'Frankie told us.' Even as he spoke the words, he felt certainty draining from them. 'It came with a certificate from an Oxford professor and everything.'

Em drew a deep breath. This would have to be handled diplomatically.

'Say what you like about our recently departed mutual acquaintance, he knew how to make a sale.'

The sofa had become very quiet.

'I'm far from an expert on these things, but I know William Shakespeare died when – the beginning of the seventeenth century? Elizabethan times? The first Queen Elizabeth. Again, I don't know for certain, but I'm pretty sure the typewriter wasn't invented until Victorian times. So, late nineteenth century? Maybe even early twentieth?'

Dan swallowed hard. Shannon put her head in her hands.

'So you're saying it couldn't have been Shakespeare's?'

'I'm saying Frankie conned you, probably to make a quick sale to cover his petrol money for the antiques fair trip or something. Sorry.'

Em maintained a respectful stillness as the reality sunk in. Their dreams of a new life of prosperity had turned to ashes. They'd been played.

'But what's contained within the typewriter might be very valuable indeed. That's why I sent Frankie to buy it back from you after he confessed what he'd done. That's why I broke into your flat after he failed to persuade you to give it up. What did you throw at me, by the way?'

Dan was stirred from his reflections by the direct question.

'Er, a chopping board.'

Em rubbed the top of her forehead.

'I see. Anyway, I was outside your flat the following afternoon, hoping for a second chance to get inside and take the flash drive back, when Bridgeman's heavies arrived with Frankie. I thought I'd missed my opportunity. From the time they took and by the state of poor Frankie when they left, I guessed they hadn't found what they were after and that you must have taken it with you. That's why I waited until you returned and followed you to your friend's last night. I was going to hang around until you all left the house, in case that was where you'd taken the typewriter, but I think your friend spotted me. I had to relocate to where I couldn't be seen. Then Bridgeman's thugs turned up again and, well... Please tell me they didn't get it. Is it still at your friend's house?'

'No,' Shannon shook her head, emphatically. 'It was never at Hermie's. We left the typewriter at her parents' house.'

Em cast her eyes to the ceiling in relief.

'That's good. It's crucial we get it back. Whatever information it contains is important enough for Bridgeman to kill, so lord knows what he'd do to your friend's parents if he found out they had it.'

Shannon winced at the thought.

'We need to keep our heads low today, but we must go to get it tomorrow.'

CHAPTER

NINETEEN

IT WAS THE LAST THING DCI CLARE LARSON NEEDED. SHE WANTED GOOD news, but life doesn't always work out the way you want it to. What she hoped would be a breakthrough, a couple of hours earlier, turned out not to be. It was a complication. Another one.

She decided to draw all available team members together for an afternoon briefing to update them on an increasingly muddied picture.

'Sorry to tear you away from what you were doing.' The door closed behind her as Larson strode purposefully to the front of the briefing room. 'I know we're all busy.'

There was fewer of them than there had been in the morning. The rest were out in the field. Larson reached her place and drew a breath. It was practically the first time she had taken a moment all day. It had been a whirlwind six hours.

'We have a few things to go over. First, and most alarmingly, we still have no idea what has happened to our couple, Dan Khan and Shannon Rafferty. We have no reported sightings in the extended area around the neighbourhood in Walkley where they stayed the night, so it's still the case that the last time they were seen, as far as we know, they were being chased by two as yet unidentified men. Could I ask you all to redouble your efforts on this one, please, because obviously the longer we go without finding them, the more concerned we should be for their safety.'

The door opened again and DI Gareth Powell walked through it, sitting quickly on the closest available chair.

'The biggest development we have is regarding the blood results at the Blackstock Road flat. We were expecting confirmation that it was Frankie Aston's blood, but the results from forensics also identified blood from a second individual. Obviously, what we were hoping for then was that the second sample would lead us to one of our suspects, so we authorised forensics to do an immediate DNA test. That did produce a match on our database, but it wasn't necessarily one we anticipated.'

Larson opened the brown card file she had set down on the table beside her and took out the top sheet. It was the print-out of an email.

'The name we have from the match is Emilia Kear, a 28-year-old female who has a conviction for hacking into the computer systems of three major oil companies ten years ago, apparently in protest at their activities. Physically, she is about as far from matching the descriptions of our suspects as it is possible to be, yet we know now she was in the Blackstock Road flat as recently as the last 48 hours, according to the samples we found. Is she somehow involved with the two men we believe are responsible for the murder of Aston, or might we have another victim? That's what we need to establish.'

'I've got an update on that if I could butt in ma'am.' DI Powell was on his feet again.

'What've you got, Gareth?'

'Not much by the way of good news, I'm afraid. There was an address for Ms Kear on the PNC which matched current DVLA records and I sent a car around there to check it out. I had a call back just as I was on my way in here to say there was nobody at the address. The vehicle registered to Ms Kear wasn't at the address either. We have a mobile number but that just rang dead.'

'OK.' Larson replaced the print-out in the file. 'A simple solution would have been nice, but let's set about finding her. I want her description and her vehicle details circulating on the PNC straight away. We also need to put a marker on the vehicle to see if it's been picked up on ANPR in the last 48 hours. We need to keep an eye on the hospitals, look out for use of her bank cards and alert port authorities in case she's on the move. Track down her close family as well to see when they last heard from her and find out if they have any idea where she might be, when she's not at home. It might be as straightforward as she's staying at a boyfriend's. Maybe she forgot her charger and her phone battery's gone dead. Let's not rule out a perfectly innocent explanation at this stage, but I would like to know her connection with Khan and Rafferty. There must be a reason why her blood was found in their flat. Was she mixed up with Frankie Aston? Is she caught up with the people who wanted Aston dead? All we're getting are a lot more questions at the moment and we need to start finding a few answers.'

The fact that Kear had also, like Khan and Rafferty, apparently disappeared was a concern. An innocent explanation would be a bonus, but Larson's hopes were not high.

'We have, at least, made a little progress on identifying our main suspects, though not enough. Descriptions from residents at Blackstock Road match those of neighbours on Eagle Street, where today's assault took place, and tally with the vague images we lifted from CCTV in and around the Asda service yard. I think we can safely say the same two men were involved in all three incidents, but we still haven't found out who they are, whether they are working alone or if they are part of an organised gang. I find it hard to believe they aren't already known to us, so we must be able to work out their identities when we have e-fits or maybe better CCTV images to go on. They were seen leaving the Blackstock Road flat with a third individual, who we believe to be Frankie Aston, and we have a description of the car they left in. A car matching that description has been found abandoned on Eagle Street. Naturally, the number plates are false and the Vehicle Identification Number has been erased, but we've taken it in to see if we can lift some prints to help us find out who we're dealing with here.'

Larson wandered to the water cooler in the corner of the room and filled a paper cup.

'The initial postmortem report is in. It makes pretty grisly reading, I'm afraid. The cause of death is believed to be asphyxiation, most likely by having a plastic bag put over his head, but our Mr Aston had a rough time of it before he died. The PM showed he had four fingers crudely cut off. Three of them were found at Blackstock Road and the fourth was in the builders' waste sacks they used to put his body in before it was dumped. It also showed burns from where live electrical wire had been applied to his torso and feet and deep wounds caused by a power drill. This is the worst kind of torture and again underlines the urgency of finding these people before they can hurt others, specifically our three missing individuals. Because of the complexity of the wounds in what appears to have been a protracted assault on Mr Aston, we should regard it as most likely the murder took place elsewhere, rather than at the Blackstock Road flat. We need to find out where.'

She took a sip of water. 'That's another question we don't have the answer to as yet, I'm afraid.'

CHAPTER
TWENTY

STICK ON THE NEXT STAIR. RIGHT FOOT. LEFT FOOT. REPEAT.

The rhythm was the same but Em climbed the stairs to the flat with an extra spring in her step this time. She was itching to get started.

Shannon and Dan trailed behind her with distinctly less enthusiasm. Each step was laboured. The load they bore was heavier.

Dan cradled the bleach bottle cardboard box in his arms, but It wasn't the bulky typewriter inside that overburdened him. It was the weight of shattered dreams and both of them felt it sapping their strength, draining energy far more quickly than any physical bundle could.

It had been nice to believe for a while that the key to a better life might have dropped into their laps. Just for a short while. Even when their present lives were turned upside down by everything that had happened since, it had still been comforting to hope they might escape and live to see a brighter day soon.

So much for that.

They had been taken in by a Fingerless Frankie con. The

stinging embarrassment hung unspoken over them all the previous evening in the flat as they watched three films on Netflix and tried not to think about how much they missed being able to play with their phones. The distraction worked for a while, but later, as they tried to get comfortable on their improvised mattress of seat cushions, their minds had the space to wander again.

The silence of that long and restless night played them through and through and through the traumas of that day like a stylus snagged on a scratched record. Not only did it remind them of the danger they had become entangled in, it taunted them with the fear of not knowing how badly hurt they had left their friend, Hermie, as they ran away and deserted her. And could they really have drawn Hermie's parents into the sights of Ronnie Bridgeman's murderous thugs? The possibility was almost too painful to contemplate. Shannon could not blank it out.

'Take it out of the box and put it on the table, would you?'

Em breathed deeply from the exertion of climbing the stairs, but anticipation had left a glint in her eyes. She leaned on her stick while the other two caught up.

They had set off to Hermie's parents' house in Totley that morning by taxi, in case anybody was looking out for the Range Rover. They didn't expect Hermie to be there. The best they dared hope for was that Melissa and Simon would be able to give them a reassuring condition update. But there she was, having discharged herself from hospital the previous night (against the doctor's advice). She was stretched out on the sofa, watching boxing on TV. A cast on her wrist, a touch of concussion, broken ribs, sore as hell, but not a complete mess. Not in a coma. Not dead.

The sight of her made Shannon cry. Hermie dismissed the flood of remorse and gratitude from her friend with a shrug.

'S'all right.'

Naturally, Melissa and Simon were much more stressed by the whole situation and wanted to know all about what their daughter had become mixed up in. Who were those men and what were they after? There was only so much Shannon and Dan could tell them. As they waited for the taxi to arrive, Em had briefed them against revealing what they knew. It would be too dangerous to say too much. The parents might pass the information on to the police and the police could not be trusted. Not for sure.

So they pleaded ignorance. Lying hurt.

At least Melissa and Simon were OK. Maybe the less they knew, the less likely they were to attract trouble. That would make the lies worthwhile.

'Just there. That's great.'

Em loitered with barely concealed impatience as Dan put the box on the floor and lifted out the typewriter, setting it on the table. She propped her stick against an armchair and stepped around the table to stand before the antique machine.

For a second or two she basked in anticipation, like a small child about to rip the wrapping off a large present, before simultaneously pressing down on two silver levers on either side of the keyboard and pulling them forward. The whole mechanism slid free of the casing.

'Would you mind? It's a bit heavy for me.'

Dan eased the guts of the typewriter all the way out and lay it carefully down on the table beside the empty shell.

'Now, let's see...'

Em reached inside the casing with her right hand. Her eyes widened as her fingers touched what she hoped and expected to find. Using her nails to work away at the edges, she began to peel away the two strips of black tape she had used to fix the flash drive in place on the back panel.

'Et voila!' She produced it with a flourish, ripping off the remainder of the tape triumphantly and rolling it into a ball between her fingers.

Her audience of two watched, unimpressed. A brushed chrome rectangular metal box. No more than three centimetres long, less than a centimetre deep. Is that it? Is that really what cost Fingerless Frankie his life and was the reason why their flat was torn apart? Were they hunted down because they inadvertently had *that* in their possession? *That?* It didn't appear as if it could possibly be so significant.

Em certainly appeared to believe it was. Or could be.

'Here we go!'

She stirred her laptop out of its sleep mode and connected the flash drive to a USB port. The computer acknowledged the connection with a chirpy two-note tune before a message box popped up on the screen.

'Ah!' Em nodded ruefully. 'Encrypted. I thought as much. Even Bridgeman isn't that stupid. This could take some time.'

She dragged up a chair and stared at the screen, beginning the process of trying to crack the code that was barring her access to whatever was on the flash drive.

Shannon and Dan left her to it. They slumped down next to each other on the sofa.

'Good to see Hermie looking so well,' said Dan, after a while. He reconsidered. 'Y'know, fairly well.'

In his own clumsy way, he was only expressing the relief they both felt; that Hermie had escaped the assault relatively lightly. She wasn't hurt as badly as they feared, for sure.

He hadn't intended to stoke a broiling pot Shannon was already struggling to contain, but by the heavy tears that instantly welled and rolled down her cheeks he knew, as soon as he turned to look at her, he had said the wrong thing at the wrong time.

'Shan?'

He reached to touch her hand but she shot to her feet and headed towards the kitchen. He weighed up whether following her was the right response and decided it probably was.

'Shan, I'm sorry. I...'

'It's our fault,' she wailed. 'We got her caught up in this. We did that to her. Us.'

He stayed back. He was fairly sure this wasn't one of those situations where he was intended to be the one to shoulder most of the blame, but he thought it best to keep his distance anyway.

'What are we going to do, Dan?' It was a frightened plea. Desperate.

There was no easy answer. 'I don't know. What can we do?'

'Well we can't hide in this flat forever.'

That was for sure, though neither of them was able to offer a viable alternative straight away.

'Maybe we should just hang tight here for a few days, like Em said,' Dan suggested.

'Huh!' There was scorn in her tone. She lowered her voice so she could not be overheard. 'Em said! Why should we take any notice of what Em said? We don't even know her. Now she's got us telling lies to Hermie, Melissa and Simon. Why are we doing what *she* says?'

'We'd have been in an even bigger mess if she hadn't shown up,' Dan whispered.

'I know that and I'm grateful, but that doesn't mean she's got all the answers. She could just be using us to get at whatever's on that flash drive and then, as soon as she's got what she wants, she might throw us to the wolves again. How do we know we can trust her?'

'We don't, not really, but what choice do we have?'

'The police?'

'What if she's right about the police being part of this? They didn't protect her brother.'

'So she said. She might be lying.'

'But it might be true.'

Shannon could not dismiss the possibility. The shock wave of disruption that had hit their lives in the last two days had made them uncertain of everything that once seemed so sure.

'Let's just stay here for a few days. Where else could we hide and be fairly sure we're safe? It might all get sorted out in a day or two anyway. The police might arrest the people who did that to Frankie and we'll be OK. It's just too risky to be out there on our own right now.'

Shannon bowed her head in resignation. 'I suppose.'

'We owe it to Em to give her the benefit of the doubt, but even if it turns out she isn't who she says she is, we can deal with that. There's two of us and she's only tiny. We could make her do what we want. How's she going to make us do anything if we don't want to do it?'

'Yeah.' Shannon leaned back against the sink. 'It's just that this whole situation is so crazy. I don't know what's happening anymore. I feel so alone.'

'Yeah, but we've got each other.'

'Yeah.' She sighed and extended her arms to invite him in for a hug. They both needed one.

A cry from the other room disturbed their embrace.

'Got you!'

They separated and left the kitchen, curious to find out what, exactly, Em had got.

'AES-256. Pretty good encryption system, but I already had the programme to disable it. Now, I just need to...'

Her fingers rattled the computer keyboard with a final burst of instruction.

'And... I'm in!'

Em's eyes did not leave the screen as she clicked and scrolled. From above her small frame, Shannon and Dan watched her open a series of folders and study what appeared to be lists of random numbers.

'Account numbers, contact numbers, policy numbers – maybe. It'll take me a while to decipher all this lot, but I suspect it will unlock lots of information Ronnie Bridgeman would rather we didn't know about his little criminal empire. This could be gold.'

The figures whizzed across the computer screen so quickly under Em's mouse control that Dan had to look away and blink.

Then she opened a folder that was different to the rest.

'Hello! What have we here?'

No numbers. Just a single icon. An MP4 video file.

Em double-clicked on it.

The image was grainy, not great quality. The picture jumped, like whoever had the camera was walking with it. That made it hard to be sure what was being filmed, at first, but it appeared to be a long corridor with doors on either side. The only sounds were of footsteps and regular breathing, as if whoever was carrying the camera was exhaling directly into the microphone. Occasionally, there was also the noise of a floorboard creaking underfoot.

Were they filming on a mobile phone? An old camcorder?

The camera stopped. It turned to face a door. A small brass plaque was mounted on the dark oak door. Three figures. Three-one-six. A hotel door? Almost certainly a hotel door.

The image dropped to a brass door handle. A hand reached to try the handle. A man's hand. It did not open. The breathing sound was interrupted by a muffled word. Probably a curse word. The knuckles rapped twice on the door.

To the left. To the right. The camera fell on the door again. The person must have been checking to make sure no one else was on the corridor.

'Come on.'

Those words were clear. A man's voice. He didn't like being kept waiting, even for a few seconds. He was anxious, maybe.

The door opened.

'About bastard time.'

The camera was on the move again, into a room. It wasn't a bedroom. No sign of a bed. It was like someone's lounge. In the corner was a L-shaped sofa. Purple or possibly dark blue. It stood out against the wall and carpet, which appeared light grey. The colour quality of the images made it hard to be sure, especially with the room's subdued lighting. There was definitely a man on the sofa, though. Waiting.

He had wedged himself into the corner, right arm draped along the sofa's low back, legs crossed. Trying a bit too hard to appear unflustered, in control. He said nothing. The camera moved towards him, step by step. He was out of shot for a second or two as the man with the camera approached the sofa and lowered himself down to sit. Then it turned towards the other man again. He was only a couple of yards away.

He was wearing a light suit and tie. The tie had been pulled loose and the top button of his shirt was opened. He was around early-fifties, maybe. Hair in need of attention. Belly curving up above the belt of his trousers. Quite tall, though, and stockily built. Looked as if he could handle trouble if the need arose.

There was nothing in his reaction to the arrival of the other man that suggested he knew he was being filmed. A secret camera?

'You got it?'

The voice was not very distinct and echoed a little because of the distance between him and the microphone. Presumably, that was also secreted. At a guess, it sounded like a local accent, though.

No reply, but there must have been some sort of response.

'Let's get on with it, then.'

The man uncrossed his legs and sat forward.

There was the sound of rustling. A bag? Plastic bag?

A large buff envelope appeared from the bottom of the camera shot and was placed on the table. Then another.

The man shuffled closer and snatched up one of the envelopes. The flap had been tucked in, rather than sealed, and he pulled it open. He reached in and drew out a bundle. A wad of banknotes.

'Is there fifty in each?' he asked.

'That's what we agreed.' It was hard not to notice the resentment in the reply.

'Good.'

The money was replaced and the envelope laid back on the table. He sat back, as if expecting the man with the camera to get up and leave.

He didn't. He waited. Then he spoke.

'Come on then. Aren't you forgetting something?'

The man smiled. 'I'll tell you where and when you can collect it.'

'No, no, no!' That made camera man cross. 'You said...'

'I said I'd get it back to you. I didn't say it'd be tonight. I wasn't going to bring it here in case you tried to pull a fast one. I know what you're like.'

The shot jumped as camera man shuffled in his seat.

'If you fuck me about, I swear to God...' Angry. Properly angry.

'Just cool it. I said I'd get it to you. That's the end of it. Can I just remind you you're in no position to tell me what to do. If that gun was to be logged as evidence, I bet there's enough on it to get you twenty to life. Without it, the case against you collapses. I reckon a hundred grand's a small price to pay for that, don't you? Now fuck off back to your hole and wait for me to let you know when and where. Is that clear?'

Camera man stood.

'Just don't you fuck me about.'

He began to turn, as if to head to the door.

The film ended.

'Now that was interesting!' Em leaned back into her chair. Dan and Shannon took a half-step away. It was certainly like nothing they had ever seen before, but they weren't completely sure what to make of it.

'I'd say the voice behind the camera was Ronnie Bridgeman and this was his idea of earning himself a bit of an insurance policy. I don't know who the other guy was, but from the way he was talking I'd be willing to bet he was a police officer.'

She turned in her chair to face the other two.

'I told you they couldn't be trusted.'

She spun back to the still image of the film's final frame on her screen.

'That looks to me like blackmail material. Some corrupt copper has taken Ronnie for a big back-hander in exchange for vital evidence not making it to court and now Ronnie has something which gives him a grip on the copper's balls! No wonder he was so keen to get it back.'

Em fell silent. A rush of possibilities were being processed through the computer of her mind. She jumped out of her seat and began to pace about the room.

'We could take Bridgeman to the cleaners with this! We can punish him for all the harm he's inflicted with his noxious dealings over the years. Revenge for Frankie, my brother – who knows how many others? We could drain him dry. I could set up accounts he would never be able to trace and we tell him that unless he pays up, this film goes everywhere. I could post it through the dark web on to every mainstream video and social media platform in the world. He refuses to pay, we bring him down. If he's sensible and he pays, we make millions! We could be set up for life – all of us!'

Millions?

It was only a matter of hours since dreams of riches had fuelled their fantasies, but Dan and Shannon were not about to get carried away again. Selling a lost piece of cultural history to the highest bidder was one thing. This sounded a whole lot more dubious. More dangerous.

'It could get us killed as well,' said Shannon. 'I say we give this to the police. They can use it to arrest Bridgeman and bring him down that way. If the other guy was a bent copper, they need to send him to prison. Hand it over. That would be the right thing to do.'

'I agree,' added Dan.

Em was snapped out of the fast flow of her plans. Incredulity filled her expression.

'What? No!'

Shannon was adamant. 'We just want this over with.'

'And then what?' Em spread her arms, pleading. 'If we hand this over, sure, they might have enough to send Bridgeman to jail for a while, but he gets out in time and we get nothing! They pat you on the head and say, "thank you" and send you back to your miserable little lives. Do you want to stay in that crappy little flat in this crappy city for ever? Wouldn't you rather live it up in luxury in somewhere the sun shines for more than one week of every year? You could have it all. Life presents this sort of opportunity to us once, if we're lucky, and we have to grab it with both hands. You want it to be over with? This way it will be over with. You get to escape your old lives and be able to do whatever you like. Nobody could ever touch you again.'

The couple looked deep into each other's eyes. It did sound tempting. But then...

'We don't agree,' Shannon declared. 'It's not right. Not honest.'

Em snorted at the suggestion honesty should be such a key part of the equation.

'You keep telling us our best option is to hide out here for now and maybe you're right,' Shannon added. 'We agree to play it your way for a few days, to give us time to see what happens. Let the heat die down a bit. After that, I reckon we should just go to the police and hand over the flash drive.'

Em skulked away, crestfallen. She stared blankly through the net curtains of the flat's window, out at the passing traffic of the busy road below.

'It's not that we don't appreciate what you've done for us,' Dan added. 'Saving us and all that. We do get what you say about making a fresh start and believe me, we want to get away as well. But what you're saying – well, it's just not us. We've only ever seen stuff like this in films.'

The sound of a double-decker bus trundling by filled the awkward silence that fell on the flat. Em sighed.

'I get it. It's a lot for you to take in. I understand.'

She sighed again. More deeply this time.

'I'm glad you've decided to stay. All I ask is that you at least think about what I've said over the next few days.'

Think about it? What's the harm in thinking?

'Sure.'

Shannon shot him a what-are-you-saying look of alarm. Dan shrugged.

'In the meantime,' he strolled towards the computer and plucked the flash drive out of the USB socket, 'I think it's best if we hold on to this. We all need time to get our heads back together.'

CHAPTER

TWENTY-ONE

It had hardly been worth DCI Clare Larson's while leaving at all. It was not as if she had been able to sleep. That had proved impossible.

She was back in the control room at just after four-thirty in the morning, having not left it until shortly before midnight. Double-checking and cross-checking everything with all the relevant information at her fingertips was a better alternative to over-thinking and second-guessing herself as she stared at the bedroom ceiling.

Day one of the investigation had been deeply frustrating. All developments had complicated the task of finding Fingerless Frankie Aston's murderers, rather than leading them closer to breaking the case open.

Forensics found no prints or DNA of consequence on the car abandoned at the scene of the young couple's disappearance in Walkley. They still had no idea where the couple had disappeared to or, indeed, if they were alive or dead. They had no idea where the woman whose blood had been found at the Blackstock Road flat, Emilia Kear, fitted into the picture. They had still not found the two men seen at both locations, though they had been able to build up pretty good profiles from witness descriptions and had used the information to establish a list of likely suspects they wanted to speak to.

But, in short, they hadn't got as far as they would have liked on day one. No one had actually said anything to Larson yet, but she felt as if she was already being judged on her lack of progress. It had been her first day as a Detective Chief Inspector with the responsibility of Senior Investigating Officer on a major case. That alone was enough to make her feel the pressure of scrutiny, even if no one was actually scrutinising her every move, every instruction, every decision. Maybe the pressure all came from within. Whatever. She felt its constricting force sure enough.

We must make real headway today.

The rest of the team drifted in early, too. Nobody said as much, but they had carried their share of the previous day's irritations into fitful night-time hours as well. Their mutual determination to get the investigation moving forward recharged the energy of the room.

Mid-morning, they took a welcome small step in the right direction.

The white Range Rover registered to Emilia Kear sparked a hit through Automatic Number Plate Recognition as part of an extensive trawl through CCTV. It was from the previous morning, close to where Dan Khan and Shannon Rafferty were last seen.

'No way that's a coincidence.'

DI Ryan Nickle read the details of the alert over Larson's shoulder.

'Nine thirty-eight, which is less than quarter of an hour after DC Short spoke to Khan on the phone and more or less the time our patrol car arrived at the address. This camera on Howard Road is what – half a mile from where the assault took place? No way that's a coincidence.'

'Agreed.' Larson drummed her fingers on the desk. 'So if it means what we think it might mean, what does it tell us? If Khan and Rafferty are in that car, are they there on their own free will or are they being abducted? We already have a connection between them and Kear through the blood found at their flat, but we still don't know if Kear is a friend or connected to the two main murder suspects. It's entirely possible the two men apprehended our couple and they all made their getaway in the Range Rover. Presumably, Kear is the driver, seeing as the two men arrived in the Mercedes SUV.'

'Unless it was stolen,' offered Nickle.

'Unless it was stolen.' Larson conceded. She puffed her cheeks. Still too many maybes.

'Let's see where we can track the vehicle to. That should be a bit easier now we've got a starting point.'

Before long, they had a route. Past Crookes Valley Park to the Ring Road, follow London Road through to Abbeydale Road, heading out towards Abbey Lane, but then all trace was lost before the road reached Millhouses Park. It was a start.

Around lunchtime, the picture became a little clearer.

'Just had a message through from DC Bower, ma'am.' Detective Sergeant Charlie McGuire bounded across the room clutching a sheet of scribbled notes.

Larson looked up from her keyboard momentarily but carried on typing.

'Yeah, go on.'

'She's out taking a statement from the young woman who was assaulted yesterday, Hermione Tyers. She's out of hospital and staying with her parents. Anyway, they had a visit this morning from Shannon Rafferty and Dan Khan.'

'Really?' He now had the DCI's undivided attention.

'And they told DC Bower there was a woman with them. They described her as a short disabled lady.'

Larson spun in her chair.

'Ryan, did you hear this?'

Nickle was oblivious, discussing the recently announced line-ups for the afternoon's United match at Bramall Lane with one of the DCs.

'What's that?'

'Khan and Rafferty paid a visit to the Tyers woman at her parents' house this morning. It sounds like Kear was with them.'

'Right!' Nickle made his way over to her desk, still carrying his coffee mug. This news was far more interesting than the football.

'DC Bower can't have missed them by very long,' added the sergeant.

Larson ignored that. 'Did DC Bower say anything else? Did they appear distressed? Was there anything in their behaviour to suggest the other woman had them there under duress?'

'The mother said they were a bit upset, especially Shannon Rafferty, but she put that down to them seeing Hermione. They're old friends. She said they weren't very forthcoming when the parents asked them about the previous day's incident, making out they didn't really understand what had happened them-selves. Nothing to suggest threat in their relationship with the other woman, who didn't say very much, apparently. Shannon said they were staying a few days at the property of the woman, who they referred to as Em.'

Larson and Nickle exchanged a look.

'No address?' asked Nickle.

'No, sir.'

Larson cupped her hands on the top of her head. 'Well at least the three of them are alive and well, but what the hell are they up to? Did they know each other already and, if so, did Emilia Kear just happen to be in the vicinity when Khan and Rafferty were being pursued? It all sounds unlikely. And why have all three of them got their phones turned off instead of reaching out to us?'

'There is an alternative we should consider, ma'am.' Nickle put his coffee mug down on the desk.

The DCI turned her head towards him. The path they were on made little sense, so an alternate view might be welcome.

'Go on.'

'Well, perhaps our three aren't the innocents they're making themselves out to be. Maybe they are in up their necks in this murder.'

Without saying another word, Larson invited him to expand.

'Take their behaviour since yesterday morning. Wouldn't the normal reaction be to call the police as soon as they reached somewhere safe? You wouldn't go into hiding and turn your phones off unless there was a reason why you didn't want the police to know where you are, would you?'

The DCI nodded slowly.

'We already know there was prior contact between them because Kear was in the flat recently and was injured in some way. Then there's the fact that Rafferty worked at the Asda store where Frankie Aston's body was discovered. Did she suggest it as a likely site to dispose of the body? We also know from Sergeant Thackeray's report after the break-in at Blackstock Road that Khan became angry and threatened to kill Aston. That was the day before Aston's body was found. We did also take a statement from the landlord of the pub closest to the flats, The Swan. He said Khan and Aston had a bad-tempered exchange in what appeared to be a dispute over a deal between the two. That was two days before the break-in and three before Aston's body was found. Maybe we shouldn't rule them out as potential suspects.'

'I hear what you're saying,' said Larson after taking a few moments to reflect on the viewpoint. 'It just doesn't sit right with me. I can't see it. There's nothing in what we know of their characters to suggest they could be wrapped up in something like this, but you're right. Nothing should be ruled out until we get them in front of us and get an explanation. Right!'

She rose to her feet.

'We need to step up our efforts to find these three. We have a broad idea of where they headed yesterday, we need to see if Comms can pick up the Range Rover on ANPR in the region of the Tyers family house and, hopefully, back in the direction of Abbeydale Road. We need to step up patrols in the area the car was last seen yesterday in case it's parked up on a back street somewhere. I also want us to monitor the three phones so that if one of them is switched on for even a second, we know about it. Where are they staying? It's not the address we have for Emilia Kear, so where is it? Somebody must have a good idea. Perhaps we ought to go early with a media appeal to see if they've been spotted in public. Nothing to suggest they're regarded as suspects. "Police believe they may hold vital information" sort of thing.'

Nickle began to move away, but Sergeant McGuire stood his ground.

'There is one more thing, ma'am,' he said. 'It might be nothing.'

'Yes, Charlie.'

'The parents told DC Bower there was another reason why the three called, other than to see Hermione. They went to collect something.'

'Like what?'

'It was an old typewriter. Apparently, Khan and Rafferty had asked them to store it a couple of days ago.'

'A typewriter?' asked Larson, incredulously.

'That's what they said.'

She and Nickle stared at each other.

Just when they were beginning to make some sense of it all.

Ronnie Bridgeman was in a foul mood.

A big shipment was coming in from the Continent in two days. They had been in the drug game so long that it normally ran without a hitch. The time three years ago when the guy in France got greedy was the last time they hit a real problem. They'd taken care of that swiftly, though, and used it as a warning to others in the organisation. Don't think for a minute you can cheat us and get away with it. You might also end your days frozen to death tied naked to a lifebelt in the middle of the English Channel.

It was always wise to stay alert to the possibility that a million things could go wrong, however, and the timing of this latest complication had not helped. They needed to treble-check that the routes they normally used to pay the suppliers without fear of detection had not been compromised because of the loss of the flash drive. His wife, Vanessa, had taken care of that. She was a lot better than he was on that side of the operation.

It still created a lot more unwanted work for him, too, and Bridgeman was at his desk, muttering expletives under his breath as he sifted through it all, when he was distracted by the high-pitched ping from within his top left-hand drawer.

The sound stilled him for a second. He should see to that straight away but didn't want to lose his train of thought. He carried on.

Ping.

That must be the same alert. It always went off again if it wasn't answered within a minute. He carried on.

The phone started ringing.

'Oh, for fuck's sake!'

Bridgeman yanked open the drawer and ripped out the phone from where it was fixed with tape under the lip of the desktop. He poked at the green answer button.

'What?'

'You got my text?' The voice at the other end of the line was unperturbed by the brusque opening to the conversation. He'd come to expect it.

'Text?' Bridgeman looked at the icon on the screen of the basic black device. 'Yeah. I haven't opened it yet. What is it?'

'Licence plate of the car you're looking for, name of the driver and last known location of the car.'

This was good. Bridgeman was almost pleased.

'Address?'

'Not been seen at the one we have. Working on it.'

'Right.'

Not ideal, but still good.

'They're close to identifying your two guys,' added the voice. 'They have lots of witnesses and strong descriptions following yesterday's balls-up. It's only a matter of time until they put probable names to the faces and then they'll come looking for your Chuckle Brothers to arrest them. They'll be doing all they can to connect this to you as well, of course.'

It was a dig. He had enjoyed that.

Bridgeman didn't bite. He was well aware how messy it got. Those two wouldn't be involved in anything where their faces might be seen in public for a long while yet. They were under orders to keep out of sight and use only the organisation's safe locations. They were his most trusted men, but they had fucked up this time. They had attracted too much unwelcome attention and, through that, had run the risk of leaving the whole organisation – including him – exposed to scrutiny. Having done so much to stay out of reach of the authorities for so long, Bridgeman was not about to take any unnecessary chances.

'Keep me informed.' He hung up.

Bridgeman keyed in the code to be able to access the message.

The driver was a woman? He hadn't expected that. Neither

had he heard of that name. He would have to put word out among a few trusted associates to see if they had come across this Emilia Kear.

Whoever she was, she'd be made to regret getting involved and the inconvenience it had cause him.

CHAPTER

TWENTY-TWO

IT WAS THEIR FOURTH DAY IN THE FLAT AND THE WALLS WERE SLOWLY, almost discernibly, creeping closer, making the space between even smaller than it already was. In time, they would surely crush the three poor souls trapped inside, but that would almost certainly be too long coming. Well before then, they would most likely be driven over the edge by a mixture of stupefying boredom and the torment of uncertainty.

This was the day Shannon and Dan had planned to move out of the flat. This day at the latest. But then, the day before, Em had pointed out that the police had put out a public appeal on the local TV news.

They stared, transfixed, at their names and faces on the laptop screen.

Keen to establish the whereabouts.

May hold vital information.

It was a bit of a shock, to say the least.

Em presented it as evidence that she had been right all along. The police were actively trying to pin the murder on them, she said.

Maybe she was right. In their heightened confusion, it seemed safer to agree to stay hidden away for a little longer. A few more days at least.

A few more days in that flat.

Em spent a lot of time in her room. Shannon and Dan had nothing to do except watch box sets on TV and worry. The tedium was getting to them. The increasing tension was getting to them. They had hardly spoken to each other at all that day.

Shannon was working her way through series four of *Homeland*. Dan had decided he preferred to take a nap.

In other circumstances, she might have found the sound of his regular breathing from their makeshift bed comforting. Cute, even. Now she just found it annoying. She was toying with the idea of making up an excuse to wake him when Em emerged from her room.

Em probably needed a stretch. She said she had to move regularly because of her condition. Fair enough – but did she have to make so much noise with that walking stick on the wooden floor?

She was not on the move for long. Em circled around the back of the sofa and lowered herself into the seat next to Shannon.

Shannon shifted uncomfortably, like the scruffy old man on the bus had slumped down and invaded too much of her personal space.

'*Homeland*. Great series.'

It was intended as the ice-breaker to a conversation. The offer was not taken up. Shannon stared blankly ahead.

Only the dialogue of the characters pierced the icy silence for a minute or so until Em decided on a more direct approach. She turned to face the figure next to her.

'Can we talk?'

No response.

'I think we got off on the wrong foot somehow, but it's just this awful situation we're in. I get the feeling that if things were different, we'd actually get along quite well.'

No response.

'Could we at least try to be civil?'

Reluctantly, Shannon tore her fixed gaze from the TV and granted eye contact.

The hostility within her began to melt. For the first time, she recognised kindness in those green eyes. Empathy. It was a gentle smile. A pretty face. How had she not seen that before? Perhaps she had been too uptight over the last few days to notice. Maybe she had simply not tried hard enough to see beyond the jerky walk, the bulbous joints on crooked fingers, the stick. For the first time, Shannon properly saw Em. Not the weird stranger, the computer geek, the jailer. The person. In that instant, her frostiness could no longer be justified.

'Sure. Why not?'

Em's smile broadened before it was overtaken by a look of deep concern.

'This must all be a terrible strain for you. How are you?'

Shannon did not intend her response to come out as a derisive snort, but that sort of summed it up. It was a simple question that had lost its value because it was the kind of thing people asked without expecting, or even wanting, an honest answer. Such a big question in these circumstances, though. So big that she could not imagine the best way to answer it. For all she had been consumed by the anxiety of everything that had happened in the last few days, she had not once stopped to consider how she could adequately sum up how she felt about it all.

'Yeah, fine,' she said dismissively with blithe wave of the hand. 'I've lost my home, I've probably lost my job, I've been chased around Sheffield by people who want to kill me for something I've not done and the police want to fit me up for the murder of a man I've only ever talked to once, in the pub, and that was to buy some knock-off hair straighteners. Apart from that...'

She glanced guiltily along the sofa. She hadn't meant it to

come out that way. That was unfair. A friendly hand had been offered and she had snapped at it.

'Sorry.'

Em shrugged. 'It's OK. I asked for that.'

'I just want it to be over.' The flash of indignant anger had subsided. Deep, pained sorrow had replaced it. 'A week ago, we were living normal lives with our lovely flat together and we didn't have much of anything really, but we were happy, you know? I just don't understand why this is happening to us. We've never done nothing to nobody. We don't break the law. We don't cause trouble. We don't ask for much. So what have we done to deserve this? It's not right. We're good people. I just want it to all go away. That's not too much to wish for, is it?'

'Of course not.' Em shuffled closer and stretched a tiny arm around Shannon's shoulder. 'You are good people. You're a good person and I'll tell you what else I see in you. I see great strength. You're a strong woman. You're indomitable and that's why you're going to come through all this. It could never break you. You're made of steel.'

'You think so?' Shannon smeared the tears from her eyes with the back of her hand.

'Yes, I think so. You deserve everything you could wish for, but I think we both understand it doesn't always work like that. It's an unfair world and it eats people like us. Sometimes it feels like it doesn't matter what we do, however much we try to be honest, decent people, the breaks just aren't there for the likes of you and me. Believe me, I know how that feels.'

'Yeah?'

'Certainly. I didn't set out to be a burglar and extortionist, you know.'

The faintest flicker of a smile danced across Shannon's sad face.

'I went to university. I had plans to make it big. I worked hard for four years, even though I was already having issues with my condition by then and got a distinction for my master's degree in Computer Systems Analysis. Top of my class, I was. I applied for jobs with all the leading companies and got lots of interviews, but, do you know what, I never got a job offer. Nobody ever said anything, of course, but I reckon they were thinking that not only was I a woman, I was a woman with a disability. I guess that made me too much of a risk. Too high maintenance. Four years of hard work and all I had to show for it was sixty thousand pounds of student loan debt.'

Em gazed wistfully towards the ceiling and drew a deep breath.

'In the meantime, bastards like Bridgeman get everything they want by doing whatever they want. They trample over good people like you, me and my twin brother, and they're allowed to get away with it. Is that fair? Of course it's not. The trick is to learn to accept that's just the way the system works. You have to reject how it's meant to be and fight back on your own terms. Everybody's in it for themselves and when you get a chance to grab what should be yours, you have to take it with both hands.'

Shannon sniffled and nodded.

Em drew her a little closer.

'I'm so glad you've decided to go along with my plan to make Bridgeman pay.'

A moment of confusion. *Did I hear that right?*

'We didn't say we would...'

'Oh!' Em pulled back her arm. She appeared startled. 'It's just that when Dan said to me this morning...'

'Dan talked to you about this?'

'I just kind of assumed he was speaking for both of you. My mistake. I probably got hold of the wrong end of the stick.'

Shannon glanced to where Dan was still blissfully snoozing on the floor behind them.

'I can't believe he'd say something like that without us both agreeing to go along with it.'

'No. You're right. I must have misunderstood.'

He wouldn't go behind my back. Would he?

'I'll wake him. We'll clear this up.' Shannon began to rise to her feet but an extended hand stalled her.

'No. Just hold on a minute. There's something else.'

Shannon sat back down.

'This is a bit awkward.' Em brought her hands together in front of her face, as if she was about to offer up a prayer.

'I don't know what sort of a relationship you two have and I don't seek to judge. People are much more open in these matters than they used to be.'

Shannon stiffened. This was ominous.

'It's just that Dan... How can I put this? I think he's beginning to... I see him looking at me sometimes. I mean, *looking*.'

'No. That's ridiculous.' That sounded harsh. Shannon didn't mean it that way. It was just that she knew she could always trust Dan. They loved each other.

'You're probably right. It's probably my imagination. I think being shut up in here with each other all day is getting to all of us.'

Yes, that was it. Dan wouldn't cheat. Wouldn't even look at another woman. Not that way.

'But...' Em swallowed the words before they had the chance to sneak out.

'But what?'

'Again, I can't be sure. I might be wrong.'

'Just say it, Em.'

She hesitated, uncertain.

'I think he might have been going through my things.'

Shannon's eyes opened wide. 'What?'

'Last night. While you were in the kitchen preparing dinner

and I was in there drying the dishes from lunch. Possibly. I'm only saying because when I went to my room later I noticed things had been disturbed. Something was missing. An item of clothing.'

'Clothing?'

'A pair of knickers. I'm sure I had three clean pairs earlier in the day, but there were only two later. I could've miscounted, but I knew someone else had been in there because they weren't laid out how I have them. I'm very particular.'

A cold wave of nausea cut through Shannon like a chill north wind.

No. It's not possible. He wouldn't.

'I only mention it because if we are going to work together in the future, I don't want anything like this hanging over us. I'd rather be honest and have everything in the open. I'm sure it's all perfectly innocent, really. I just want you to know that I've done nothing to encourage Dan. However open you two choose to be in your relationship is your own business, but that's not my style. It's too complicated for my tastes. Anything between the three of us in the future will be strictly professional. We can all be friends, of course. But that's it.'

He wouldn't. He just wouldn't.

'Anyway, I'm glad we've cleared the air. Don't think badly of Dan. Anybody would behave a bit out of character if they've gone through what you two have been through in the last few days.'

Not my Dan. He wouldn't.

'I've said enough. I'll leave you to *Homeland*. Oh, that episode has finished.'

He just wouldn't.

CHAPTER

TWENTY-THREE

'Rendall James Farrell, aged thirty-two, six feet and two inches tall, strongly built.'

DCI Clare Larson pressed a button on the remote control and the image projected on to the large screen changed from a photograph of a surly black man to a photograph of a surly white man.

'Christopher Gamson, aged thirty-four, a little shorter at five feet and eleven inches and of stockier build.'

Another press of the button. The next slide was a composite of two E-fit pictures: one of a black man, the other of a white man.

'These are the images you'll have become familiar with over the last couple of days, based on the descriptions we took from witnesses at both the Blackstock Road and Eagle Street locations. As you can see, allowing for the additional facial hair in one case, they bear a reasonably strong resemblance to Farrell and Gamson. Having fed the information from witnesses into the database, we now regard these two as our most likely suspects in the Frankie Aston murder case.'

She left the images on the screen and turned to face the rest of the team in the briefing room. It was the start of day four of the investigation.

'Some of us are already too well acquainted with the activities of Messrs Farrell and Gamson, but for those of you who haven't had the pleasure as yet, let me enlighten you. Both independently built up long records of involvement in violent crime before joining forces in the organisation of our city's most notorious and elusive criminal, Ronnie Bridgeman.'

Larson clicked the remote control again and a photograph, taken at distance as if it was part of a surveillance operation, came up on the screen. It was Bridgeman in a dark blue suit, walking and talking animatedly into a mobile phone.

'These days, they are regarded as Bridgeman's go-to guys when he wants an opponent eliminating or a victim leaning on. They are his enforcers, linked to a string of unsolved murders and the disappearance of at least a dozen missing persons in the last four or five years, but, in common with their boss, frustratingly out of reach of the law. We've been chasing evidence to put these three dangerous men away for good for too long now and that's largely because they're usually a lot better at covering their tracks than it appears they have been in this case. Whether they've become a little cocky or Farrell and Gamson just got sloppy, they've given us an opportunity to make this one stick and we have to take that chance. I want those two arrested and then, when we get our witnesses to give us positive IDs linking them to the crime scenes, we can work on pinning the Aston murder on them and, ideally, dragging Bridgeman down with them by association. Where are we up to on that, Ryan?'

DI Ryan Nickle was at the back of the room. Fourteen heads turned to see what he had to say.

'Surprise, surprise, it looks as if they've gone to ground since they were last seen at the Eagle Street incident three days ago. We're keeping a close watch on all known hang-outs and places within the Bridgeman organisation. We've also opened surveillance on Bridgeman himself on the off-chance he has a careless moment and leads us to Farrell and Gamson, but nothing yet.'

Fourteen heads turned back to the front of the room as Larson prepared to pick up the thread of the briefing.

'The shocking cruelty of the Aston murder has all the hallmarks of a Bridgeman gang killing, going by the evidence of previous bodies that have shown up over the years which we also strongly suspected were down to their handiwork. If we can get them for this one, it may help us tidy up a few other outstanding murder cases, so in a lot of ways this is about so much more than finding who was responsible for killing Frankie Aston. We have the chance to take out a very big target here. That is now our top priority, but I don't want us to lose focus on these three.'

Click. It was the three images they had used in the public appeal, launched the day before. The photo of Dan Khan was far too old. He appeared boyishly young and startled. Shannon's was up-to-date and caught her in a half-smiling, almost coy, pose for her Asda personnel record. Em's was more of the mug shot variety and had been taken for her last blue badge application.

'None of them have, as yet, emerged from wherever they've been hiding and so we still don't know why it is Bridgeman and his cronies appear so keen to get hold of them. Until we do find them, we still can't say for sure whether or not they are actively connected to this murder as well so, until we find them, they remain potential suspects. What they are for sure are key witnesses who hold crucial information that could, potentially, go a long way to helping us get the convictions we are after regarding Bridgeman, Farrell and Gamson. We still have every reason to believe they are alive and in Sheffield, but the last time they were seen was when they visited Hermione Tyers, the woman who was injured in the attempted abduction at Eagle Street.'

Larson had already decided not to make further mention of

the typewriter they had apparently gone there to collect because they could still make no sense of the information, had no idea where it fitted into the overall picture and, as such, it would only serve to confuse.

'The appeal hasn't turned up anything useful so far, although one caller suggested that before he flew back from holiday on Saturday night he'd seen all three of them in a bar in Malaga and could even send us a photo he'd taken on his phone.'

The detail was greeted by shaking of heads around the room. The perils of public appeals.

'We checked. It wasn't them.'

Mock surprise all round.

'One outstanding lead we have is that we still need to establish how our three travelled to and from the Tyers home in Totley. We have them connected to the white Range Rover we believe they used to get away from the incident at Eagle Street but came up with no ANPR hits for the journey to Totley the following day. Since then, DS Senior has been leading a team visiting the city's taxi companies to see if any of them have records of transporting passengers to and from that address at the times we know they were on the move, but no luck yet I believe, Paul?'

A shaven-headed man in a maroon shirt half-rose from his seat to give confirmation.

'No, ma'am.'

'Ask them all again. The Tyers father said he thought he saw a silver saloon car waiting outside the house while the three were visiting, so a taxi is the most logical possibility. You might come across somebody more helpful this time. You know as well as I do that it wouldn't be the first time we've been turned away with nothing just because the person on the desk has lost his licence and holds a grudge against authority.'

DS Senior half-bobbed up again. 'Yes, ma'am.'

Larson surveyed the room. It had not been an easy investigation, but the picture was beginning to come clearer.

'Unless anybody has anything more to add, that'll do us for now. We're getting closer. Let's make sure today gets us closer still.'

CHAPTER
TWENTY-FOUR

DAN STAYED UP LATER THAN THE OTHER TWO THAT NIGHT. THE afternoon nap had passed an hour and a bit of another boring day, but it left him feeling wide awake until well after midnight, so he watched a bit more telly. It wasn't until twenty past one, during a third consecutive episode of *Game of Thrones*, that his eyelids began to feel heavy.

He sneaked under his half of the spare duvet as carefully as he could so that he did not wake Shannon beside him and listened for the steady rhythm of her breathing. She was still asleep. Good.

At least he thought she was.

How could she sleep, with all that going through her mind?

It was bad enough that Em suggested Dan had been giving her the eye. Shannon could kind of dismiss that. Em might have misinterpreted a perfectly innocent look. It might even have been wishful thinking on her part. They'd seen nothing to suggest Em had a bloke of her own and Dan's a good-looking guy. Other women do fancy him. She'd see them looking him up and down sometimes and there was the time just recently when she'd had to warn off that bitch who was coming on to Dan in the pub up town. He'd laughed it off and accused Shannon of being jealous. In truth, she was a bit.

But the other part. That was different.

Dan? A perv? Stealing a pair of knickers?

The very idea made her feel sick. However hard she tried to dismiss that accusation, it was so disgusting, so abhorrent, that she could not suppress it for long before it came bobbing back to the surface.

She thought about confronting him that night, but would that be enough to settle her mind for good? Of course he'd deny it. He was bound to. Then, if he had done it, he would get rid of the evidence somehow and she would still not know for sure. As much as she wanted to believe Dan was incapable of doing such a horrible thing, she had to prove it to herself. If she didn't, Shannon knew she would always have that tiny, destructive demon in the back of her mind taunting her.

What if he did it? Can you really be certain he didn't?

So she pretended she was asleep and waited. Waited until Dan drifted off. Waited until his breathing became slow and regular.

She lifted the covers and edged slowly off the seat cushions. If he woke up and asked her where she was going she would say she was nipping to the toilet. He didn't. She made sure she was well clear of their makeshift bed and eased to her feet.

Shannon tip-toed around the foot of the bed, pausing for a few frozen seconds when a loose floorboard creaked under her weight. Alongside him, she stopped and gazed down. There was no light in the room, but the curtains were inadequately thin and yellow hue from the streetlamps outside had percolated through. It was just enough for her to make out the shape of Dan's profile against the pillow; his mouth slightly open, his deep, dark eyes hooded in sleep, his black hair ruffled. He was adorable. She wanted so badly to believe she could look at him the same way for ever more. She had to put her mind at ease.

He had discarded his clothes in a semi-neat pile a few feet from where they slept. Shannon picked up each item and frisked it to make sure nothing else was concealed. When she came to his jeans, she slipped her hand into the pockets. Nothing in the left. All there was in the right was a few loose coins and – oh yes! That. Dan had carried the flash drive with him since he took it out of Em's laptop two days ago.

Only two days? It seemed longer ago.

She ran the flash drive between her fingers. The cause of so much trouble. She dropped it back into the pocket.

So far, so good. Shannon would have loved that to be enough to allow her to slide back into bed and drift into a long, unburdened sleep, but it was not enough.

Where else could he have hidden them?

They had brought nothing. Em had ordered them a few essentials off the internet, but their bag was still at Hermie's house. Gathering their stuff together had not been a priority when Bridgeman's heavies came calling.

There was not much furniture in the flat, but Dan might have found a little cranny somewhere to hide them. A place where Em would not go looking. That could be anywhere. Searching for such a place would take ages and seriously risk making a disturbing noise. There had to be other options she could dismiss first.

Jacket. He had his jacket on when they escaped from Hermie's. He wore it again when they picked up the typewriter. Where is it?

Shannon scanned the room through the dim half-light. Was that it, on the back of the folding chair? She hurried over to see as quickly as she dared.

Yes, it is.

She felt into the side pockets. A crumpled tissue, a twenty

pence piece and a folded sheet of paper. An official letter, maybe. That's all.

Inside pocket?

She unzipped it, noiselessly. Her fingers brushed against something. Cotton-like cloth. She hesitated, then pinched it between two fingers and a thumb to slowly pull it out.

She wanted to believe it was a handkerchief. But Dan doesn't use handkerchiefs.

It wasn't a handkerchief.

CHAPTER
TWENTY-FIVE

IT WAS DEFINITELY GETTING WORSE. DAN WAS NOT SURE HE COULD STAND it for very much longer.

If they were all getting along OK, that might be a different story. They might just about be able to muddle through. But Em had barely said a word to him since he confiscated the flash drive and even Shannon was giving him the silent treatment now.

Last night was bad enough. It was just the two of them in the living room watching telly. As usual. Em was in her room. As usual. He had tried to get Shannon to join in what was normally one of their favourite games, slagging off the cast during *Geordie Shore*, but when he said something about lip fillers that he thought was really funny, she barely acknowledged him.

She just said: 'Uh?' and then when he repeated it, 'Oh, yeah.'

It was as if she wasn't even watching it. She was kind of distracted, like she was somewhere else. He could understand that. He wished he was somewhere else as well.

But this morning! Jeez! This morning, she had gone way beyond behaving a bit distant and was being downright hostile. He asked her if she wanted him to make her some toast and she bit his head off.

'I can make my own toast.'

Fine. No probs.

At first, he thought she was just being a bit cranky. She was sometimes, especially in the morning. This wasn't normal morning crankiness, though. This was more than that. She wouldn't even look at him. He walked into the living room, with his tea and toast, and she went into the kitchen. He went into the kitchen to wash his plate and empty cup and she turned her back on him. He said something harmless about not being sure whether it was Tuesday or Wednesday today, and she stormed out and shut herself in the bathroom.

She was in there again now. She had been out in the meantime, once he had finished clearing up and had put the telly on in time for *Cash In The Attic*, but she'd stomped straight through the living room and into the kitchen again. She usually really liked *Cash In The Attic*.

Normally, he would have gone to her, wrapped her in his arms and asked what was wrong. That usually worked. It was the same when one of them got mad with the other. They never stayed mad for long. They said sorry and made up with a hug. Sometimes with more than a hug.

But when she stormed out of the kitchen again and locked herself back in the bathroom, he thought: 'To hell with her!'

Being shut away in that tiny flat day after day was getting to all of them, big time, but Shannon was being a complete cow. She was behaving like a stroppy kid. There was no excuse for that. She was just making a bad situation even worse.

Dan started to stew and the more he stewed, the more bitter he became. The more bitter he became, the more intolerable was the thought of staying in that flat for even one more day.

He had to get out.

Dan left the TV playing to itself and sauntered towards the window. He pulled back the net curtain to peek outside. People were doing their normal stuff. Driving up and down the road, going to the shops, just walking around. Maybe they didn't have anything in particular to do. It was a nice Autumn day. The sun was out. It looked quite warm, judging by what people were wearing. Perhaps that was reason enough for them to be out. They didn't realise how lucky they were.

He let the curtain fall back into place. Looking just made him feel worse.

Close by, to the left of his feet, was the stuff Em said she and Fingerless Frankie had stolen from Ronnie Bridgeman's house. He'd seen the huge TV – you could hardly miss that – and the stupid framed painting that just looked like lots of rows of coloured dots, but he'd not had a look at what was in the black bin bags which were piled up beside them in the corner of the room. He'd not even asked what was inside. Maybe he should look. There might be something interesting.

The first bag was very interesting. He'd never seen so much cash. It was bundled and bound with elastic bands, like you see in the programmes about drug cartels, rather than neatly stacked with a bit of paper around the middle, like you get when a gang has pulled off a bank job or someone is preparing to meet a ransom demand. He picked up a bundle of tenners in one hand and a bundle of twenties in the other. It hardly seemed to diminish the bagful at all. There must be thousands and thousands and thousands in there.

He put the money back and opened a second bag. Papers, documents and around half a dozen passports. Watches and jewellery mostly, though. He had no idea if it was the really top-class stuff, but he assumed it was good quality, seeing as it used to belong to a gangster.

In the next bag was some sports gear. He wasn't much of a sports fan but decided to investigate anyway. One boxing glove. What use was one boxing glove? He tossed that away. A flag with the number eighteen on it and the words 'St Andrews 2000'. It had got a signature on it. Tiger something. A cricket ball stuck to a wooden base. A rugby ball that had 'Sheffield Eagles 1984' written on it in marker pen. A shirt. He pulled the shirt out. It was red and blue stripes and bore a badge on the left breast. FCB. Never heard of them, but the colours were nice. There was some sort of pen mark on one of the red stripes, but never mind. He looked down at the front of the once-white tee-shirt he had been wearing for the last six days. It was getting scruffy, not least because he'd spilt macaroni cheese down it a couple of teatimes ago. He peeled off his T-shirt and pulled on the red and blue striped one. It fitted OK.

'Cool.'

The last bag annoyed him. There were three laptops and a tablet, one of the new type of iPads. Why didn't Em say these were there? Him and Shannon could have used them, for games and stuff. Em wouldn't let them anywhere near her laptop. Dan frowned deeply. He tried to spark the tablet into life but it needed a passcode and he didn't have it. He thought about knocking on Em's door and asking her if she could unlock it, because she seemed pretty good at that sort of thing, but didn't want to talk to her and she obviously didn't want to be friendly with him either. It wouldn't have hurt her to let them use the computers, though. They weren't even hers.

Holding it in his hands cranked up his frustration levels even higher than they already were. Here was a portal to the wide world. The internet. Social media. Funny videos. Denied to them for so long. It was cruel.

Dan put the tablet back in the bag and felt more isolated than ever. Already on his knees so he could do his rummaging, he let his chin fall to his chest and his shoulders slump. He was truly alone.

From outside, a car horn blast stirred him. It was an awakening. Don't let the inside beat you, it said. Come back to the outside.

Outside.

He stood. Must go outside again, if only for a short while. Maybe the police and the Bridgeman gang were chasing them and the public had been alerted to keep an eye out too, but going out for a bit wouldn't do any harm. It's not as if the two people he was shut away with cared at all.

On the dining table was the blue baseball cap Em had been wearing when she rescued them. He adjusted the strap at the back and put it on. There was a small oval mirror on the wall close by and he checked his look, bowing his head so that he could barely catch sight of his reflection from under the shade of the peak. Wearing the cap and his new red and blue shirt, nobody would ever recognise him. If he was to go out, a disguise was a must.

Where could he go?

What Dan really craved was a proper meal.

A KFC! That's it! I'm going for a KFC!

Where is the closest? He didn't know this part of town at all. He wasn't entirely sure what part of town he was in. He couldn't just go wandering in hope of finding a KFC. He might get lost and would be increasing his chances of being spotted.

He couldn't use the laptops or the iPad to search, but... Next to the door to the stairs which led to the back of the shop was a glass bowl. That was where Em had made them put their phones, with their batteries removed, until it was safe to use them again.

Surely it was safe now. Until he could find the location of the nearest KFC at least.

He moved eagerly to the bowl and fished out his phone, then worked out which battery was the right one. It clicked back into place and the screen sparked into life. A short time later, it had found its bearings and picked up a signal.

Dan keyed in the search. *KFC near me.*

The map was filled with a dozen or more little red pins, each bearing an inviting knife and fork symbol. He tapped on the one that was nearest to the blinking blue dot that pulsed over his current location. One-point-eight miles away. That was a bit far to walk.

However.

The bowl wasn't only a useful receptacle for disabled phones. It was also a good place to keep car keys. He picked them out but was suddenly not so certain. Sneaking out on foot was one thing. Taking Em's car without permission was another. This might be going too far.

Dan had never actually passed his test. That was another factor. He'd never officially had a lesson, but that wasn't really an impediment where he grew up. He'd first driven a car when he was fourteen. That wasn't his either, but that didn't seem to matter then. Driving Em's specially adapted car should be a breeze anyway. Automatic gearbox, just push the lever on the steering wheel one way to accelerate and the other to brake, like he'd watched her do. He'd figure out which was which soon enough. One press of the keypad to open the automatic roll-over garage door and you drive away. Easy.

But dare I?

From his right he could hear the sound of the shower being turned on in the bathroom. Shannon wasn't coming out anytime soon. He hadn't heard a peep from Em's room all morning.

He wouldn't be missed. Drive around for a bit, enjoying cruising in the nice big motor, then go for some food. Maybe he could bring a KFC back for the girls as well, as a kind of peace offering.

He walked back to the black bin bags and opened the one with the money, peeling off four ten-pound notes from one of the bundles. Sunshine pierced through the net curtains and made him squint. He hadn't felt its warmth on his skin for an age. He shielded his eyes and, through the curtain, spotted two young mothers chatting on the opposite side of the road, one with a young girl on her hip and the other with a slightly older-looking boy in a pushchair. It seemed so nice out there.

He shoved the money into one pocket and his phone into the other, then gripped the keys firmly in his hand.

'D'you know what?' he said under his breath, 'fuck it!'

CHAPTER

TWENTY-SIX

The overhead sign said they were approaching junction twenty-eight for the A12 Chelmsford and the A1023 Brentwood. Ronnie Bridgeman relaxed in the back seat of his brand new Audi Q8 and watched through the privacy glass window as they sped past the exit.

He held not even the slightest desire to visit either place. He didn't like southerners and never did business with them, so he had no reason to go. In his view, both towns sounded like shit-holes anyway.

They were only an hour and a half or so into a five-hour journey and though Bridgeman was normally the world's worst passenger on long trips, he was unusually becalmed this time. The driver and the minder in the front passenger seat had noticed this, too, but they weren't about to say anything. The driver was making the most of being able to do his job without the dubious benefit of a constant stream of advice in his ear.

Part of the reason why Bridgeman was so strangely quiet was because it had been a successful trip. He had concluded his deal with the Turks and reckoned he had, through his mastery of negotiation and status as the key to the north of England, shaken on an agreement that was more in his favour than theirs. The Turks couldn't get the better of him.

He didn't like having to deal with those people, but business is business. He didn't trust the Turks. Neither did he trust the Serbs, the Greeks, the Tunisians, the Afghans, the Russians, the Americans, the Central Americans, the South Americans, the Nigerians, the Indians, the Chinese or the French. Especially the French. Needs must sometimes if you want to increase your prominence in the markets.

There was another reason why Bridgeman was subdued, other than the fact that he'd knocked back too much whisky negotiating with the Turks. He was concerned. Some would say worried. His domestic issue in Sheffield had still not been resolved. The flash drive was still out there, in the wrong hands, and though it had not yet developed into an immediate threat to his security, the possibility still existed that it might. He didn't like that. The longer it dragged on, the less he liked it. If it went badly wrong, it could ruin everything. Everything.

There was still time to rescue the situation, but his extensive network of eyes and ears had failed to come up with a result so far. Where were those three bastards? They had to show themselves soon.

Ping.

It wasn't his normal phone; it was the other one. He'd taken to carrying it everywhere with him lately. He retrieved it eagerly from the inside pocket of his jacket. This could be it.

You have half an hour head start, then police will be all over it.

There was an address with it. A flat above a closed-down shop called *Tech Two* on Abbeydale Road, it said.

Bridgeman's hangover was swept away in a surge of adrenaline.

Think fast. The two he'd normally turn to were out of

commission. Who could he trust to get it done? Who was close enough to get there quickly?

He checked his watch. Nine fifty-three. His guy who ran his gentlemen's club on Chesterfield Road was usually in place by now. That couldn't be far from this address. He was good. Dependable.

Bridgeman took his other phone from his other inside jacket pocket and found the number.

'Boss.'

'Take a couple of men to the address I'm about to send you and go now. There are three people I need you to apprehend. Two women and a man. Take them to the depot. Faz and Gammo will be waiting for you.'

'Got that.'

'This has to be done *now*. No fannying about. We have a very tight time frame. And listen, they've got a flash drive...'

'A flash drive?'

'Yes, a flash drive. You know what a fucking flash drive is, don't you? It's absolutely imperative you find it and bring it with you. Don't take any shit if they play dumb. I don't mind what you have to do to them to get it, but don't hang about. The place is going to be crawling with cops in less than half an hour. Do you understand?'

'Got it. On my way.'

He forwarded the text message with the address details. Next, he had to call Faz and put him in the picture. They knew what to do, but he wanted to be there.

'How far away are we?' he barked.

The driver checked the satnav. 'Two-and-a-half, two-and-three-quarter hours taking it steady.'

'Well put your bastard toe down. Move it!'

The driver accelerated and drifted to the outside lane. Maybe it wasn't going to be such a peaceful journey back after all.

CHAPTER
TWENTY-SEVEN

One of the young Detective Constables was the first to spot the alert.

'Message from Comms Room. The Range Rover is on the move,' he announced.

It sent a prickle of expectation around the Incident Room. They had been waiting four days for Khan, Rafferty and Kear to break cover and now, at last, it seemed they might have. DCI Larson brought up the alert on her laptop and DI Powell stepped over from the adjoining desk to look over her shoulder.

'Right,' said the DCI, quickly assessing the information. 'We've got a first hit on a camera on Abbeydale Road close to Millhouses Park, so it looks as if they're heading for Totley again until, see, they're picked up again on Whirlowdale Road and then heading west on Hathersage Road. Are they making a run for it, do you think?'

'Looking that way,' Powell added with a grimace. 'Could be an idea to get in touch with Derbyshire to let them know we might need their help to intercept the car if they're on their way out to the Peak District. Not a huge amount of camera coverage out there.'

Her phone rang. The name on the screen told her it was DI Nickle.

'Yes Ryan.'

'The taxi driver came up trumps,' said Nickle. 'He's given us the address on Abbeydale Road where he picked up our three missing people and dropped them off again after ferrying them to the Tyers home in Totley.'

They had been optimistic of such a result the previous evening when DS Senior reported they believed they had found the taxi driver they had been searching for. Nickle had gone to interview him at the start of his shift. Hopes were raised for a major breakthrough.

'Great, give it to me,' she said, scribbling down the details. 'Cheers, Ryan.'

Larson hung up and threw her head back in exasperation. 'Bloody hell! Talk about London buses! We've got an address.'

Powell had overheard the conversation and rolled his eyes. It was the news they wanted, but had it been superseded?

'OK. Let's get out to this address now anyway, even if it turns out nobody's there anymore,' she said. 'Put Derbyshire in the picture, please Gareth, and we need to get our cars out looking for the Range Rover before they get too far. Get word out on the PNC. Where are they up to now?'

They gazed back at the laptop screen.

'Ringinglow Road heading east?' said Powell, quizzically. 'Is that right?'

'Seems so,' Larson confirmed. 'Are they heading back into town? What's going on?'

～

St Albans 5
Watford 11

Heathrow 30

Progress was slow. Much slower than he wanted. They were not even on the M1 yet. The long stretch of sixty miles per hour restriction for road works was pushing Bridgeman to the brink of implosion. Normally, he would have told the driver to charge through regardless, but traffic was heavy and they had spotted a blue and yellow chequered police BMW prowling the inside lane at a steady fifty-eight, ready to pounce on the reckless. They couldn't risk being pulled over.

It felt an eternity since he issued the order. He needed news. They must have done it by now. Not knowing was giving him a bad feeling.

Was it a trap? He had to believe his source wouldn't dare do that. He'd be a dead man.

Had they taken too long and been picked up by the coppers? That couldn't be ruled out.

The phone rang.

'Thank fuck.'

He answered it. 'Yeah.'

'Got two of them, boss.'

'Two?'

'Only two of them there. They said the other one, the bloke, had disappeared. They claimed not to know where he'd gone.'

Bridgeman screwed his eyes in barely supressed fury.

'What about the flash drive?'

'Not there.'

'What do you mean, not there? Didn't I tell you to show them you were being serious until they gave it up?'

'We did. They kept saying it wasn't there. They said the bloke had got it with him.'

Bridgeman released an angry roar from the depths of his being and punched the headrest in front of him so hard that the driver jolted forward and almost swerved into the path of a small hatchback in the outside lane.

'Boss? We couldn't push it too far. We needed to get out of there. We heard the coppers arriving just as we were driving off.'

He was fighting to regain his composure. Think. There was a way.

'Take them to the depot, as planned, and hand them over. Wait there for my instructions.'

He hung up.

Bridgeman poked at the phone with a stubby finger.

Recent calls. Scroll down.

When was it? Friday. Friday morning.

Scroll down.

That it?

He selected the information button. An unattributed mobile number in Sheffield, England. September the ninth, a call at eight minutes past nine which lasted four minutes.

That's the one.

It was the number his source had passed to him that Friday morning. The number he'd called, pretending to be from the police so they could trick Khan into telling them the address where he was hiding. The address Faz and Gammo should have nabbed him at if they hadn't fucked it up.

He had Khan's number.

This time, the little bastard would be left with no option but to give himself up and hand over the flash drive.

'Sergeant McGuire on line one, ma'am.'

Larson snatched at the phone and dabbed at the flashing button. It must be news from the Abbeydale Road flat. McGuire was in one of the cars dispatched there.

'Yes, Charlie.'

'No sign of them, ma'am.'

Damn. At least that should mean they're all in the Range Rover.

'There has been a forced entry from the rear of the building and indications of a struggle inside the flat. Some personal effects lying around, so if they have made a run for it, they left in a hurry. We've come across two phones and a laptop that was still switched on. I don't like it. If I was to hazard a guess, I'd say someone else got here before us and I don't think they were friendly.'

Larson sighed. 'OK. Stay there, Charlie, and see what you can turn up. Let me know if you find anything useful.'

DI Powell had stayed within earshot.

'You hear that?'

'Hmm,' he said. 'Don't like the sound of it.'

'Me neither. Where are we up to with the Range Rover? Somebody must be close enough to spot it soon, surely.'

They checked the screen again. The car had taken a few diversions which had confused them, but it had gone through Hunter's Bar roundabout and was heading towards St Mary's Gate. Still travelling towards the city centre.

It couldn't be long until one of their cars made visual contact.

TWENTY-EIGHT

THE START OF THE SHIFT ALREADY FELT A LONG TIME AGO. PC DAVE Wood's stomach growled as the patrol car turned the corner and he caught sight of the drive-in. The prospect of food was hugely appealing, but his partner, PC Mark Campbell, was not governed by his stomach to the same extent and he was at the wheel.

Besides, they were on the look-out. The alert, issued to all units about an hour ago, said it was high priority and there had been nothing on the radio since to suggest a resolution had been achieved, so they carried on looking.

Still, nipping in for a drive-through coffee and maybe something to nibble on wouldn't hurt, would it? Tide them over until they could take a proper break. He thought about suggesting this to Campbell but didn't want it to look like his mind wasn't on the job and so he let it slide. As if to taunt him further, the queue at the lights left them tantalisingly close to the car park entrance. His eyes drifted longingly towards the restaurant. So near, yet so far.

The lights changed and Campbell put the car in gear, ready to move on.

'Hang on!' Wood called out. He checked the registration plate number on the description they had been sent through the Police National Computer.

'White Range Rover, black roof. That's it!'

'Where?' Campbell was scanning the traffic ahead.

'Parked up in the KFC,' he pointed. 'There!'

Campbell swung into the car park and accelerated towards the Range Rover, braking sharply to a halt across its rear bumper so there was no way the driver could reverse out and escape them. He switched on the blue lights and reached for the radio on the right shoulder of his black police vest.

'Two-three-zero-four to control.'

'Two-three-zero-four go ahead.'

'We have intercepted suspect vehicle yankee papa two zero mike oscar victor in the car park of the KFC restaurant on the corner of Queens Road and Charlotte Road. We're about to approach.'

'Do you require assistance two-three-zero-four?'

'Not at present. We will update as soon as we've established if there's anyone in the vehicle.'

'That's received.'

Wood was already out of the car and walking to the driver's side of the Range Rover. Campbell got out and looked around in case any of the restaurant customers who had noticed the burst of activity appeared to be attempting a swift getaway.

Wood tapped on the window. A young man was behind the wheel. He held a mobile phone in both hands in front of him. He was staring, eyes fixed on the phone in frozen terror as if it was a bomb set to explode at the slightest movement.

'Can you wind the window down for me please, mate?'

No answer. No reaction at all.

Wood tapped again, more firmly this time.

'Can you wind the window down please?'

Campbell cupped his hands to his face to peer through the

dark glass of the rear door. There didn't appear to be anyone else inside.

Wood was running short of patience. He tapped a third time. Hard.

The young man flinched and turned with a jolt, wide-eyed, to the source of the sudden noise.

'Window,' mouthed Wood and made a winding motion with his hand.

This time the message got through. The young man scanned the buttons on the inside of the door for the one most likely to operate the windows and pressed it. The window lowered smoothly with a gentle buzz.

'Is this your vehicle, mate?'

It took the young man a couple of seconds to recognise he had been asked the question, like he was on a time lapse. The officers began to suspect he was on something else.

'N-no. Not mine. I borrowed it.' There was deep fear in his startled eyes. If he was under the influence of drugs, they appeared to have taken him to a dark place.

Wood opened the car door.

'Can you get out of the vehicle for me please, mate?'

Both officers stepped back to give him room to climb out. Slowly, timidly, the young man complied, once he remembered he had to unclip his seat belt first.

'What's your name, mate?' Wood asked. Campbell took out his notebook.

'Dan. Dan Khan,' stuttered the young man.

The policemen exchanged a glance. They recognised the name.

'You know you've got half of South Yorkshire Police looking for you, Dan?'

He was horror-struck again, as if he had been plunged back into a bad dream.

'They've got her!' said Dan. He grabbed Wood's bare forearm, agitated to the point of desperation. 'They've got both of them!'

Campbell reached instinctively to his side, in case this got out of control and he had to do something to restrain the young man.

'Woah, steady down!' Wood gently prised the hand from its grip on his arm. 'Who's got who?'

'They've got my Shannon. And Em.' A thought flashed through his panicked brain and he moved back towards the open car door. 'I've got to go.'

'You're not going anywhere,' said Campbell, planting his hand firmly on Dan's shoulder. Dan recoiled at the contact and turned sharply in fright, as if he had only just realised there were two policemen with him. Campbell eased him gently away from the door so his colleague could close it.

'Talk to me, Dan,' said Wood. 'Who's got them? We can help you.'

The suggestion struck home. Yes. The police. They can help.

'Somebody called Ronnie Bridgeman,' Dan blurted. He hoped he didn't have to explain who Bridgeman was because he didn't really know a lot about him.

The policemen knew who he was.

'Bridgeman?' said Campbell. 'Bridgeman's got your friends?'

'He says he's going to kill them unless I get to where he told me to go at twelve o'clock. I've got to give him this.' Dan reached into his trouser pocket to produce the silver flash drive. 'Then he says he'll set them free. That's why I have to go.'

Wood checked his watch. Eighteen minutes to twelve.

'Where have you got to go – to meet him?'

'The car park of a pub called the Falstaff, just off Derbyshire Lane.'

Wood knew it. Large pub on the corner. It had been boarded up for a couple of years. He tried to calculate how long it would take to drive there. Ten minutes? Maybe twelve? Could be cutting it tight.

The officers looked at each other. Without saying a word, they both acknowledged this was a decision that had to be taken by someone above their pay grade. Campbell backed away and began to speak into the radio on his shoulder.

Dan appeared close to being swept away by the overwhelming tide of panic.

'Listen to me, Dan.' Wood stared intently into the darting eyes of the young man, attempting to lock him into a fixed gaze. 'Listen to me.' He placed both hands on Dan's upper arms and this time got his attention.

'You're going to have to be calm and you're going to have to be strong. If Bridgeman has got your friends then you're going to have to do as he says for now, but we will have your back. You'll not be going into this alone, do you understand, Dan?'

He nodded frantically. 'But if he sees you, he'll run. He'll kill them.'

'He won't know we're there.' Wood immediately realised the flaw in his bold assurance. Their transport wasn't exactly unobtrusive. 'We'll stay out of sight.'

No doubt plans were being formed with his partner on the radio which involved unmarked cars being sent to the meeting place, but what if they didn't get there in time? He didn't like the thought of sending this frightened kid in alone when they would have to stay so far back that they couldn't be spotted. They couldn't afford to let him out of their sight, so if they couldn't keep in visual contact...

'Your phone,' said Wood. 'What type is it?'

The question momentarily confused Dan, like he couldn't understand why the policeman had randomly chosen to start a conversation on the various merits of phone brands.

'Err, iPhone eleven.' He raised his hand to show the device. 'I've been wanting to upgrade but I haven't...'

'Perfect,' Wood interrupted. 'Can you unlock it and go to *Settings* for me?'

Dan did as he was told.

'Give it to me for a sec.' The officer began to scroll through the options. 'I've got an iPhone as well. I used to have this on my daughter's phone when she was younger so I could keep tabs on her when she went out.'

He reddened, guiltily, and looked up. 'You'll understand one day, if you ever have a daughter.'

Wood tapped and scrolled some more.

'That's it. *Location Services* on. I just need to share it now and key in my Apple ID. That's good. Great.'

He handed the phone back, reached into his trouser pocket for his personal mobile and went straight to the app he needed.

'Perfect.' He showed Dan the screen. 'See. Now I can follow you without having to keep you within eyesight.'

'Oh, OK,' Dan replied, less than convincingly.

Campbell re-emerged from the other side of the Range Rover.

'I've just spoken to DCI Larson. They're putting officers in unmarked cars in place so they can apprehend the suspects once we know the two females are safe, but we have to be sure there's no risk.' He turned to face Dan. 'That means we will have to send you in there, Dan. If you don't show, that could blow it. Are you all right with that, mate?'

'Yeah, yeah.' His heart was thumping. He felt as if his legs were about to give way under him.

Wood checked his watch. Thirteen minutes to twelve. They had to move.

He gripped Dan's shoulder firmly. 'You've got this, mate. We'll get you and your friends out of it unharmed.' He opened the car door and surveyed the cabin. 'Is there a satnav?'

'Dunno,' said Dan. 'I don't need it. I know where it is. I'm pretty sure.'

'OK.' Wood grimaced. He would have preferred to have more reassurances in place but there was no time. 'We've got your back. Best set off, mate.'

The two officers moved swiftly to drive the patrol car out of the way. Campbell manoeuvred it so that he could be ready to follow as Dan reversed out the Range Rover and then moved slowly forward towards the exit.

'Give him half a minute.' Wood gripped his phone. The blue dot began to move on the map as the Range Rover pulled out onto the main road. 'I've got him on this.'

He spoke into his radio.

'One-five-six-four to control.'

'One-five-six-four go ahead.'

'The target has set off for the rendezvous point and we are in pursuit, keeping a short distance away. We have a trace on his mobile phone.'

'That's received.'

A knot of nervous apprehension had taken over where only recently there had been hunger pangs. Wood watched the screen. There was so much at stake.

'OK,' he said. 'Let's go. Right at the lights on to Queens Road.'

The lights were still at green for them. They could see the Range Rover turn left at the next lights ahead.

'He's going towards Heeley.' The blue dot steered the right course. The lights had changed this time and the gap between them began to lengthen. When they set off again, half a mile back, Wood noticed the dot was no longer moving.

'Bugger.'

'What is it?' asked Campbell.

'Not sure, but I think he's stopped.'

They took a ninety degree turn in the road and, squinting,

Wood caught sight of a large white car, pulled in to the side with a left indicator on.

'What's he doing? He's going to be late.'

Campbell slowed down so that his partner could peer in and see what was happening with Dan in the Range Rover. Had he lost his nerve?

'He's talking on the phone,' said Wood. 'What's going on? Pull in a bit ahead.'

An angry driver behind them sounded his horn as the patrol car was bumped up on to the kerb. They ignored it. Campbell peered into his rear view mirror and Wood turned in his seat to look back.

Dan was still on the phone. They watched and waited. Suddenly, the Range Rover pulled out into the traffic again, making a red hatchback pull up sharply, and lurched across the road into a side street. The white reverse lights lit up and the tyres squealed as the car was whipped around the corner to face the opposite way.

'Jesus! He's going back on himself!'

Campbell shoved their car into gear and shot out, causing the red hatchback driver more consternation. He had to bump the front wheels onto the opposite kerb to complete a U-turn.

'One-five-six-four to control.'

'One-five-six-four go ahead.'

'Target has changed direction and is heading back towards Queens Road. Repeat. Target heading back towards Queens Road.'

'Maybe they know we're following,' said Campbell. 'Maybe there's been a change of plan.'

CHAPTER
TWENTY-NINE

ONE MALE OCCUPANT.

DCI Clare Larson heard the words over the radio and her heart leapt. It had been four days since they lost contact with three of the key figures in the murder investigation and now it seemed they had one of them.

But only one of them.

Where were the other two? Then she found out. Then she knew for sure this investigation had taken a darkly sinister twist.

She and DI Gareth Powell had headed to the small office, away from the general hubbub of the incident room, as soon as the first call came through from the Constable in the patrol car. Larson had chosen, from the start of the investigation, to station herself at a desk among the rest of the team. She wanted to make herself accessible to all ranks, but she found it useful to shut herself away in the tiny ten-by-ten side room when she needed thinking space. Now was definitely a time to be free from distraction.

Larson paced, like a stressed animal in a holding cage. Dan Khan had been told Shannon Rafferty and Emilia Kear were being held by Sheffield's most notorious criminal, according to the information relayed by the Constable. It was what they most feared when they found the flat at Abbeydale Road empty. An empty flat with signs of a forced entry and a hurried exit. Not a good combination. They'd suspected the hand of Ronnie Bridgeman was all over this case and now they had confirmation.

Bridgeman was calling the shots. He had apparently threatened to kill the two women hostages and Larson had no doubt he was capable of such brutality. Their safe recovery was paramount. That was why she had taken the decision to allow Khan to comply with Bridgeman's demands. She was sending him into danger. She felt she had no choice, but she hated doing it. There was far too much that could go horribly wrong.

Their chances of a happy resolution depended on getting officers in place at the closed-down pub on Derbyshire Lane, without their presence being detected, and then pouncing on the criminals after the exchange had taken place. The two women for a flash drive? What was that all about? Right now, they could not concern themselves with that. All that mattered was that nobody got hurt.

If it did go horribly wrong, three lives could be lost and that would be on her call. It seemed absurd to measure what might be about to happen in terms of how it could impact her career, but she knew if this did end badly, her judgement would inevitably be called into question. An ignominious end to her short career as a Detective Chief Inspector was the last of her concerns at that moment, though. Especially when the officers in the patrol car radioed in an unexpected development.

'*Target has changed direction and is heading back towards Queens Road. Repeat. Target heading back towards Queens Road.*'

'What the hell?' Powell, who had been perched nervously on the edge of a chair, shot to his feet.

Larson snatched up the radio.

'One-five-six-four, this is DCI Larson.'

'Yes, ma'am.'

'Have you seen anything to explain the change of direction?'

'The target was pulled in to the kerb and on his phone when we passed the car. Our suspicion is he's been issued with new instructions. By the speed he's travelling, it looks like he's been told to get a move on as well. We've still got the phone trace and we're in pursuit.'

Larson swore under her breath. The pub rendezvous was a distraction. A decoy in case the police were on to them. Unmarked cars were heading in the wrong direction. Powell realised that too and quickly left the office to issue the recall. Where was Bridgeman sending Dan Khan to now?

'Stay with him and keep us in the loop.'

'Understood, ma'am.'

Powell burst back into the office. 'All units heading back towards town.'

Larson nodded.

'Do you think Bridgeman realises?' he asked.

'Could be that he's just making sure he stays a step ahead,' she replied with a shrug. 'We've got to hope that's the case. How far out are the unmarked units now?'

'Ten minutes. Quarter of an hour.'

The radio crackled into life again.

'One-five-six-four, we're on Bramall Lane approaching the football ground and the target has turned left on to St Mary's Gate.'

The inner ring road. Khan could be heading anywhere in the city from there.

'Target filtering left on to London Road.'

Larson plotted the route in her mind. If he carried on in that direction it would be easier for the unmarked units returning from the first location to intercept him sooner. They were heading more or less straight towards him.

'Now turning off London Road with a right at the lights down, what's that, Boston Street?'

Boston Street? Larson searched for it on her phone. She hadn't expected him to get off the main roads this soon.

'Right turn again. We are about to enter London Road. No visual contact.'

Larson studied the map. Can't be the first right. That's a dead end. Second right. Napier Street? Where's he heading? A short cut?

'Another right. He's pulling in to – that's a car park, isn't it? The Waitrose car park.'

'That can't be the new rendezvous, surely?' said Powell. 'It has to be too public.'

'I can't see any alternative exits out of there to get him back on to the ring road. Just one road out. What are they sending him there for?'

She spoke into the radio.

'Larson to one-five-six-four. Proceed with caution. If this is the meeting point we can't risk you being spotted because it might put the hostages in danger. Back-up is on the way, but it's still ten minutes out.'

'Understood, ma'am.'

'We should cover the exit,' said Powell.

The DCI considered. 'We'd be showing our hand. I don't think we can afford to do that until we know everybody is safe. Let's see where this is heading.'

'Approaching the supermarket entrance. The target appears to have come to a halt at the far end of the car park. What do you want us to do, ma'am?'

'Pull in and park up out of sight. Proceed on foot. Get eyes on the target vehicle and let us know what's going on; but be careful.'

'Copy that.'

~

Campbell swung the patrol car right into the car park approach road with a squeal of the front tyres. The first line of parking spaces were all taken.

'There. Pull in there.' Wood pointed towards a space just up ahead.

Campbell stepped heavily on the brake as a young woman with a child in the seat of her trolly wandered across their path, struggling to control the trolly and its heavy load of shopping. She shot them an irate stare for daring to drive too fast and made sure they had to wait for her to get out of the way, just to make her point. Finally, they were able to pull in to the gap and the two officers jumped straight out of the car. The young woman quickened her pace, worried her petulance had landed her in trouble.

'You go that way, I'll go this,' said Campbell.

They set off on separate routes to the same destination, slipping between the neat lines of stationery cars and dodging the moving ones when they crossed the snake of connecting roads, crouching low all the time. As they approached the last block of parking spaces, Wood pulled up, taking cover behind a scruffy metallic blue people carrier, and waved his colleague over.

'There,' he said, breathing heavily. 'See it?'

'Got it,' Campbell confirmed.

The white Range Rover was on the furthest row of spaces with no other car on either side of it. They couldn't see Dan Khan – or anyone else – close by.

'The driver's door's open,' Campbell added.

Wood squinted. He was right. It was only open a little, but it was open.

'One-five-six-four to DCI Larson,' he reported into the radio. 'We've found the vehicle. No activity around it. I'm going to find a spot where I can observe if the vehicle is still occupied.'

The officers exchanged a brief glance and Wood set off, skirting the line of cars to where he could get a sideway view into the Range Rover. It was empty. He was sure it was empty. He looked around quickly, to be sure he was not being watched, and darted towards the car.

Nobody there. Campbell joined him.

Wood pulled out his mobile phone from his trouser pocket.

The blue dot was nudging across the map. It was out of the car park and heading back towards the main road.

'Shit!'

He fumbled for the radio.

'Target is on the move again. Repeat. Target on the move. The vehicle has been abandoned. He's approaching London Road in another vehicle, but we have no idea as to its identity.'

They sprinted back to the patrol car. No need to keep a low profile now. They didn't want to allow the new car, speeding away with Dan Khan on board, to get too far ahead of them.

Campbell, younger and leaner, reached their car first and dived into the driver's seat. He had started the engine and was beginning to reverse out by the time his red-faced and panting colleague caught up. Normally, Campbell would have made a cutting comment, but this was no time for banter.

Wood had started to get his breathing under control as they sped left out of the car park. Campbell switched on the blue lights and siren. They would have to make themselves less obvious again soon but cutting through any traffic build-up before reaching the inner ring road could save them valuable seconds.

'Target is on the inner ring road heading in the direction of the University Square roundabout. He's got a bit of a jump on us, but we're making up ground.'

'OK one-five-six-four, this is Larson again. We have Sergeant Panapa in an unmarked unit only a minute or so behind you. Drop right back when he is in a position to take over and we'll need you to communicate directly with him to relay the movements of the target.'

'Understood, ma'am.'

Wood and Campbell were relieved to hear that back-up was arriving, but they were shooting in the dark. The inner ring road was rarely anything other than very busy. Cars and vans darted between the three lanes to dodge slower drivers or in tardy realisation that their exit was almost upon them, with newcomers filtering in at every junction to add to the confusion. How could they possibly know which of them was now carrying Dan Khan? He could be in the back of a truck or riding pillion on a motorbike, for all they knew, and they didn't have a clue where it was heading, other than where the blue dot was leading them.

The blue dot was their lifeline. Their one hope for keeping Dan safe.

The dot was making its next move.

'Target heading right at the Shalesmoor Roundabout east in the direction of the Parkway.'

Campbell was doing his best to weave through the traffic, but it was stop-start all the way and his increasing frustration was manifesting in more frequent swear words at a higher volume. He was considering giving it another burst of blues and twos so they could cut another chunk out of the gap between them and the target when the call came in.

'One-six-one-six, we have you in view one-five-six-four. Disengage and we'll take over.'

In his rear-view mirror, Campbell could see the powerful black BMW X5 closing on them, blue strobe lights dancing across its front grille and along the top of its windscreen. It cut through the traffic easily as drivers noticed its advance and yielded submissively. With a flash of its headlights, it was soon past the patrol car too and away towards its prey.

'We see you, one-six-one-six. The target is approximately a mile ahead, still heading east on the A61. He is approaching the lights over the river. We'll stay with you as close as we can and keep you up to date on its progress.'

'*That's received.*'

The X5 was out of sight almost as quickly as it had appeared. It was time for the interceptor to do some intercepting and the two officers in the patrol car felt a weight lift off their shoulders. But they still had a big job to do.

'Target is filtering left on to Savile Street, one-six-one-six, and approaching the lights at the crossroads.'

'*Understood.*'

The blue dot hovered at the junction. The lights were against them. That could only help the X5 to catch up some more. It jolted forward again.

'He's staying on Savile Street heading towards Brightside.'

Brightside. It was once as pleasant as it sounds, but not for a long time. Not since it became a main artery to the heart of the steel industry that clung to the contours of the River Don and made Sheffield famous around the world. Though the dense smog exhaled by the vast heavy steel mills had long since dissipated, it remained a busy industrial area.

'*What's the latest on his position, one-five-six-four?*'

'I have him moving past the junction with Carwood Road, still heading north-east. Are you close to establishing visual contact?'

'*We're almost at Carwood Road. I see half a dozen or so vehicles ahead of us. It could be any one of them.*'

Even allowing for the time delay as the signal from Dan's phone bounced back off the satellite, the two officers in the patrol car felt a surge of optimism. They were getting closer. All they needed now was for their suspect vehicle to reveal itself, either by making a move off the main road or by the others dropping out of the line of traffic.

'*One of the cars, a silver Toyota Corolla, is turning left on to Atlas Way. Please confirm, could this be our target?*'

Wood stared intently at the blue dot as it faltered along the main road, teasing them by stalling for a second before jumping past the junction with Atlas Street. It wasn't that car.

'Negative. He is still proceeding north-east on the A6109.'

Still, one down. With luck, they might narrow the field down to a single possibility before the pursuit got much further. Heading in their current direction, they would be on the motorway in less than three miles and that could add another layer of complication to keeping track of them.

'*There is a dark blue Volvo SUV moving into the lane at the lights to turn right off the A6109 on to Newhall Road. Get ready to advise.*'

The blue dot came to a stop. That might just mean the suspect was also waiting at the traffic lights, maybe to carry on straight ahead. Wood was willing it to head right, along the thin white strip of the map off the main road. Come on! Be the one!

'*Lights have changed and the Volvo has completed the right turn. What do you see, one-five-six-four?*'

Come on! Come on! The dot seemed to take an age to catch up with real life. Come on!

Finally. It moved. It went right.

'That's the one. Target confirmed heading right on to Newhall Road.'

'*Understood. We have him in sight. Control, stand by to direct back-up when we're able to identify the vehicle's destination and I'll have a registration for you as soon as we get close enough. Thank you, one-five-six-four. Good work.*'

Wood punched the air, as much in relief as celebration. That had been an intense last hour. Campbell gripped the wheel a little less tightly and turned the car off the main road. There was the familiar reddish brown sign of a Costa up ahead.

'I don't know about you, Woody,' said Campbell, 'but I could kill for a coffee.'

THIRTY

The pain around Shannon's left cheekbone had eased. It throbbed and hurt like hell at first, so badly that she tried to keep her eye shut. Opening it worsened the shooting stabs of agony that felt like dull needles being shoved into her brain.

She had never been hit as hard as that. The man who did it was one of the three who barged into the flat, shouting and scattering stuff around like it was their task to break as much and make as much noise as they could before a hooter sounded. She had been in the kitchen, making a cuppa not long after having showered and dressed. They'd dragged Em out of her room. Both of them were terrified. Of course they were. God knows what the men were going to do to them.

After doing their best to tear the place apart in what must have only been a few minutes but felt a lot longer, one of the men turned his fury on the two of them. They had attempted to hide away in the corner of the room, screaming, huddled tightly while the turbulent violence of wanton destruction exploded around them.

'Stand up!' he demanded, spit glistening on his lip.

They rose timidly from a crouch. Snivelling fearful tears,

bodies braced against potential impact like they were caught in the headlights of a car hurtling their way.

'Where is it?'

Neither of them could answer, even if they had known in that moment what it was he wanted.

'Where is it?' he roared again.

Shannon attempted to respond.

'What...? What...?'

'The flash drive!'

The flash drive! The flash drive! Jesus! That damned flash drive!

'We haven't got it.'

She wasn't being defiant, flippant or deliberately obstructive. It was the truth. If she'd got the wretched thing, she would have happily handed it to them so the men would go away and the ordeal would be over.

That was when he hit her the first time.

It was an open-palm slap but there was some force behind it. There was no wonder it hurt. He was a big man, at least twice her age, with muscles that strained the stitching of a buttoned grey suit jacket. His face was red from the boiling rage that sent darting bolts firing from his bulging blue eyes and his nose was crudely misshapen, like a boxer's. A boxer who had taken too many punches. Perhaps his opponents had not usually been young women half his size.

She yowled from the impact, shocked. It was astonishing she stayed upright. Em mumbled 'Oh my god! Oh my god!' and shrank even tighter into the wall in case the next blow was heading her way.

'Where is it?' He stretched out the word 'where' this time and turned up the volume of the delivery another notch.

'It's not here!' Shannon blubbed, pleadingly. 'My boyfriend's got it.'

'And where's he?'

There was no way she could answer that and make their situation better.

'I... don't... know!'

That was when he hit her the second time.

This one felt harder, even though it was again an open palm to her left cheek. Maybe that was because her pain levels were already high from the first slap. Her knees gave way under her this time and she crumpled to the floor, holding her face and bawling like a baby.

Em cowered into the corner, left exposed now. She shook uncontrollably.

The man appeared ready to unleash, but one of the others approached over his shoulder.

'Boomer,' he said. 'Time.'

That one word jolted him to his senses. Time. They had none.

'Grab them,' he commanded the other two. 'We've got to go.'

That was maybe two hours ago. It might have been less than that. Time had been irrelevant since. The area around Shannon's left cheekbone still hurt, but it was more of a throbbing ache now. When she was able, she had touched the point of impact gently and was surprised it had not broken the skin. It was starting to swell now, though. It had already puffed up enough to reduce the lid of her left eye to a narrow slit.

She couldn't touch it anymore. Her arms were tied behind her back with gaffer tape. Her legs were bound, too. So were Em's, she assumed, going by the sounds of stretching and tearing when they were first brought to the room and pushed into plastic chairs, side by side. They were blindfolded, so had not been able to tell where they were going in the car and didn't know much about the room they were now in, except that it smelled cold and stale. Shannon had also noticed that the area under their feet, under the chairs, crinkled like it was covered in plastic sheeting.

The more she thought about why it might be covered in plastic sheeting, the less she liked it.

The tears had dried now, but they were no less terrified. Neither of them had dared say a word since they had been dragged from the flat. They listened, absorbing the sound of two men – two other men than the ones at the flat, they thought – making plans across the other side of the room, straining but not wanting to hear clues as to what their fate might be.

Then Em spoke, in no more than a whisper.

'Shannon.'

Shannon heard it clearly enough but hesitated, wondering if it was safe to answer.

'Yeah?'

'I'm sorry,' Em added.

Sorry? This was not her fault. If it hadn't been for Em, she and Dan might have been in this position – or worse – several days ago.

'You've nothing to say sorry for.'

'Oh, but I have.' Em's hoarse voice was cracking. 'I should've let you two go straight to the police, like you wanted to. You'd have been safer there.'

Shannon's head dropped. That was obvious now. She already regretted that they hadn't been firmer in standing up for themselves, but Em's suggestions that the police couldn't be trusted, that she and Dan might be fitted up for Fingerless Frankie's murder, had sown just enough of a seed of doubt to keep them in the flat. Just until they could be more certain.

'There's another thing,' Em said, faltering. 'I lied.'

'What?'

'About Dan.' She held back, finding it hard to release the full confession. 'About him coming on to me. He didn't, of course. I made that up.'

'But what about the...'

'I put them there, in his coat pocket. I had an inkling you wouldn't be able to stop yourself searching, just to make sure.'

Shannon flushed with shame and anger. She'd been led on. She'd been shown up for what she was; a dumb bitch blinded by jealousy. Even Em had seen it in her and had played on it. How could she doubt her Dan? How could she be duped into doubting him so easily?

'Why would you *do* such a thing?'

There was quiet between them. Shannon wondered if she might not be granted the courtesy of a full explanation. Surely, that was the least she deserved.

'I was selfish,' Em said at last. 'When I saw what was on that flash drive all I wanted was to use it to hurt Bridgeman but hurt him in a way that profited me. Bring him to his knees. Ruin him, but make him grovel first, for what he did to my brother. If you two had your way, the police would have been handed the information they needed to send him to prison, but that wasn't enough for me. What would have happened to all his wealth? I wanted it. Dirty money or not, I could have put it to good use.'

She stalled. This was hard to say.

'The two of you were rock solid – I could see that. I knew you weren't going to come over to my way of thinking and that sooner or later you were both going to leave the flat and take the flash drive to the police. There was only so much longer I could persuade you to stay, so I had to come up with something quickly. I realised I had to come between you. Divide and conquer if you like. You're a strong woman, Shannon. Dan is more vulnerable, I think. My idea was to make you so cross with him that you walked out and that's why I came up with the story about the knickers. Once you left, I expected Dan to want to come running after you to win you back. That was when I reckoned I could persuade him to leave the flash drive with me, for safe keeping, until you two had patched it up.'

'But he would have explained everything to me and I would have believed him. You must have known then we wouldn't come back to you. We'd have gone to the police.'

'Yes, but you'd have had an interesting story to tell them and no evidence. By the time you'd led them to the flat to gather the proof, I'd have long gone.'

She paused. 'I didn't reckon on Dan being the one to leave first. I got it all wrong.'

Em swallowed hard. 'I know what I did was terrible. I'm so ashamed.'

Shannon could hardly believe what she was hearing. Em had fed her poison and she had been stupid enough to swallow every drop.

The last time she had seen Dan, she had been so disgusted with him that she couldn't stand to be in the same room. There was no way she could have looked him in the eye and confronted him but if she had, she would have seen the truth. She would have known that Dan could never do anything like that to her. Never.

She wanted him so badly now. She wanted to tell him she was sorry for doubting him. She wanted to hold him and tell him she had always loved him and that she would love him for ever.

But where was he?

They were not going to get out of this alive. She knew that. They were going to end up dumped in a bin like Fingerless Frankie. That's why there was plastic under the chairs, to help contain the mess after the men killed them. She thought about Dan again. Part of her was glad he was not there when the men broke into the flat; that he had escaped this horror. Part of her – most of her – wished he was with her now. They should be facing this together. If it was the other way round and he was tied to this chair while she was still out there, she knew she would want to be with him, whatever the consequences. She couldn't stand the idea of having him taken from her. He would feel the same way. How could either of them live without the other? It was not possible.

Yet the last time they were together, she had treated him so cruelly. The last time ever.

She began to sob again.

A voice bellowed at them from across the room.

'Will you shut the fuck up?'

Shannon tried to compose herself. She stifled the sound, but not the tears that were blotted by the black cloth covering her eyes.

'I'm really sorry,' Em whispered. Then they said no more.

Even the men had stopped talking. Stillness echoed off the walls of that musty room, intensifying the prolonged agony of their wait. The empty silence was draining all hope from Shannon. She began to wish it was all over.

Why don't they get on with it?

Beside her, there was sound. Em had been shuffling in her seat almost the whole time they had been there, but she hadn't been this vocal before. It was a quiet sound, but hard to block out once you tuned in to it. A sad whimper. Like a wounded fox hiding in its burrow away from the hounds. She was in pain.

'Are you all right?' Shannon breathed.

'Struggling a bit.' Em moved again and let out a gasp as if she had brushed against something sharp. 'Staying still this long is no good for me and I'm overdue my meds. My joints are seizing up.'

Shannon resented Em for the deception she had confessed to, but her initial anger had fallen into the shadow of the anger she directed at herself for allowing herself to be deceived. She knew she should hate Em for what she did, but she couldn't. All she felt now was pity. Em shouldn't have to suffer like this. It wasn't right.

'Hey!' she called.

Em flinched. 'What are you doing?'

'You two!'

The men were bent over their phones, trying to ease the mounting tedium of their vigil. One of them rolled his eyes in irritation.

'What?'

'Can you cut my friend free?'

'Shannon!' Em hissed, trying to silence her.

'Yeah, right!' snorted the man.

'She's got rheumatoid arthritis. She needs to be able to move because it affects her joints if she has to stay still. She's in a lot of pain.'

The other man piped up. 'Would she like us to run a bath and pour her a glass of wine as well?' He imagined he was being witty.

'Look, I wouldn't worry about it, if I was you,' said the first. 'If it wasn't for the fact that the boss wanted to be here personally, you wouldn't be in no pain no more.'

There we have it. We're going to die here.

The confirmation should have crushed Shannon, but it didn't. It emboldened her.

'Well, what's it matter then? You're going to kill us, OK. All we want is that you let her get up and walk about for a bit while we're waiting for you to do it. It's not much to ask, is it?'

Em fed on the new brazen mood of her fellow prisoner.

'I'm hardly likely to charge over there and try to beat you up, am I? Ten minutes to get my joints working again. That's all it takes.'

'Come on!' Shannon added. 'Ten minutes.'

'Oh, for fuck's sake,' muttered the first man. They heard footsteps approaching from across the room. Em felt breath on the back of her neck before the knife sliced through the tape and her arms sprang free. He circled to the front to release her legs and pulled off the blindfold.

He glared fiercely into her face, pointing a finger inches from her nose.

'Ten minutes.'

She blinked. Even the dim light given by the single bare bulb in the sparse room was too much at first. She twisted and flexed her arms and legs to encourage blood to circulate before making a slow, tortured attempt to rise to her feet. It was torment, but it was better than the alternative.

'Thank you,' she said to the man, but he was already stomping away from her, back to his accomplice on the other side of the stark, windowless room. She recognised them. The two she had seen hauling Frankie away from the Blackstock Road flat. The two she had seen outside the house on Eagle Street.

A sharp rap on the door made both women jump. The bearded white guy and the taller black guy exchanged an 'are-you-going-to-get-that' look before the white guy took the hint that it was his turn to move. He sauntered to the door and pulled back the bolt to open it. The boxer with the bent nose stepped into the room.

'Boomer,' greeted bearded guy.

'Gammo,' replied boxer. He glanced towards black guy. 'Faz.'

'Sorted?' asked Faz.

'Yep.' Boomer reached into his trouser pocket and pulled out a small rectangular computer flash drive in a brushed chrome metal sleeve. He handed it over.

'Sweet,' said Faz, dropping it into the inside pocket of his coat. 'And?'

Boomer gestured with a twitch of his head towards the door. 'Lads are bringing him from the car. Where's the boss?'

'Got caught in a hold-up on the M1 south of Northampton,' Faz replied, unable to keep the mischievous smile off his lips.

'I bet that went down well.' Boomer raised his eyebrows. They had both witnessed Bridgeman's impatience too many times.

'You know it. He messaged me to say he'll be here...' Faz consulted his watch, '...in about half an hour.'

There was activity at the door. With heavies on either side gripping his arms, Dan was steered reluctantly into the room. Since being bundled into their car in the supermarket car park he had been dreading what lay ahead. It would surely be nothing good. They had taken his bargaining chip and had reneged on their side of the deal. It was hard to see a way this turned out well.

But then he saw her and suddenly none of that mattered any more.

'Shan!'

She heard his voice and her heart leapt.

'Dan?'

He wrestled free of the two men's grasp and ran to her, dropping to his knees so that he could wrap his arms around her, bound and blindfolded in the plastic chair.

'I thought I was never going to see you again,' he cried, tears of relief rolling down his cheeks.

'Me too.' She was overwhelmed. 'I love you so much.'

'I think I'm gonna puke,' muttered Faz.

Dan kissed her ravenously on the lips and then pulled her tight to him again, squeezing his cheek against her's. She winced and let out a yelp of pain. He noticed it and pulled back, alarmed. He gently lifted the blindfold. Her beautiful face made grotesque by a purpling swollen welt. One of her gorgeous eyes almost completely hidden behind puffy inflamed lids.

The shock of it hit him in the chest with such force that it knocked him back to his childhood. He remembered his mum. He wanted to kill his dad for doing that to her. If he had been bigger, he might have tried. Thankfully, his dad walked out on them soon after it happened, but Dan never forgot that sensation of utter helplessness. He swore he wouldn't let that happen again.

'Who did this to her?' He spun, his eyes filled with fury, to face the five men.

They laughed at his outrage, scornfully.

'Who did it?'

Boomer stepped forward, preening.

'What you going to do about it?'

Dan rose to his feet and moved forward, meeting the challenge. It was not an even match, but he didn't care. He was ready to throw everything he had into it anyway.

'Big man,' he said. 'You must think you're so tough, hitting a woman like that. Make you proud, does it? Big man. Tough guy.'

He moved closer.

Boomer shortened the gap between them with another step.

'You're heading the right way for a slap yourself, son.'

Dan was undeterred. He stuck out his jaw, striding boldly until they were practically nose to nose.

'Come on then, big man. Show me what you got.'

He didn't see the short right-hand punch, but he felt it. Straight to the solar plexus. It took all the wind out of his sails and every breath of wind out of his body, too. He crumpled like a drinks can that had been stamped on. Only after five, six, seven seconds of complete immobility, curled in a foetal, eye-bulging ball on the floor, was he able to suck in a first wheezing lungful of air, like a swimmer desperate to break the surface from a deep dive. After the trial of drawing breath came the hacking cough and the nausea. The challenge, such as it was, was over.

Boomer adjusted the sleeves of his jacket and backed away. Much as he kind of admired the balls of the kid, that had to be done. There was only so far he could be pushed.

'Tie him to the chair, for fuck's sake,' Faz ordered the two who had brought Dan from the car. They hauled him up by the arms and dragged him towards where Shannon had watched the whole, short, futile episode in horror.

'Dan! Dan! Are you all right? What have you done to him?' she bawled.

The two wrapped gaffer tape around his legs and arms, securing him to the chair next to Shannon. Even if he had wanted to resist, it would have proved beyond Dan. He couldn't even sit up straight or control his coughing spasms.

The five men huddled on the opposite side of the room to share their amusement at the brief entertaining interlude. Their mood changed when a moment of clarity struck Gammo.

'Where's the other one?'

They all stared in the same direction. Two chairs. Two hostages.

Em had gone.

The door. It remained slightly open.

'Shit!' Faz kicked at an empty cigarette packet on the floor. The other four watched him.

'Fucking go and find her! She can't have got far. She's a cripple.'

They burst into action at last.

'I'll stay with these two.'

The four men piled through the door and split off in separate directions to scour the warehouse building and try to find their missing captive. So much of it was filled by stacked pallets and boxes that all they could see was a vast choice of ideal hiding places.

'Shit!' screamed Faz again. He looked at his watch. The boss was expected in no more than twenty minutes. The last thing he needed was to explain to Bridgeman how they had managed to lose one of his intended victims.

Then he heard different voices and he realised that was not quite the last thing he needed.

'Armed police! Stay where you are! Stand still! Get on the ground!'

In no time they were at the door. Bristling with noise and no-nonsense intimidating menace, dressed in heavy black from their Kevlar helmets to their hefty boots to the tips of their Heckler and Koch assault rifles. Soon there were five of them in the room, all pointing their weapons at the man holding a handgun to the head of a borderline hysterical young woman strapped to a plastic chair.

'Put down your weapon! Now! Put it down!' they yelled at him, five voices all bombarding Faz's frenzied mind with the same message. He planned, as well as you can plan anything in the face of such a paralysing assault to the senses, to use the hostages to negotiate a way out, but he soon understood it was a hopeless ambition.

He dropped the gun and cupped his hands on top of his head.

'Fine, fine.'

It was over. The Specialist Firearms Officers swarmed over him, pressing him to the ground, frisking him for other weapons and wrenching his arms behind his back to tighten the handcuffs.

One of the officers crouched in front of the two petrified innocents in the drama. He pulled up his balaclava to reveal his face in hope of easing their trauma.

'It's all right now,' he said, calmly. 'We'll soon have you safely out of here. Are you OK?'

CHAPTER
THIRTY-ONE

THE ATMOSPHERE HAD BEEN TENSE IN THE INCIDENT ROOM MOST OF THE morning. The team knew this was their big chance to break the case open. When the news came through, it was as if a huge firework had burst in the air and had showered those below with rose petals.

The two main suspects in the Frankie Aston murder, Farrell and Gamson, as well as three more of Ronnie Bridgeman's goons, were in custody.

Most importantly, Shannon Rafferty, Dan Khan and Emilia Kear were all safe and well. They were on their way to be checked out medically, but it would not be long until DCI Clare Larson and her team would have the answers to so many questions that had lain open for the last five days.

Larson stayed in the small side office throughout. She sagged into her seat as the news spread and cheers sounded around the incident room, lacking the emotional energy to join in the celebrations.

'Well done, ma'am,' said DI Powell, who had been with her throughout. He could appreciate what this meant to her. First major case as Senior Investigating Officer, well on the way to a major result inside a week.

'Shall we join in?' He gestured towards where the others were congratulating each other with handshakes and hugs.

'Just give me a minute,' she said. 'You go.'

He flashed a brief understanding smile and headed for the door, closing it behind him.

Larson exhaled. She was drained. Nothing beat the sensation of seeing a case to a successful conclusion but this was different. Only now did she fully comprehend how much she had taken on her shoulders, as the SIO. It can't be like this every time. Surely she would learn to handle it better in the future, with the benefit of experience.

God, I hope so or I'll end up in an early grave, like Jim Pendlebury.

She shook herself after allowing in such a gloomy thought. The team deserved – she deserved – to toast this triumph and the team needed to be told, by her, that they had done a good job. It was time to get out there.

But they also needed reminding that it wasn't all over yet. There was so much work still to be done. Everything had to be rock solid to give them the convictions they needed and they still had to gather evidence to get the one they really wanted. The ringleader. Bridgeman.

One step at a time. Larson coaxed life back into her limbs and went to join the rest.

'Ryan.'

The room was still buzzing, but not in celebration anymore. They were back to business. The DCI had said a few words and then the focus was back on. Everybody was driven to finish the job. The light at the end of the tunnel was only closer. Larson was heading over to consult with one of her Detective Inspectors, Ryan Nickle.

'What's happening with the surveillance on Bridgeman?'

He frowned. 'Still looking to re-establish contact, ma'am.'

'Re-establish?' She was taken aback.

'Yeah, we followed him yesterday morning when he drove to his casino on Dickinson Lane, watched him go in, kept his car in sight in the car park all the while, but he never reappeared. We've still got people out there, but nothing so far.'

Larson tried to work out whether she should be annoyed at hearing this for the first time.

'You didn't think to bring this to me?'

'I've been out all yesterday afternoon and all morning working on it myself. The situation was in control as far as it could be. I figured you had enough on your plate. Sorry, ma'am.'

She was irritated but he was right. Nickle was an experienced officer. They had been in CID for just about the same number of years. She had to show trust.

'That's fine. Let me know when you pick up on him again.'

'Sure.' He turned back to what he was working on.

Larson began to go but stopped.

'Another thing, Ryan. Our three wanderers should be heading in soon from the hospital. I want to talk to Kear and Gareth Powell will lead the interview with Rafferty and Khan. I'd like you to carry on with what you're doing, but I'll need you when we start interviewing Bridgeman's gang later.'

He gave a thumbs-up.

Bridgeman was just approaching the motorway junction for Meadowhall when word came through. It sucked the air out of him. The last he had heard, all three of the people who had caused him so much strife had been taken. The flash drive was back in their hands. They were on track again. A crisis had been averted. All that was left to do was to guarantee that the three stayed silent forever. He was looking forward to witnessing the final act. He was five minutes away.

He was so relishing the anticipation of what was to come that he almost ignored the message when he heard the phone ping in his pocket, but he decided he should see.

The news was bad enough. It couldn't have been much worse. What did make it worse, though, was not hearing soon enough. If he had been told earlier, he could have warned Faz that he needed to get everybody out of there pronto, before the cops arrived. They'd been caught cold. Five good men had been nabbed.

His contact had let him down.

Bridgeman could not afford to think about retribution, though. His troubles were clearly much, much bigger than that.

He had to prepare to fly. It was too dangerous for him to stay around. He had to get out before the net tightened around his neck and choked him.

Vanessa. His wife needed to be told. They had contingency plans ready, just in case this day ever came, and now it was time to put them into action. He phoned.

'Yes, Ronnie.' She sounded in a good mood. She soon wouldn't be.

'Where are you?'

'Home. Why?' She picked up on the tone in his voice straight away.

'Grab what we need and get out of there. We're exposed. You know where and when to meet. I'll see you there.'

'Shit. Right.' She was absorbing the warning, recalling what they knew they must do, even though this was what they had always dreaded. 'They're not heading this way, are they?'

'Don't think so, but the house is being watched. You'll have to be a hundred per cent sure you've slipped them. Be careful.'

She hung up. They had much to do and no time to do it, but the procedure was in place. She'd be all right. Soon, they'd be on their way.

CHAPTER

THIRTY-TWO

'So tell me again.' Detective Inspector Powell leaned forward, as if anticipating a big secret was about to be revealed. 'What made you want to buy an old typewriter from a man in the pub?'

Shannon and Dan, calmer for having been given a short time to recover from their ordeal, had just run through the start of the sequence of events as they unfolded over the last nine turbulent days for the benefit of the two policemen sat opposite them in the interview room. It was a tale that began with the ill-fated transaction in The Swan and took them via two break-ins at the flat and being chased from Hermie's house to, so far, arriving at Em's.

'Is that important?' asked Shannon, the bruise on the left side of her face now a deeper reddish blue.

'No, not really,' Powell admitted. 'I'm just curious.'

It was not a subject the couple were especially keen to expand on. Their deluded belief that they possessed a priceless piece of literary history had been rudely shattered. Since it was explained to them that the typewriter wasn't invented until almost three hundred years after William Shakespeare died, they had come to an unspoken mutual understanding to stop themselves sounding – and feeling – a little bit silly.

Don't mention the S-word.

'I just thought it looked nice,' suggested Dan, lamely.

'Oh!' Powell leaned back, neither enlightened nor amused by the explanation.

Dan picked up the white mug off the veneered table in front of him and took a slurp of tea. He put it down and chose another biscuit from what started out as a plateful. Under the table, he and Shannon gripped each other's hands a little tighter. They had hardly let go for a second since being rescued.

'And you say you'd never met Ms Kear until she pulled up in her car to save you from the two men who were pursuing you.'

'That's right,' Shannon confirmed. 'Dan had kind of met her before when he threw the chopping board at her to stop her robbing the flat.'

'That's true,' Dan chipped in.

'But he didn't know it was Em. He only found out when Em told us it was her.'

'She had a cut on her head.' Dan spoke through a mouthful of biscuit and drew a line on his forehead to indicate the precise location of the cut.

'I see.' Powell scribbled a note to himself. 'But Ms Kear – Em – made it her business to seek you out because she knew the computer flash drive was hidden inside the typewriter.'

'Correct,' said Shannon.

'The typewriter Frankie Aston sold you in the pub.'

'Uh-huh,' said Dan.

'The typewriter that was one of the items stolen when Frankie Aston and Ms Kear – Em – broke into the house of Sheffield's biggest criminal gang boss, Ronnie Bridgeman.'

'Spot on,' said Shannon.

'We didn't know it was stolen then.' Dan felt he should make the point. 'We didn't know about the flash drive either.'

'How could you have?' Powell stared at the pad in front of him without writing another note. He was glad to have clarified the story because he wasn't sure he would have believed he'd heard it right first time otherwise.

'So why didn't you come to us after escaping from the two men? You must have known you could have just called us and we would have come to collect you, to put you in protective custody. Why did you turn off your phones and go dark on us?'

Shannon picked up her mug of tea but delayed taking a drink.

'Because Em told us you were trying to blame us for Frankie's murder. She told us we needed to lay low for a bit. I think she was also dead keen to find out what was on that flash drive.'

'Which was still hidden in the typewriter.'

'Yeah.'

'Which you'd taken to...' Powell consulted his pad. '...your friend Hermie's parents' house. For safe keeping.'

'Yep.'

'Because someone – Em – had tried to steal it from your flat.'

'Correct.'

Powell nodded. 'Right.' That's all clear then.

'So what *was* on the flash drive?'

It had been recovered from the possession of one of the men arrested at the depot, but the police IT experts hadn't yet been able to get past the encryption code.

'Well.' Shannon took that drink at last as she prepared to enlighten the officer. 'It was mostly long lists of numbers that Em said might mean something but meant nothing to us, did it Dan?'

He picked up another biscuit. 'Not a thing.'

'But what was really interesting was the video.'

That caught Powell's interest. 'A video?'

'A *secret* video,' Shannon expanded with relish. 'It was like somebody was walking and recording on his phone, only it can't have been that because then it wouldn't have been a secret video, would it?'

'I guess not,' Powell accepted.

'It was this man going into a room and Em reckoned the man was Bridgeman. Then there was another man sitting down. He was quite big – you know, got a bit of a gut on him – and pretty old. At least fifty. Anyway, the one who was filming handed over a load of money. What was it, Dan? A hundred grand?'

'A hundred grand,' he affirmed with a nod.

'Then he got a bit annoyed when the other man didn't give him what he wanted in return. A gun was mentioned. Something to do with it being evidence that could land the guy with the camera in prison for a long time. Em reckoned that was Bridgeman bribing a policeman and that Bridgeman had filmed it so that he could blackmail the policeman. That was what Em reckoned.'

'She doesn't much like the police,' added Dan.

Powell's eyes had widened. This was big. They had to get access to that video. He needed to talk to DCI Larson straight away to put her in the picture.

He glanced towards the young Detective Constable who had been by his side through the interview.

'I think we'll take a break there,' said Powell and the DC took the cue.

'Interview suspended at fifteen eighteen,' he said and stopped the recording.

'We'll finish up shortly, but if you want to freshen up a bit or stretch your legs, DC Crowther here will show you where to go.'

The DC gave them a friendly smile. He pointed to Dan's front, to the red and blue-striped Barcelona football shirt he had changed into at Em's flat.

'I hope you don't mind me asking, mate, but I've been trying to make out the signature on your shirt.' he said. 'Is it Messi?'

Dan peered down his nose at the shirt and wiped away biscuit crumbs with the back of his hand.

'Not as bad as my other one was.'

Em had her arms crossed. She had answered all DCI Larson's questions politely and concisely. DI Powell, who had been asked to sit in on the interview after telling the boss what he had learned from Shannon and Dan, was satisfied her account was not at odds with theirs. She was co-operating, but you would not have called her co-operation whole-hearted.

Especially now they were on the subject of the flash drive and its contents. That was still a sore subject, as far as Em was concerned.

Larson didn't really do charming but had turned it on as much as she knew how to. Powell had warned her what Em thought of the police and, as if to prove that the information was not flawed, Em had spelt out her feelings at the start of the interview.

Larson had bitten her tongue and had made allowances, not only because of the trauma this woman had recently been through but also because they needed her help. The word from IT was that they would need more time – possibly a lot more time – to decrypt the flash drive, yet they knew from Shannon and Dan that Em had already cracked the code.

They wanted to see it for themselves, and now Larson's patience was being stretched thin.

'Why should I help you?' said Em, indignantly. 'You lot didn't help my brother when he needed you.'

The DCI sighed. They'd been here already.

'As I said to you, I'm sorry for what happened to your brother. I don't know what went wrong, but I can only assure you your impression that we fed him to the wolves deliberately is totally unfair. It's not the kind of behaviour tolerated by the vast majority – all, in my experience – of the officers in the force. All we want is to put away the bad guys and, right now, we have a chance to put away the baddest of the lot. I don't understand why you won't help us do that.'

Em glared back across the table, unmoved.

'What you've seen on that flash drive could be the difference between sending Bridgeman to prison for the rest of his life and him wriggling off the hook again. Surely you don't want to see that happen any more than we do.'

The face remained stony. Larson had seen it for long enough.

'Right, I've tried reasoning with you, it's time to start talking personal consequences if you refuse to comply with our requests.'

Em did not flinch.

'Let's talk burglary, for a start. We recovered quite a haul at your flat, which you stole from Bridgeman. Art, electrical goods, jewellery, not to mention a substantial amount of cash. That's easily enough to take the case to Crown Court and put you in line for what, three to six years? Then we have withholding evidence, wasting police time. And how about kidnapping? Taking away of one person by another by force or fraud. Two people, in this case. That's up to seven years.'

Em cocked her head. 'You're bluffing.'

'Am I? Try me. You'll soon see if you carry on standing in the way of what I want. I'm not a woman who likes to be messed about.'

She softened her expression. 'Look, I don't want to get all heavy-handed with you. You don't trust me; you don't trust the police in general. You had a bad experience. I get it, but I might also point out that if it hadn't been for us doing everything we can to protect the innocent, you and your two friends might well have been lying dead in a shallow grave right now. It suits neither of our purposes to have gangsters like Bridgeman roaming free, so give us a break here. Help us get the evidence we need to put him away, for good.'

Em was reassessing.

'And no charges are brought against me.'

'No charges. I promise.' Larson held her breath.

'I'll need my laptop,' said Em.

'We have it in the building.' The DCI could have cried out with relief. 'We brought it from the flat along with all of Bridgeman's stuff.'

Powell rose to his feet to fetch it. 'I'll get the flash drive from IT as well.'

'No need,' Em shook her head. 'I downloaded everything on to the laptop while I was running it through my decryption programme. I can unlock it with a password now.'

The two women were left alone. Larson stayed quiet, sensing Em was ready to tell her more. Show off a little about how she did in a few key strokes what a whole IT department had so far not managed in an hour or more.

'I didn't mind if Dan and Shannon kept believing they held the whip hand on me just because they had the flash drive, so that's why I didn't point out that I'd made a copy. What was a potential problem for me was if they left the flat with the flash drive, because then I knew they'd come to you with it and there was a good chance your people would access it eventually. That way, I would lose my opportunity to take Bridgeman for everything he's got. That would have been a waste. I had to make sure I had the flash drive as well.'

She eased back in the chair, relaxing into her new alliance.

'I've been working on the data for a few days. I shut myself in my room so the others wouldn't get curious about what I was doing. There's a lot of data on there, but I'm almost through it. At first I thought it was just account details and such, but then I realised not all of the numbers fitted the pattern, so I wondered if it was a cipher. It was quite a well-constructed one, but I began to unpick it. It started to give me not only accounts and amounts but names and locations. It was quite exciting. I'll show you when I have my laptop.'

Larson beamed. She was unquestionably impressed, not to mention completely excited by the potential implications. They could take down a whole network of dangerous thieves.

'Great. What I'd like to see first of all, though, is the video.'

Em appeared crestfallen. The video? Sure, it was good, but it was nowhere near as monumentally remarkable as the work she'd done on the data.

'Of course.'

Powell burst back into the room with the laptop and slid it across the desk to Em. She lifted the lid and was straight away locked into the task. In seconds, she spun the computer around to face the two officers opposite her.

'Just double-click to play,' she said.

They looked at the frozen image of a long corridor with doors on either side. Larson tapped twice on the laptop touchpad and the image began moving. They watched and they listened, silently. Agog. When it had finished they stared at each other.

'It is, isn't it?' said Powell.

'It is,' said Larson. 'Hetherington.'

THIRTY-THREE

When Clare Larson was in full stomp mode, you did not want to be in her way. A man armed only with a hand-held stop paddle sign would stand a better chance of halting a runaway train. The DCI had hit her most purposeful long stride almost as soon as she burst through the door of Interview Room Five. The steely resolve of her expression and the laptop tucked under her arm made her look like a rugby prop forward who had a rare sight of the try line and was not going to let anyone stop him planting the ball over.

She was angry. Very angry. It had been such a shock that it took a few seconds, but once she accepted the evidence before her own eyes, the fire was burning.

Grant Hetherington was bent. Recently-installed Detective Superintendent Grant Hetherington was bent. She had worked under him for years when he was one of CID's most respected senior officers. She had looked up to him. Admired him. Only a few weeks earlier, he was on the three-strong panel when she was interviewed for the Detective Chief Inspector job. Effectively, they named her his successor. He had been the obvious, logical choice to move up to DSU when Bob Haley retired.

Larson did not want to believe it was true, but she had

watched him on film, pocketing a bribe of a hundred thousand pounds from the odious crook Ronnie Bridgeman in return for burying crucial evidence in a murder case.

It was unequivocal. Not open for interpretation. The date stamp on the film said that was eight years ago. Eight years! All this time she had worked with him, looked up to him, admired him – and he was the worst kind of corrupt.

She set out to confront him straight away.

DI Gareth Powell was doing his best to keep up as she took the stairs two at a time, but even for a person who enjoyed his regular gym sessions, it was not easy. He was still trailing as she closed in on the DSU's office and bore down on his personal assistant.

'Is he in?' asked Larson, without breaking stride.

'Yes, but he's on a call...'

She charged straight through the office door anyway.

Settled behind an L-shaped walnut veneer executive desk, reclining into his black leather executive chair, was the hefty bulk of a man in his late-fifties. He was one of those people who appeared permanently bedraggled, no matter how much effort he made to smarten up, and breathed with the persistent wheeze of a man who was carrying too much weight and had smoked too many cigarettes. A phone was pressed to his ear and, caught mid-conversation, it seemed to have been a happy exchange, but his face dropped when Larson and then Powell invaded his space. Slightly irked bemusement gave way to concern as he clocked the stern gazes of the two detectives now in front of him.

This must be serious.

'I'll have to call you back, John,' he said and hung up.

'I know I said my door was always open, Clare, but you might have knocked.'

She said nothing. She simply opened the laptop lid, planted it, facing him, on the desk and double-clicked the touchpad.

Hetherington watched, instantly recognising the footage,

instantly comprehending what this meant. He did not bother watching it all. He knew how it went.

'I suppose this is where I should say something glib about this not being how it looks.' His voice was heavy with acceptance. 'I think that would be a waste of time, though, wouldn't it?'

Larson stared at him. It was plain for all to see that the evidence was utterly damning, but she wanted more than that.

'Is that all you've got to say?' For the first time in her career, she did not feel the reflex need to address him as 'sir'.

Hetherington shrugged. 'What more is there to say?'

'You could start by telling us why.'

'Why?' Her anger was still raw and the mocking tone of his response did nothing to ease it. 'Greed. Pure and simple. That's why. I would've thought that was obvious. Look.' He rubbed his fingers into his brow and screwed up his eyes. 'I was stupid. I saw a way to make easy money and I ended up in over my head. It was meant to be a one-off, but obviously the recording changed all that. I knew I'd landed myself in a world of trouble. It was too late then. He had me by the balls.'

'You still had the option to come clean.'

'That's an easy thing to say.' Hetherington suddenly appeared weighed down by the burdens of the world. 'I had too much to lose. Family, career, status – I couldn't just give it all up. I knew this might come back to bite me one day, of course I did, but for as long as it was still in Bridgeman's interests to keep up our arrangement, I thought I might get away with it. Stupid, I know.'

Larson was simmering, barely able to contain her contempt for the figure facing her. Annoyed with herself for not somehow seeing through him before.

'So you were OK with letting us all down, trashing the reputation of all the good coppers you worked alongside for 40-odd years, betraying the public trust to help a dangerous criminal stay above the law? You were OK with that as long as you thought you might get away with it?'

'It wasn't all one-way, you know.' Hetherington was back on the defensive. 'My arrest record, my conviction rate, was consistently the best in the department. That's how come I earned the right to wear the crown on my epaulette. I put a lot of crooks in jail and you know part of the reason for that? It was because of Bridgeman giving me information. Sure, he only did that because it helped him get rid of the competition, I'm not that naïve, but it did help keep down the crime rates. There will always be criminals, but what I was doing was, in effect, regulating them. We were effectively policing the criminal fraternity between us. That has to be worth something, surely?'

'What?' Larson was incensed by his twisted logic. 'How can you even think that? While you were letting Bridgeman feed you the small fish you were, in return, turning a blind eye to him dealing with the bigger fish himself. He was doing whatever the hell he liked. You were letting him operate above the law. You were complicit in murder, drug dealing, extortion – the list goes on. That's completely unjustifiable. My god, all these years we've been trying to put him away and we were never able to make anything stick. He always seemed to be one step ahead. We've had that again this week. We turn up to collect two key witnesses and Bridgeman's thugs have been there first. We finally get an address for where they've been hiding and turn up only to find – surprise, surprise – Bridgeman got there before us again. There's no bloody wonder. He had friends in high places all the time.'

He stared blankly back at her as she vented. He waited for her to finish and then stood.

'Come on then. Get it over with.'

Larson could no longer speak. Her disgust choked her. She spun away and waved a hand at Powell for him to complete the formalities.

'Grant Hetherington, you're under arrest on suspicion of assisting an offender.' Powell spoke while he was on the move to the other side of the desk. He saw no practical need to put on the handcuffs but wanted to anyway. 'You do not have to say anything, but it may harm your defence if you do not mention when questioned something which you later rely on in court. Anything you do say may be given in evidence.'

Hetherington kept his gaze on Larson throughout.

'You know, for what it's worth, Clare, you weren't my choice to get the DCI job,' he said. 'Nothing personal. I was outvoted. I suppose you've proved me wrong now.' He reconsidered that last bit. 'Looking at it another way, you've actually proved me right.'

She turned. 'What's that supposed to mean?'

He wrestled with the thought of expanding but decided against.

'Never mind.'

THIRTY-FOUR

DISGRACED DETECTIVE SUPERINTENDENT HETHERINGTON WAS HANDED over for another team to interview and establish how many more charges he should face. Clare Larson and her colleagues had enough with the investigation they were still deeply involved in to keep them busy for the rest of the day.

The interviews with Em Kear, Dan Khan and Shannon Rafferty were completed and gave them plenty of fresh information. They were edging nearer to closing the case.

They also had the five men picked up in the depot raid to deal with. None of them were at all talkative. They expected no less. It mattered little. Farrell and Gamson were charged with Frankie Aston's murder and the other three were on the hook for a whole string of lesser, but still very serious, offences.

It had been a good day, but not the perfect day.

Bridgeman was still out there. They had enough on him to bring him down at last, but they had still not found him – and that was a big concern. A nationwide alert had been announced on the Police National Computer and measures had been taken to prevent him getting out of the country, but would that be enough? He had the means to take flight without going through official channels. The big prize they really wanted to secure, the biggest prize, could still slip through their fingers and all the team's available resources were diverted to the effort to make sure that didn't happen.

Larson and the two Detective Inspectors, Gareth Powell and Ryan Nickle, stayed back after the evening briefing to go over everything again, just to be sure there was nothing they had overlooked. After that, the energy between them was practically spent. They were running on fumes. It was time to call it a day.

'Pub?' suggested Powell.

'Not tonight, mate.' Nickle cupped his hands behind his head in a stretch. 'I've got to get off.'

'Chief?' Powell switched to Larson for support.

She turned the invitation over in her mind briefly.

'Yeah, maybe. There's just a couple of other bits I need to take care of first. Hannah Short has sorted out rooms at the Waterside Hotel for Shannon, Dan and Em. I want to make sure there'll be a couple of uniforms on watch all the time they're there. They can't go home yet, not while Bridgeman could still be around, and I don't want to take any chances. I need to organise a car to take them as well.'

'I'll drive them there myself,' offered Nickle.

'You sure?'

'Yeah, the Waterside's more or less on my way home. I can check to make sure everything's secure before I leave them for the night.'

Larson stood. 'That'd be great, Ryan, thanks.'

The other two also got up to go.

'No probs,' said Nickle. 'I'll take them there straight away. They must be knackered. I'll hold on at the hotel until the uniforms are in place.'

An hour later, Larson and Powell were the only two left in the Incident Room. After the bustle and buzz which had filled the space for the previous few days, the still calm took on a quality that was almost eerie. The two detectives sat at desks on opposite sides of the room and the only sound between them was the distant hum of a vacuum cleaner down the corridor.

Powell closed down his last document and signed off the computer with a flourish.

'I'm done. How about that pint?'

Larson exhaled wearily.

'Nah. You go on without me.'

Clare Larson turning down the offer of a pint? This was out of character. Powell collected his jacket from the back of his chair and wandered towards her desk. He knew her well enough to realise she was holding back on something. Just because she was his senior now didn't mean he should stop being a mate. He took a seat and waited, to see if she wanted to offload.

'Something's bothering me,' she admitted at last. 'You know when we were about to lead Hetherington away and he said about me not being his choice for the DCI job?'

Powell scratched his head. 'Yeah, I remember.'

'Well, it's what he said after that. He said I'd proved him wrong, presumably by us all doing a decent job, but then he said something about I'd proved him right from another perspective. What did he mean by that?'

'Dunno,' said Powell, pulling a face. 'Was he having a dig, seeing as we'd just nicked him?'

'Can't be just that. I've proved him wrong, yet I've proved him right. I could tell he was thinking about explaining why, but then he thought better of it and kept it to himself. Proved him right about what? I can't work it out. It's like a riddle.'

'Maybe think about it in the morning? It's been a long day.'

Larson rejected the proposal. 'I can't leave it there. It's going to bug me all night unless I figure it out.'

'Righto.' Powell rolled his chair closer to her desk. They were going to work this out together. 'How did he say it? As I recall, it was kind of "you proved me wrong because you weren't my choice to be promoted to DCI, but then you proved me right – unfortunately". You know, like it was a cause of regret to him that you'd proved him right.'

'Yeah, I'd agree,' nodded Larson. 'That was the inference I read into it as well. So what was it he was trying to guard against by blocking me for the job? The fact that the video came to light wasn't down to anything I did especially. The flash drive could have been recovered whoever was in charge of the investigation. Somebody would have recognised Hetherington in the footage once the drive was decrypted and then it would have been game over for him anyway. What did he mean? There's something we're missing.'

'OK, let's take it back,' said Powell. 'There's still something we don't know and maybe we won't know it until Hetherington is interviewed. He might not even say then. So, instead of speculating on what we don't know yet, let's go over what we do know again and see if the answer's there.'

That made sense to Larson. 'We know Hetherington black-mailed Bridgeman for a pay-off in exchange for the non-disclosure of crucial evidence in a murder case eight years ago. We know Bridgeman made a secret film of the money being handed over, giving him leverage over Hetherington. We believe he probably used that leverage in the intervening years to gain valuable information about police investigations into his activities, enabling him to stay one step ahead and avoid being arrested.'

'Sure,' Powell added. 'And we know this because we have the video. So let's watch the video again and see if there's anything on it we didn't pick up on first time.'

Neither of them had watched it through since Em showed it to them in the interview room. Larson had asked for a copy of it to be sent to her before handing the evidence over with Hetherington. She searched for the file and opened it. Powell manoeuvred his chair next to hers and they both leaned forward to scrutinise the footage.

The corridor. The door. Room three-one-six. Knock on the door. It opens. The room. The sofa. The man on the sofa. Hetherington. Bridgeman walks over and sits down. They...'

'Woah!' said Powell, suddenly. 'Pause it there.'

Larson clicked. The image froze. 'What've you seen?'

'The table, see?' He pointed. 'Two pint glasses, both more than half full.'

There they were. Two glasses on coasters, one directly in front of Hetherington and the other between him and where Bridgeman now was.

'Can't be there for Bridgeman because somebody's clearly drunk some of it,' he added. 'So somebody else was in the room before Bridgeman arrived.'

Larson said nothing. She clicked to play.

The envelopes are handed over.

'Why was he so specific about two envelopes with an equal share of the money in each?' said Larson. 'He's got an accomplice. We don't get to see him or her, but they're still in the room. Remember the door? Bridgeman doesn't let himself in. You can't do that with a hotel door unless you've got a key. Somebody opened the door for him and it wasn't Hetherington.'

The video was playing to itself now. The minds of the two detectives were racing ahead.

'Bridgeman had two of them on the payroll, not just Hetherington.' Larson was on her feet. 'Might that be why he didn't want me to get the DCI job? Did he want his oppo to get the job instead? That way they would have had an even tighter grip on the department so they could shield Bridgeman and protect themselves from being exposed. Is that what he meant by being proved right? He knew that if I was the new DCI and not his preferred candidate, he wouldn't have the same level of control. That was his fear – and he was proved right!'

Powell slumped so deep in his seat that he was practically horizontal. 'Christ! So who were the other candidates?'

'All external,' said Larson. 'Except...'

'What?'

She swallowed hard. 'Ryan Nickle.'

Powell jumped as if an electric charge had been put through the chair.

'Ryan? He never said he was going for it.' The broader implications hit home. 'Ryan? No!'

Larson did not want to believe it either, but she was processing the possibility. 'Think about it, though. This video was taken eight years ago. Hetherington was a DI. Who was his regular sergeant back then? Who, as his regular sergeant, was most likely to be in that room with him? Who, as his regular sergeant, was most likely to agree to a scheme to extort money from Bridgeman and agree to withhold evidence? Probably evidence they'd found together.'

They both knew the answer to those questions.

'Christ!' Powell exclaimed. He peered towards the clock on the office wall. 'Twenty past seven. He'll have reached the hotel by now. The witnesses! What if he's still in contact with Bridgeman?'

He was not alone in feeling the hollow sensation in the pit of his stomach.

'Let's not get ahead of ourselves,' warned Larson. 'We can call him and tell him to bring them back to the station. Tell him – tell him Bridgeman has been spotted and that they're safer spending the night here. If we're wrong, he'll head back.'

'But what if we're right? He'll know we've got wind of something and that might be the last we see of him – and them.'

Powell was spot on. They couldn't risk it.

'We need to get cars out there,' said Larson. 'We've got to get to the hotel as soon as possible.'

THIRTY-FIVE

Dark clouds rolled in mid-afternoon and hung immovably over the whole city, consigning it to evening gloom long before the sun had the chance to declare the day done. That suited Ronnie Bridgeman just fine. It suited his mood and it suited his purpose.

He sat in the driver's seat of his Audi Q8, waiting. It was time. Vanessa should be with him very soon. He hoped it would be very soon because he had parked half on the grass verge on the main road, close to the entrance to Handsworth Cemetery, and he didn't want to attract any unwanted attention.

Since word reached him of the police raid on the depot, he had been busy. Once he dropped off the two men who had accompanied him on the trip to Kent he had taken himself away to a place he knew the police would not come searching for him. There were plans to be set in motion, funds to be secreted away, tracks to be covered. He had done as much as he could to make sure they were able to get out of the country swiftly, unnoticed. There was just this one last thing to do and then he and his wife would be on their way to make a fresh start.

A car was approaching down the hill. Bridgeman bowed his head to conceal his face and to shield his eyes from the headlights' glare. The car pulled in, on the opposite side of the road, close to the cemetery entrance. It was a taxi. Shortly after, he watched as Vanessa climbed out from the back seat, carrying one of her larger handbags. The type you could pack plenty of useful and valuable items into without it attracting attention. She did not acknowledge her husband's presence across the road until the taxi had pulled away. Then she walked over and got into his car.

'No problems?' he asked.

She wrinkled her nose. 'They were outside the house. I let them follow me into town and trailed them around the shops as if it was just a normal day. I finished off at the hairdresser's when I thought they might be getting a bit bored by it all, then I sneaked out the back way and caught a taxi. They really should teach policemen to be better at surveillance. Amateurs.'

Bridgeman started the engine and drove across the road, through the gated entrance to the cemetery.

'So what happened then?' She knew it was bad enough to initiate their long-prepared emergency flight plan, but she wanted details.

'They hit the depot,' he replied, bitterly. 'They got Faz, Gammo and three of the others. The three bastards who stole the flash drive are still alive. I can only assume the cops have it now and are trying to break the security.'

He drove slowly along the narrow road between the neat rows of headstones. Frustration overtook him and he punched the steering wheel hard with an open fist to purge his emotions in a flash of violence.

'We were so close! We had it back. Another half an hour and they'd have been dead. We wouldn't be having to do this.'

Vanessa allowed time for the steam levels to settle. 'Why weren't you warned?'

'I was, but too late.' He was calmer now.

'Do you think your contact has turned?'

He had considered this. 'I don't know. I don't think so. Something must have gone wrong. We're not the only ones in deep shit because of this, you know.'

She drew a deep breath. 'I suppose so.'

Bridgeman pulled in and set the gear lever to 'park', then turned off the engine. They had arrived. He flicked a switch to open the tailgate.

He got out and walked to the back of the car. Inside the boot was a large bouquet of flowers in cellophane. He lifted them out by the stalks, then closed the tailgate.

Without saying a word, they walked towards the corner of the cemetery that was enclosed by a low white iron fence. The family plot.

At the head of the one grave in the plot was a large marble carving of a sorrowful angel reposing on a pile of rocks in eternal vigil, its right wing wrapped around the outer edge of a smooth white stone. Chiselled out of the stone were the words:

Rose Elizabeth Bridgeman
27.11.1949 – 26.05.2008
Gilbert Bridgeman
21.09.1947 – 07.02.2011
Together again
Forever missed by their loving son

Bridgeman clutched the bouquet to his chest in a moment of silent reflection.

'Ah, poor Rose and Gil,' he said, mournfully. 'Worked hard all their lives for nothing and died without knowing what it was like to taste the sweetness of what money can give you.' He paused. 'That's where being honest gets you.'

Vanessa hugged her coat closer around her with her hands in the pockets.

'I've heard the speech before, Ronnie. Let's get on with it, shall we? It's getting chilly.'

He sighed and bent to lay the flowers on the grave, but before placing the bouquet flat, he reached a hand between the roses and lilies and drew out a long metal crowbar.

'I'll lift the stone if you take the box out,' he said, letting the flowers drop to the ground.

Bridgeman dug the crowbar between where the end of the marble plinth met the turf and grunted as he prised it up, tearing at the grass roots. Vanessa crouched beside it and waited until it was raised high enough for her to put in her hand and drag out a metal box, long and thin like the type found in bank security vaults.

Bridgeman let the plinth fall back into place, breathing heavily from the effort. He took out a key from his trouser pocket and handed it to her.

Vanessa twisted it in the lock and opened the lid. Inside was a clear plastic bag with two passports in false names, a blue velvet bag containing gold bullion coins and a few jewels, a small bunch of keys and a black CZ 75 handgun with two spare clips of ammunition.

'Right,' he said, picking out the gun and pushing it down the back of his trouser waistband. 'Time to get moving.'

She closed the lid and they began to walk back to the car. The silence of the empty graveyard was disturbed only by the growing swirl of the wind as the evening grew darker, so they both heard the ping from his inside coat pocket.

He took out the phone to read the message.

'What is it?' She knew it was the phone he only used when he was contacting his insider.

Bridgeman began reading and stopped still. He read it again.

'Well?' she demanded.

'He's taking the three witnesses to a hotel. Says he can give me access to them at seven-thirty.'

'Which hotel?'

'The Waterside, just out of town.'

Vanessa pulled back the sleeve of her coat to look at her watch. 'Nearly forty minutes.'

He gave her a quizzical stare. 'What?'

'Nearly forty minutes,' she repeated. 'Plenty of time.'

Bridgeman turned to face her. 'You're kidding, right?' From her blank expression it was plain to him that she was not.

'Do you still trust him?' she asked.

'Well.' He was finding it hard to believe they were having the conversation. 'He fucked up, but it's still in his interests to stay onside, so yes. I suppose.'

'There we go then. You should do it.'

He was temporarily lost for words, on the brink of exasperation. 'It makes no sense. We've got the plan. We're ready to leave.'

She shuffled closer and looked him square in the eyes. 'It makes perfect sense. They're loose ends, Ronnie. We don't leave loose ends. What's that you are always telling me? Dead witnesses can't testify. He's handing them to you on a plate. Sort yourself out. Be a man. Where does he suggest he'll take them for you?'

Bridgeman was thrown by her words. By her apparent conviction that this was a good idea.

'The hotel car park.'

'Perfect. It'll be dark by then. Get it done. Get away quickly.'

'You mean it, don't you?'

Vanessa was becoming angry at his lack of enthusiasm for her strategy.

'Of course I fucking mean it! You have to do this. We're not going anywhere unless you do. In fact, if you've not got the nerve to do it, give me the gun. I'll do it.'

She pushed her hand into his chest. He was being challenged. He never backed down from a challenge, but his usually solid belief in his invulnerability had been shaken. Normally, he would have agreed with her sentiments totally. He wouldn't have needed challenging. He would have gone ahead and done it. He would've proved he was still the king.

'All right, fucking hell,' he said. 'Come on, then.'

CHAPTER
THIRTY-SIX

Detective Inspector Ryan Nickle glanced into his rear view mirror for the umpteenth time. The three of them hadn't gone anywhere, of course. They just sat there, like a row of hungover revellers the morning after a big blow-out. Hardly moved, hadn't spoken at all since they began the twenty-five-minute journey across town from police headquarters towards the Waterside Hotel. No doubt they were exhausted, after everything they'd been through. Dreaming, maybe, of a nice room service meal, a long soak in a hot bath and then curl up in a soft, warm bed to let sleep carry them far away from the madness their lives had become.

They have no idea.

Nickle could not believe his luck when this opportunity fell into his lap. Up to the point where he had volunteered to drive the three of them to the hotel, his best plan was to slip away unnoticed. Leave work as if nothing was out of the ordinary, maybe throw in a few 'see you tomorrows' for good measure, and then disappear without trace before the shit really hit the fan.

It would mean abandoning his wife and family to cope with the fallout, which was harsh. That couldn't be avoided. He felt bad about it, but any option that gave him a chance to avoid being dragged through the disgrace of public humiliation followed by a long stretch in prison was a price worth paying. Prison. As an ex-copper, life inside wouldn't be worth living.

Before putting himself forward to do the hotel run, he watched as his cover was picked apart by the prevailing wind and knew he had to leave while he still could. But how? He could barely imagine how to begin plotting an escape on his own but could see no alternative. This gave him an alternative, though not one he would have ever considered attractive. He could never have imagined Bridgeman might be his last remaining ally, but that was the low point this whole messy scenario had brought him to. Desperate times make for strange bedfellows.

Maybe it was the slimmest chance, the last throw of a doomed man, but he had to take it. He could not see how he could avoid being caught otherwise, sooner or later. The question was, could he convince Bridgeman to help him get away?

That wouldn't be easy. Their arrangement had failed last time. That wasn't his fault, though. If he had been able to send out a warning about the raid on the depot in time, he would have. He hadn't made a mistake. It was sheer bad luck, that's all. Bad luck that he had been out of the loop for a crucial period. Surely, Bridgeman couldn't suspect he'd done it on purpose. That would make no sense. They all had too much to lose. However reluctantly he and Hetherington had been dragged into it in the first place, the alliance between them relied on all sides keeping their end of the deal. They had evidence that could bring Bridgeman down, he had material that could ruin them. Understanding that, maintaining the status quo, guaranteed they would all stay out of jail. It was mutually assured survival. That's why he couldn't possibly have deliberately held back on issuing the warning. All that would have done was put them all in adjoining prison cells.

As far as Nickle was concerned, he had done all he could that morning. He bought Bridgeman an opportunity by feeding him the address he got from the taxi driver half an hour before he announced it to his colleagues. That should have been the game-changer, drawing all the nervous uncertainty of the previous few days to an end. Bridgeman could send his men to take the three witnesses from the flat first and nobody would ever see them again. Not alive, anyway. The irony was the only way he could manage that situation was by interviewing the taxi driver himself and that was the reason he was out of the loop for a while. When he got back to the station, expecting a subdued atmosphere because Bridgeman had beaten them to the punch again, the Incident Room was more highly charged than a metal pole in a lightning storm. He texted the warning almost as soon as he'd worked out why, but it was too late.

Even though Nickle had done all he could, he knew Bridgeman would not be happy. Maybe he had a right to be, but do you know what? None of this would have happened if Bridgeman hadn't lost flash drive. If blame was to be pinned anywhere, how about there?

But blame was for another day. Escape was a more pressing concern and reaching out to Bridgeman again gave Nickle his best chance of getting away. That was why he set up the rendezvous at the hotel. It was a sort of offering. He was delivering the three witnesses for Bridgeman to deal with, practically gift-wrapping them. He could do no more. That surely had to be worth a seat on the private plane taking them to somewhere abroad, away from the grasp of recriminations.

That's the way he hoped it would go, but he was far from confident of success. Bridgeman might not even be there. There had been no confirmation text.

'We'll be at the hotel soon,' he said to the rear view mirror.

None of them acknowledged him. Shannon and Dan were still holding hands as if to let go would be to release a balloon into the wind with no hope of getting it back. Em sat apart from them, as close to the door as she could be. She was embarrassed by her confession to Shannon, made when their outlooks were at their most grim in the depot. More specifically, she was embarrassed by everything she had confessed to. She could see now how twisted her priorities had been.

Nickle checked the time on the in-car screen. Just before seven. The satnav said they were due to arrive at three minutes past. He had told Bridgeman he would make sure they were in the car park at half past. Not knowing where Bridgeman was meant he had to allow him a reasonable amount of time to get there. It made his timing was a bit awkward, though. They couldn't just hang about in the car park and wait for Bridgeman to show up. He would have to take them into the hotel and then come up with an excuse to get them out again. He'd figure that out.

Soon, the sign for the hotel stood twenty yards ahead. Nickle indicated left.

A narrow unlit road was flanked by mature trees and bushes which shielded them from sight of the hotel until the driveway opened into a drop-off area for the reception. The Waterside was an elegant mid-nineteenth century stone mansion which was once the status statement of a wealthy Victorian steel baron. It stood two storeys high and was solidly stone-built to last. Much longer than the industrialist's fortune, as it happened.

In other circumstances, Nickle would have ignored the warning of the No Parking area shaded out in yellow lines and pulled in as close to reception as he could. Not this time. He wanted to see the lay of the land for the next part of his plan. He drove on. A raised barrier marked the point at which they would be leaving the hotel grounds to head back towards the main road, but before it was the car park. He slowed down. In the evening gloom it was dimly-lit, secluded, quiet. Ideal.

'We're here,' he announced and the three figures on the back seat stirred, relieved to have reached the end of their journey. Nickle parked the car.

Two uniformed officers were already waiting in the hotel, sitting at a table in the corner of a bright, over-modernised reception area. They rose alertly to their feet as the DI pushed open the heavy wooden outside door, his three weary charges trudging close behind. Nickle acknowledged them with a nod and a half-smile. They both appeared exceptionally young to him. One female, one male. More babysitters than bodyguards. It would not matter. He wandered towards them to begin the introductions and find out how well they had been briefed on their assignment, just to keep up appearances.

Em, Shannon and Dan huddled patiently a couple of yards away. They just wanted to get to their rooms but lacked the energy to protest at the delay.

Nickle turned to draw them into the dialogue.

'This is Shannon, Dan and Em,' he pointed them out in turn for the benefit of the two PCs. 'These are the officers who are going to stay here tonight to make sure you have everything you need. This is PC Grace Price and PC Matt Thompson...'

'Max, sir,' the male PC tentatively corrected.

'Sorry, Max. How about I leave you to get to know each other a bit while I sort things out with the receptionist?'

He took one step and delayed. 'Actually,' he said to the two PCs, 'it might be a good idea if you put together a list of stuff they're going to need. Toiletries, that kind of thing. They've not been able to bring anything with them.'

Nickle left them to their task and strode towards the light wood panelled reception desk. At the bottom of the three steps that led to it he stopped and took out his phone. It said seven thirteen. Close to time. He touched the text messages icon and opened up the last conversation on the list to post an update.

All set this end. Are you here yet?

The message was sent. A reply would be good, but he wasn't banking on one. He would keep his end of the deal all the same.

After checking in the three guests and making sure the most senior person on duty at the hotel was aware why it was necessary for two police officers to stay on guard for the night, Nickle started to make his way back towards the group. He glanced at his phone. No reply. Seven twenty-four.

'How's that list?'

The female officer held up her notebook to show him her scribbled notes.

'I tell you what,' he added, as if struck by an idea. 'You two go and get everything now. There's a big Tesco just down the road. I'll make sure everything's OK with the rooms and stick around until you get back with the supplies.'

'Are you sure, sir?' The male PC was uncertain. 'We were told not to leave the hotel until we were relieved in the morning.'

'Yeah,' said Nickle, making light of the objection. He found the young officer's keenness to follow orders to the letter strangely endearing. 'It'll be fine. Anybody attempts to pull you up for it and you blame me.'

The officers left.

'Right.' Nickle turned his attention back to the other three and flourished door key cards in paper sleeves with the hotel logo printed on them. 'Let's get you to your rooms.'

He began to lead them towards the main staircase but came to a sudden halt. They shuffled to a stop behind him.

'My phone,' he said, reaching for his inside jacket pocket. He turned to face them so they could not see the phone screen as he held it. There had been no incoming call or message but he pulled an inquisitive face as if there had been.

'It's my boss. Bear with me a sec. I'd better take this.'

He stepped away from the group as if to seek privacy while he apparently answered the call, leaving them with a casual 'Yes, ma'am' to add to the deception.

They watched as mounting concern spread over his expression during the brief faked conversation. His demeanour said something was wrong. They were meant to sense it. He hung up and hurried back to them.

'Look, stay calm,' he began and instantly they were anything but calm. 'We've had a tip-off. The hotel might not be safe. We need to leave. Follow me.'

THIRTY-SEVEN

MAYBE THE TEMPERATURE HAD DROPPED A DEGREE OR TWO NOW THAT the sun had finally sunk below the horizon and the dark of evening had deepened. Maybe it was because the chill shadow of fear had again loomed over them. Whatever the cause, Shannon and Dan shuddered as they followed Nickle out of the hotel. There was a new danger in the cool September air and the threat of it had injected a prickle of fresh nervous energy through their minds and bodies. They didn't care to know the nature of this new peril. They only wanted to get away from it.

'Please.' A small breathless voice stalled their progress down the road leading to the car park. 'Not so fast. I can't keep up.'

Em was ten yards behind. In their haste, they had forgotten she could not walk as quickly as the rest of them. Dan dropped back.

'Put your arm around my neck.' He stooped towards her and she took hold as he scooped her fragile frame into his arms.

Nickle checked ahead as they approached the car park. No people. Five other vehicles. No way of knowing if one of them was Bridgeman's. Was he even here? Anxiety tingled in his stomach.

This is it, he thought. *Either he shows now or I leave them here and make a run for it alone.*

Dan lowered Em carefully down onto her feet as they reached the Nickle's car. 'Thank you,' she said quietly. Shannon took hold of his arm and pulled herself close. They turned towards Nickle.

'Damn,' he said, patting and reaching into each of his pockets in turn. 'I can't find my keys. Where did I...?'

It was a charade. He was buying time. Then he heard the scrunch of footsteps on the car park gravel and his heart jumped.

A squat, shaven-headed figure in a dark, knee-length overcoat was stepping towards them. Bridgeman. He reached around his back with his right hand and pulled out the gun from the waist-band of his trousers.

Em saw him first and gasped. Shannon and Dan responded to her alarm and turned. They saw the gun being pointed at them and scrambled hastily around the back of the car for cover.

Nickle moved towards him. Bridgeman extended his gun arm and aimed straight at the advancing policeman.

'Not one more step,' he warned.

'Woah!' Nickle raised his hands in subjugation. Perhaps he hadn't been recognised in the dim light of the car park. 'It's me.'

'I know who you are,' Bridgeman growled. 'Back away. Now!'

A clammy chill drained the colour from Nickle's face.

'Hey, come on! We've got an arrangement.'

Bridgeman seared him with a contemptuous scowl. 'Not any more we don't.'

There was nowhere for Nickle to go. To back away would be to surrender his only remaining realistic hope. He was pleading for survival.

'I've done all I could – look!' He gestured with a flick of the head towards the three figures cowering behind the car. 'I was the only one who could have brought them to you. I've risked every-thing for you. I've helped keep you out of prison for eight years and now I need your help. Just get me out of the country. That's all I ask. Do that one thing and you'll never see or hear from me again.'

There was no concession in the angry face glowering towards him.

'Come on, man! You owe me!'

Bridgeman's expression darkened like pinched fingers had snuffed out the last barely flickering candle in a room. His hand squeezed the grip of the gun, increasing pressure on the trigger to the point where one more ounce of intent would have propelled a bullet towards its target.

'*Owe* you?' Incredulity dripped from his tone. 'Owe *you?*'

He took a half-step closer until Nickle almost felt the barrel of the gun reach out to touch his nose.

'Because you fucked up, I've got to give up everything I worked hard for all my life. Because you fucked up, five good men are in the nick. Because you fucked up, a deal that would have made me one of the most powerful men in the north of England has gone up in smoke. You think just because you've finally brought me these three arseholes that makes it all better?'

Bridgeman shook the gun at the policeman to hammer home his point.

'I don't owe you a bastard thing!'

Nickle slumped to his knees. His only hope of escape now was to get away from there alive. He did not rate those chances very highly.

A police siren sounded, close enough to make all five of them stare wide-eyed towards where it had come from.

Bridgeman turned back to Nickle and bared his teeth like a Pitbull ready to strike.

Nickle realised with horror the conclusion that had been drawn.

'No. I didn't...'

A single shot was all it took. It tore through Nickle's skull an inch above his left eye and exited in a shower of blood, tissue and splintered bone. The force of it threw his upper body back and he hit the ground, his legs still bent under him.

Three screams ripped through the evening gloom. Bridgeman had no interest in them. He had to get away, fast. He turned, ready to run, towards the far corner of the car park.

From behind the dense greenery that isolated the hotel grounds from the main road, the emergence of a high-speed pursuit police car in a burst of blue lights stopped him in his tracks. It screeched to a stop, blocking the far exit. Two officers jumped from it, drawing side weapons as they crouched to protect themselves behind the car's open doors.

'Armed police! Armed police!'

Running was no longer an option for Bridgeman. He would be taken down before he could get two steps away. He swung his shooting arm in the direction of the police and dipped behind the back of Nickle's car, unaware that he had stepped into the thick trickle of blood that seeped down the hill from the former owner's lifeless body.

He shuffled, crab-like, to where three petrified figures grovelled in the dirt, barely able to function, never mind move. Bridgeman grabbed Shannon by the collar, yanking her upright so that he could clamp her close to him, her neck fixed in the crook of his left arm. He dragged her out into the open, still pointing the gun towards the police vehicle. She clasped both her hands on the arm around her neck, scrambling to find her feet to stop herself being choked by his stranglehold.

'Put down the weapon and let her go!' demanded the officers.

A second police car sped towards them with lights flashing, this time from the direction of the hotel reception. It swung around to pick out Bridgeman and his captive in its headlights as two more officers with handguns burst quickly out to fix him in their sights.

Bridgeman squinted. Both exits were blocked. His options were diminishing.

From the far end of the car park an engine roared, headlights beamed. The wheels of an Audi Q8 ripped through the loose surface as it accelerated rapidly towards the desperate gangster and his panic-filled human shield. It skidded still beside them.

The last card to be played. The police still shouted out their instructions, but he was in a position to make his own demands.

'Back off!' he bellowed, jabbing the end of the gun against Shannon's skull. 'Back off or I'll blow her head off!'

A third police car was bearing down on them from the hotel direction.

Bridgeman was assessing his options. He had to clear an exit.

'You!' he shouted, pointing the gun towards the first police car to arrive. 'Out of the way. You've got thirty seconds to move that car or I put a round through her knee.'

Shannon shrieked. The two officers looked at each other through the empty cabin of the car. They had little choice. The older of them, a Sergeant, took the decision.

'Get in, Joe. We can't risk it.'

Reluctantly, they reversed the car away from the exit.

Bridgeman grinned. He had control again. They could never get the better of him. He inched back towards the Q8. Soon, he and the girl would be in the back seat and Vanessa could drive them away from here. Shannon dug in her heels to try to stop him, but she was not strong enough.

As Bridgeman reached to open the rear door with his gun hand, through the dark evening he saw a figure flying towards him from the back of Nickle's car. Instinctively, he twisted and fired. The figure dropped in a heap, but in the turning motion, Bridgeman surrendered his grip around the neck of his captive.

She slipped free, off-balance, and fell. He froze in the headlights, realising his protection had gone. Four shots rang out, two each from the two officers who now had an unhampered line of vision. All four thumped into the torso of their target. He went down.

For a stunned second, there was total silence, but then the tyres of the Q8 spun, searching for traction on the gravel, sending the car hurtling forward.

It was heading for the newly-created opportunity of the open exit. A chance to escape. But the officers in the first car read the intention and pulled forward again, plugging the gap. The Q8 rammed the police interceptor at an angle, lacking the momentum and the direction to bump it cleanly out of the way. It struck with a glancing blow, diverting it into the trunk of a mature oak.

Steam rose from the crumpled bonnet of the crashed car. It was over.

Two officers rushed to the cabin of the Q8. The driver, a woman in her mid-forties, was no longer trying to get away. The double impact with the car and the tree had stunned her. She groaned, arching her back away from the pressing presence of the inflated airbag, blood trickling from her left nostril.

The four other officers approached Ronnie Bridgeman with their weapons still drawn, but their caution was unnecessary. He was plainly dead, as was a third victim they discovered close by, hit by a single bullet to the forehead.

The one who had been shot attempting to get to Bridgeman lay where he had fallen. A young woman of similar age knelt by his side, her bloodstained hands caressing his cheeks, her anguished wails splitting the night.

'Oh god, no! Please don't die, Dan! Please don't die!'

. . .

Clare Larson and Gareth Powell had listened to the events unfolding on the police radio on their torturously hampered drive through city centre traffic from headquarters. They heard the urgent appeal for an ambulance to assist a male, mid-twenties, who had sustained a gunshot wound to the chest and feared the worst.

By the time they arrived, there were two ambulances and six police cars on the scene.

They headed towards a gap in the blue and white incident tape and Larson flashed her ID card to the officer who was making sure no one unauthorised made it any further.

'Who's in charge?' she asked.

The Constable surveyed the scene of becalmed pandemonium behind him until he was able to point out an officer in a peaked cap and bright yellow jacket.

'Sergeant McDermott, ma'am.'

She and Powell made their way towards a man who was issuing instructions to two junior colleagues.

'Sergeant.' They both showed their IDs again. 'I'm DCI Larson and this is DI Powell. Walk me through it. What've we got?'

'Well.' The Sergeant blew his cheeks. There was a lot to take in. 'We've got two dead, one seriously wounded, one a bit shaken up but otherwise OK. One of the fatalities was hit just before we got here. I believe he's one of ours.'

Larson could just make out the form of a body in the direction where McDermott led her with his eyes.

Jesus Christ, Ryan. How did you let yourself get caught up in all this?

'The other is over there.' McDermott turned to his right to indicate a shape on the ground, now covered by a sheet. 'Ronnie Bridgeman, I understand. The driver of the crashed Audi is his wife, Vanessa. She's being checked out by paramedics, but I've got officers with her, ready to take her in.'

Larson winced as she looked to where two more paramedics were working on Dan. 'What about the lad?'

She recognised Shannon and Em standing a couple of yards further back, helplessness contorting their tear-stained faces as they hugged each other for whatever comfort they could find.

'We did all we could for him before the ambulances arrived, but it's a nasty one,' said the Sergeant. 'He lost a lot of blood.'

'Is he going to make it, do you think?' asked Powell.

'Hmm.' McDermott pondered. 'Not sure.'

EPILOGUE

Getting shot really hurts.

It's not like when somebody on the telly gets shot, where they fall down and hold their hand to where the bullet went in, then sit up and talk about how it'll be all right and they probably don't even need to go to the hospital or anything. It's not like that at all.

It is the WORST PAIN EVER!

It's been two months now and it still hurts. Not as much as when it first happened, though. When it first happened I thought I was going to die.

I've been told I was lucky. The doctors said it could've been a lot worse. The bullet hit me in the right side of my chest, broke one of my ribs and made a hole through one of my lungs. Another couple of inches either way and the bullet could have killed me, the doctors said, so I suppose that is lucky. You know what, though, if I'd died it would've been worth it, as long as I stopped Bridgeman taking my Shan away.

That's all I wanted to do. I wasn't trying to be a hero, like some people have called me since. All I knew was if Bridgeman had got Shan into that car with him I might never have seen her again and I wasn't going to let that happen. I had to try to stop him. I've never been one for thinking much and I didn't really think through what I was doing then either. I just did it. I kept Shan safe and that made everything else worthwhile.

Do you want to know what it was like? People have asked me that question a few times, but I can't tell them much because I can't remember a lot about it. When the bullet first hits you, it's like getting a whack on your chest, like somebody thumped you dead hard. I was running forward when I was hit and it literally knocked me off my feet. There was no way I was going to get up again, let me tell you. I lay on my back and I could hardly breathe – probably because, as I know now, there was a hole in my lung. I touched where it hit me and looked at my fingers. They were covered in blood. I think I passed out then and everything after that until the next day is a bit of a blur.

I do remember bits, like Shan crying (a lot) and a policeman pressing on my chest and me wondering why he was pressing down when that only made it hurt even more. I remember being in the ambulance (I've never been in one before) and lots of people around me in the hospital, but they're like little film clips in my memory. It's like when you're fast-forwarding through a programme to get to the good bits and then, when you come to another boring bit, you fast-forward again.

I can't remember anything about the operation I had that night. They told me they sewed up the hole in my lung so they could fill it with air again, sorted the broken rib, gave me some more blood to replace what I lost (which was a lot) and cut some little bits of bullet out. I was a bit disappointed they didn't give me the whole bullet as a souvenir, but it carried on through my chest and came out of my back. I don't know where it ended up after that. Perhaps somebody parking their car at the hotel one day will find it. I hope if they do they hand it in.

I'm nearly back to how I was before, but my arm and my hand still don't work like they should. Something to do with the nerves.

I hope they get better eventually because it's a bit irritating when you keep dropping stuff like you're clumsy, but Shan understands and doesn't tell me off all the time.

Shan's been great, considering. I was the one who got shot, but she had it rougher than me that day, I reckon. She had a gun put to her head twice, she watched two people get killed right in front of her and she saw me get shot and thought I was going to die. That's a lot to deal with, but she's been incredible really. It's not been easy, by any means. We've both had bad nightmares since, though we don't get them as often now as we did at first, thankfully. When they do come we help each other and then it's all right. We've always got through bad stuff together like that, but we're even tighter now, if anything. I reckon that's because we both know how close we came to losing each other.

I don't know how I'd have coped if I'd lost Shan that day. Sometimes, my mind starts wondering what it would've been like if Bridgeman had managed to get Shan into the car and driven away and it scares the shit out of me. I don't like to think about it, but you can't help yourself sometimes. Shan says she has the same kind of thoughts. We've been to talk to a counsellor lady the police put us in touch with and she says it's normal to think that way after going through what we went through, but we want those feelings to go away now. We'd just like life to be normal again.

Shan did go back to work at Asda a week ago and the counsellor lady called that an important step forward. I miss her when I'm in the flat on my own, but I don't need her to do as much for me now, not like when I first came home from hospital. She was fussing around me and making me cups of tea all the time then, even when I hadn't asked for one. I'm glad she's not like that anymore. She even moaned at me the other day when I left the breakfast things in the bowl without washing them before she got home. I reckon that's a sign we're getting back to the way we were before all this and that makes me happy.

We're so lucky to have each other. I feel sorry for Em that she doesn't have somebody close like that, but she does have us now. We've seen her a few times since that day, at the hospital and at the flat, and we've become good mates. Em told us she's starting her own business, designing security systems for companies and people with posh houses. She said because she's so good at breaking in, that makes her better qualified than anybody to build systems that criminals aren't able to figure out. She lost me a bit when she explained more about it, but she seems to know what she's doing. She's definitely better at doing stuff with computers than anybody else I've ever met.

Talking of computers, Em gave me the laptop I'm writing this on. It was one of those her brother did up and it's great. It's tons easier to use than that stupid typewriter. We got rid of that, by the way. Shan didn't want to keep it and neither did I, to be honest. It reminded us of poor old Fingerless Frankie and sad times. We got thirty quid for it from a junk shop in Heeley Bottom and bought an Indian takeaway with the money.

Now I've got the laptop instead and I'm starting to feel better I've made my mind up I want to crack on with writing that book again. I've already got the plot figured out and if you're wondering if it's going to be based on what happened to us – you'd be right! I'll change the names, of course. I'm thinking of making Peaches McPlenty my main detective.

Peaches McPlenty and The Curse of The Mysterious Typewriter.

I quite like the sound of that. I reckon it could be a best seller.

Even if the writing thing doesn't work out, that's OK. I never really wanted to be rich anyway. It was nice for a time when we were dreaming about all the money we could've got if the type-writer had once belonged to you-know-who, but all that feels less important now. Things are different for us somehow. We're the same but we're not the same if that makes sense. We never had much before, in terms of money and nice stuff and all that, and we haven't got much now, but so what? We don't need it. Me and Shan have got so much to look forward to. This is like getting a second chance, a fresh start. The council found us a nice new flat and, like I said, we're tighter than ever. After everything we've been through, I reckon we're unbreakable.

I'm not saying I'm glad it happened or anything daft like that. It was a horrible experience I wouldn't wish on anybody, but it didn't finish us and we came out of it stronger in the end, just like Batman in *The Dark Knight Rises*.

Isn't that really the only thing that matters? As some cleverer bloke than me once said, all's well that turns out all right.

ACKNOWLEDGMENTS

The journey to completing a novel can take you to some strange places.

Never before – and I did have to pursue some very odd lines of inquiry in my previous career as a journalist – have I needed to have a conversation about the best way to go about dumping a dead body in a supermarket service yard. Neither, I suspect, had the manager at my local branch of Sainsbury's, but he gamely humoured me and answered all my questions. He even seemed to be getting quite into it by the end. Thankfully, he didn't call the police.

On the subject of police, I dropped really lucky when I met Jo and Ducky Mallard at a talk I gave to promote my last novel, *The Murder of Miss Perfect*. Jo is a former CSI and Ducky a former senior detective, and they could not have been more helpful in allowing me to tap into their vast experience in the effort to keep the plot of this novel vaguely plausible. I only hope we didn't put anyone off their lunch when we met up to discuss gory matters at the café.

Former newspaper colleague Paul Wyatt was also a great help, in his capacity as a member of the Derbyshire Constabulary media team. For an Ipswich Town fan, he's a great bloke.

Two other specialists were subjected to phone conversations they didn't expect. George Blackman told me everything I needed to know about the inner workings of vintage typewriters and Glenn Carter cheerfully gave me a steer on how it might be possible to crack the sort of security systems he installs. Thanks for not thinking I was the world's most brazen burglar.

A decision I took in planning this novel was to incorporate a character with a disability. This was not to tick an inclusivity box, but was inspired by my fellow author Penny Batchelor, who has campaigned fervently for positive disability representation and recognition in the industry. She deserves to be heard more widely.

Thank you again to family and friends for necessary encouragement, especially my chief sounding board, Sue. Huge thanks also to Sumaira and Nikki at SpellBound Books for their continued faith in providing a vehicle for my scribblings.

ABOUT THE AUTHOR

Mark Eklid's background is as a newspaper journalist, starting out with the South Yorkshire Times in 1984 and then on to the Derby Telegraph, from 1987 until he left full-time work in March 2022.

Most of his time at the Telegraph was as their cricket writer, a role that brought national recognition in the 2012 and 2013 England and Wales Cricket Board awards. He contributed for 12 years to the famed Wisden Cricketers' Almanack and had many articles published in national magazines, annuals and newspapers.

Writing as a profession meant writing for pleasure had to be put on the back burner but when his work role changed, Mark returned to one of the many half-formed novels in his computer files and, this time, saw it through to publication.

The Murder of Miss Perfect (July 2022) was his first novel for independent publisher SpellBound Books, but Mark had previously self-published *Sunbeam* (November 2019), *Family Business* (June 2020) and *Catalyst* (February 2021).

All four are fast-moving, plot-twisting thrillers set in the city of his birth, Sheffield.

Mark lives in Derby with his partner, Sue. They have two adult sons and have been adopted by a cat.

ALSO BY MARK EKLID

THE MURDER OF MISS PERFECT

Detective Chief Inspector Jim Pendlebury almost died at the end of his last big case.

Three years later, he is struggling to cope with forced retirement and the frustration of failing to convict the teacher accused of killing an 18-year-old student after seducing her.

Now, he must try one more time to search for the vital piece of missing evidence the police failed to find during the initial investigation and make sure justice is served for the cruel murder of the beautiful young woman the media dubbed Miss Perfect.

CATALYST

Sheffield is being steered towards an ecological disaster which will put thousands of lives at risk by an unscrupulous city council leader who is chasing one last big backhander before he gives up power.

With time running out to avert a potential catastrophe, fate takes a hand.

An old lady is injured by a falling branch from a tree during a storm. It is the unlikely spark for a chain of coincidental events which sets one man on the path to save the city.

FAMILY BUSINESS

Family historian Graham Hasselhoff thought there were no skeletons in his cupboard. That is, until the day he met the son he never knew he had.

Getting to know Andreas, who is now the boss of a road haulage firm, soon leads him to a trail of arson, beatings, mysterious warnings – and murder.

Can his son really be behind this deadly business?

Graham has to quickly work out if Andreas is an impetuous eccentric – or a dangerously ruthless criminal.

SUNBEAM

John Baldwin has been on a downward spiral to self-destruction since the day he witnessed the murder of his best friend, Stef. It has cost him his marriage, his business and his dignity.

One year on from the day that turned his world upside down, he sees Stef again. John fears he has finally lost his mind but Stef is there to pull his friend back from the brink, not tip him over it. He offers John a fresh start, a new destiny.

John rebuilds his life. He has everything again but there is a price to pay. The killer is still on the loose and Stef wants revenge.

Visit his website, markeklid.com, for further details.

Printed in Great Britain
by Amazon

31565960R00162